Acknowledgments

Charlotte Bennardo

To everyone mentioned in *Sirenz*—ditto.

Thanks to all the people who've touched my heart with their enthusiasm for our writing success. There are so many, but I only have room for a short list: my parents Jeanne and John Zurawski, my sister Brenda Garretson, Aunt Dolores, the United Methodist Church bell and singing choirs, Pastors Vicki and Christina, Roni, Loretta, Arline, Dawn, Anita, Jeannie B., Gina, members of the Society of Children's Book Writers and Illustrators, the bloggers for taking time to read and review, and most importantly, to Natalie: co-author, co-conspirator, co-defendant, co-star, co-worker, and co-creator.

Natalie Zaman

To my friends and family, especially Raz, Asim, Mari, Vin, and Mom.

Huge thanks to Brian Farrey-Latz and Sandy Sullivan at Flux for once again making *Sirenz* sing, Natalie Fischer-Lakosil for believing in my not-so-many projects, and Kirsten Cappy and The Curious City for helping us share Meg and Shar's story. A thousand loves to the NJ-SCBWI and blogging communities whose members supported us from day one.

And, of course, to Char, the calm yin to my raging yang (and vice-versa!).

About the Authors

Charlotte Bennardo

A moderate shoe freak, Charlotte Bennardo divides her time between writing, her three sons, writing, her family and friends—and writing. When she's not wearing out her laptop keyboard, she likes to swim, garden, play with her cat, and hang out with her best friend and co-author, Natalie. Married, she lives in Bridgewater, New Jersey. Visit Charlotte at charlottebennardo.com and charlottebennardo.blogspot.com, and on Twitter at charbennardo.

Natalie Zaman

Natalie Zaman learned that it's hard—but not impossible—to farm in high heels. When she's not chasing free-range chickens, she's writing, knitting, or plotting a road trip. She lives in New Jersey with her family—about five minutes from Charlotte. Visit her online at nataliezaman.blogspot.com.

Visit Meg, Shar, and Hades at www.thesirenz.com

SIRENZ
Back in Fashion

Also by Charlotte Bennardo and Natalie Zaman:
Sirenz

SIRENZ

Back in Fashion

Some gifts aren't worth the price!

Cha...

xx
Just in case! Nat

Charlotte Bennardo & Natalie Zaman

flux
™

Woodbury, Minnesota

First Edition
First Printing, 2012

Book format by Bob Gaul
Cover design by Lisa Novak
Cover illustration © Annabelle Metayer/Heflinreps Inc.

Flux, an imprint of Llewellyn Worldwide Ltd.

Library of Congress Cataloging-in-Publication Data
Bennardo, Charlotte.
    Sirenz back in fashion/Charlotte Bennardo & Natalie Zaman.—1st ed.
        p. cm.
    Summary: High school seniors Meg and Shar are separated when Hades tricks them into a second assignment, taking Shar to the Underworld with him while Meg tries to get her new roommate to don the golden fleece that will send her to her fate.
    ISBN 978-0-7387-3187-2
    [1. Sirens (Mythology)—Fiction. 2. Mythology, Greek—Fiction. 3. Hades (Greek deity)—Fiction. 4. Fashion—Fiction. 5. New York (N.Y.)—Fiction.] I. Zaman, Natalie. II. Title.
    PZ7.B4352Siu 2012
    [Fic]—dc23

                                                    2011052166

Flux
Llewellyn Worldwide Ltd.
2143 Wooddale Drive
Woodbury, MN 55125-2989
www.fluxnow.com

To the real Estelle Eberhardt, a fashion maven in her day.
See you on the other side of the River…xoxo
—*Char*

For my dear Miss Emma Coleman, who always encourages, dispenses advice both practical and fashionable (and fashionably practical), and gave me the perfect person to man the counter of New York's finest sweetshop.
—*Nat*

MEG

Odd Couple

"What do you think, Meg, chartreuse or lime?"

I finished the paragraph I was reading and turned my head slightly. Shar towered over me in spiked heels and yellow and green striped PJs. She held up two hangers; the dresses on them looked nearly identical, as did the colors.

"Lime," I said, and went back to my page.

"You didn't even look!"

"Yes I did." I kept my eyes on my book; I had to finish reading another act of *Julius Caesar*, and this had to be the ninth ensemble she'd put together that required a second opinion. Each one was a different shade of green, the "it" color for spring, or so she said. At least she'd settled on what shoes to wear. *Some things never change.*

"I know," she said brightly. "You can do a reading for me! That'll help me decide."

I take it back. A lot has changed.

Experience and I had made a believer out of Shar; she'd added an astrology app to her phone and carried more lucky charms than a gypsy in her purse. I warned her that over-doing it could be counterproductive—less is more—but she was a newbie in the world of the occult and still dazzled by its mysteries.

"Shar, you don't do a tarot reading to pick an outfit," I said as she went over to my desk and started fishing through the litter of books, papers, highlighters, and pens.

"Fine." She plucked the tarot deck in its black drawstring bag from behind my laptop. "Don't tell me what to wear. Tell me what's going to happen today. Then I can narrow down my choices."

I gave her a droll look. "You're going to meet a stranger and fall deeply in love. Go for the lime green."

She ignored me and pushed the deck into my hands.

"That's really what's going to happen—I don't need to do a reading to tell you that," I offered hopefully, but Shar pouted. Only a reading or a thorough analysis of her extensive wardrobe would appease her, and I didn't feel like discussing the finer points of boot-cut versus flared jeans. Not today; I needed to finish my homework before we went downtown.

I slid the cards out of the pouch. *Shar, here's what's going to happen this afternoon: we're meeting Jeremy and Ian for lunch. I get to see Jeremy, and you get to meet Ian, and we're all going to live happily ever after. The End.* I flipped through the deck quickly, then handed it to her.

She proceeded to shuffle the cards, touching each one carefully just like I'd taught her. Her lips twisted into a self-satisfied grin, pleased she'd gotten her way.

"Remember to focus on the question," I sighed.

Shar's features quickly knit into an expression of fierce concentration. While she worked at forcing her will into the cards, I gazed past her and out the window. Our room was on the third floor of the dorm that housed seniors like Shar and me—talented students chosen for the Academically Independent High School of New York's Fourth Year Live-In Program. It overlooked a tree-dotted courtyard, but from my vantage point on the bed, all I could see was the dull brick wall of the opposite building. In fact, unless I walked right up to the window and leaned out, there wasn't much else to see. Scenery-wise, the window was useless. Nothing like the view from that posh pad we'd lived in while working for Hades ...

Damn!

It had been just about two months since we'd kissed the Siren life and Hades goodbye, and I thought that with every day that passed, the experience would become more and more distant and eventually fade into a hazy memory. The world, however, was full of reminders. Inevitably, I'd walk down the street and pass someplace where Shar and I conspired, planned, or shopped. Then there were the mornings when I'd pull an impossibly priced top or jacket out of my closet—something that, in my normal life, I could never afford. The simple act of taking the subway—the place where it all started—conjured memories of the deal we'd made with the Lord of the Underworld. He'd tricked us into becoming his Sirens. I'd never felt so stupid in my life, but it all happened so quickly...

I shut the thought out of my mind.

It was done, over, *finis*, and Shar and I were back to suffering through boring bagged lunches, pinching pennies until they screamed for mercy, and settling back into our old odd-couple life in the Live-In dorm. It was hard to believe senior year was almost over. We only had a couple of months left until graduation. Then summer. Then college. It felt like we'd only just started.

"Okay, I'm ready." Shar straightened the cards into a neat stack and placed them on the smooth stretch of coverlet between us.

"What's going to happen... *later today?*" She said the last words in a Hollywood-mysterious voice.

Shar wasn't the only one looking forward to this afternoon—I was too. Now that my boyfriend Jeremy was free of Arkady Romanov—our Siren assignment and his over-demanding employer—he was re-enrolled at NYU, and between his classes and mine, we saw less of each other than when his doomed boss had kept him on a short leash. Our meetings were few and fleeting, and no longer seemed to pass in slow motion like when we'd first met. Still, I always counted the minutes until I saw him, and right now there were about 246 left.

Shar hadn't met anyone who interested her since we'd come back to our normal lives, but hopefully that was about to change. Jeremy told us he met Ian in film class and said he was nice, good-looking enough to have done some modeling work, and most importantly, unattached. He suggested the four of us do something together. After hearing this, Shar promptly embarked on a crusade to find an "I'm meeting a former model that I could possibly start dating" outfit.

I turned the first card over, revealing a picture of a heart being pierced by three swords.

Shar picked up the card and peered worriedly at it. "That doesn't look happy."

"That's the past," I said, taking it from her and placing it back into position. "Broken heart, love triangles."

She nodded grimly—we'd both been interested in Jeremy when we first met him. And then, of course, Hades tried to recruit her to be his spring-slash-summer lollipop and she'd been caught between him and his wife, Persephone. Still, Shar looked doubtful as she said, "Makes sense … you sure that's the past?"

"Yes. It's what your experiences were, not are or are going to be."

She nodded and tapped the next card. "Good. Moving on."

I flipped it over. Death.

"Oh, great!" Her shoulders slumped.

"Shar," I started. We'd been through this before—many times. "Remember what I told you about the Death card. It means—"

"Sudden change," she said, cutting me off. "But couldn't they express it in a different way? Why all the skeletons and dead people?"

"Look past it," I said with a dismissive wave. "You want change, don't you? Never be afraid of the Death card."

"Next," she grumbled.

I flipped the card over and Shar let out a little squeal. The Lovers.

"Interesting," I mused.

"Obvious!" she bubbled. "Do you think I'm runway ready? Maybe I'll have an actual date for the Spring Fling." She got up and twirled around, catching her stiletto heels together and nearly falling over.

"Better work on that twirl, Naomi," I said, trying not to laugh. Shar was usually graceful in everything from sky-high stilettos to chunky wedges, but she was giddy, and when she was giddy, she got clumsy. "Remember the Death card? Things aren't always what they seem to be, so don't take them at face value. I wouldn't pick out his 'n her towels just yet."

Her lips squished together into a tight and disappointed pucker.

"It's not bad," I said. "The Lovers indicates that there'll be choices to make."

She brightened. "Like what to wear!" She got up and sashayed over to her dresser. She pulled out another green ... something. I couldn't tell what it was. *Please, no more outfits! I have to finish my Lit reading!*

"Does abrupt change call for skinny jeans and flats or a mini-dress?"

"I'd do the jeans," I said as seriously and with as much authority as I could. "If you fall down you won't embarrass yourself."

"As if!" she huffed, pulling a few more things out of

her dresser: a scarf, a different top. She arranged the things precisely on her bed, smoothing out wrinkles, adjusting the position and angle of a sleeve, a collar.

"Perfect!" she said, stepping back and surveying her work. Despite myself, I looked up again. Shar had put together a pair of form-fitting dark jeans and a slinky blouse the color of new grass. *With a pair of fierce bronze heels and a stack of glittery bangles ... um, wait a minute ...*

A chill breeze flitted through the window, which was open a crack to compensate for the baseboard heaters; Maintenance must've cranked the temperature up to 90 degrees. Shar grabbed a bathrobe and kicked a neon pair of pink flipflops out from underneath her bed with her toe.

"Going to take a shower. Are you done with the bathroom?" She looked me up and down with a critical eye. "We're going to be right by Century 21 and—"

"I know, you want to stop in before we meet the guys," I finished for her. "I showered earlier, just have to get dressed. I promise I'll come up with something that meets with your approval."

She nodded and whooshed her way out of the room, closing the door behind her with a soft click. I leaned over and squinted at my laptop; the little clock on the bottom read 9:47. I guessed I should get ready. Getting up, I stretched and sauntered over to the closet. Without thinking, I slid the door open to my half, and a pile of shoes, boots, CDs, and clothes gushed out, making a little swamp of stuff around my feet.

"Crap," I said aloud.

We usually kept the closet door shut in fear of an avalanche; this situation was more the result of our indulgent Siren shopping sprees than my general lack of tidiness. I kneeled down and scooped up an armful of things from the pile, then paused for a moment and surveyed the room. For the most part it looked as it had from the beginning—a kind of yin-yang, my brooding darkness against Shar's perky lightness. Her coordinated bedding was bright and neat, her desk clear, her dresser orderly. On my half of the room clothes hung out of every drawer, and the desk was a burial mound of textbooks and half-finished papers. But here and there were tiny signs of welcome intrusion—rosy scarves draping my bed, a glittery cat bank with a raised paw watching over Shar's workspace like a guardian. I felt a surge of comfort wash over me. Shar and I were the same people who had met back in September, but now we were friends.

I got dressed: black skirt, semi-clingy black tee, a denim jacket. Out of the mess of my top drawer I got some glittery socks. I pulled them on and started looking through the jumble of stuff on the floor for my shoes when Shar breezed in, her hair done up in a towel turban.

I could see her, out of the corner of my eye, sizing up my clothes.

"A little predictable, but I guess it's all right. I like the socks—a nice jolt of bling."

The muffled tones of a synthy electronica song came from her bag. She sighed and walked over to the purse that rested at the foot of her bed.

Digging out her phone, she said "Alana" and slid it open to read a text.

"She wants to go out later." Shar tapped in a reply and tossed the phone on the bed, then took the towel off her head. Almost immediately the song started up again.

Shar read the new text and shook her head.

"What's up?" I asked.

"Going out with your vampire roomie again?" she read.

Shar, Alana Dean, Kate Jones, and Caroline Cerillo were known as the Fashion Foursome; all of them were going to the Fashion Institute of Technology after graduation. They weren't thrilled when Shar had the unlucky fate of being paired up with me last fall. I hadn't been too pleased with the situation either, but when we returned to school after winter break—and our alliance with Hades—Shar tried to bring me into the fold. But it just didn't work. Slowly, she cut down on hang-time with her former BFFs in favor of studying, shopping, and hitting the occasional club with me, the vampire roomie.

Shar grinned as she replied to the message.

"What'd you tell her?" I asked.

"That I can't go out because I'm meeting a former model for a lunch date and hoping it'll turn into something."

I brushed aside a twinge of hurt that Shar didn't mention me in the message, rationalizing that if she had, it might have resulted in Alana coming down to our room for a "talk," like she did when things first started getting back to normal. None of my friends would do that, but then, I wasn't part of a posse where if one member went astray, eyebrows were raised and questions were asked.

As if on cue, the music started again. Shar looked at the message and nodded. *"Go for it, girlfriend! We want a full report!*" she read. "That means I won't be hearing from her again today, but watch out tomorrow." She started getting dressed.

I found my shoes at the bottom of the heap and started strapping them on.

"Oooo!" Shar cooed when she saw them. "Are those…"

"Vivienne Westwood."

"Where did you get them? *How* did you get them?" She picked up the shoe I hadn't slipped on yet. "They look like you've had them forever."

"Vintage store. They were cheap because of the nick on the side here," I said, turning it so she could see.

"Ewww! Foot germs! I would *not* wear someone else's shoes!" Her hand jerked away.

"But they're designer!"

She squinched up her face. "At least it's a leap up from all your previous choices. With such decadence, how can you live with yourself?"

"They're old," I started, putting on the other shoe, "but even if they were new, they're not made in the third world, so I know the person stitching them together is being paid a living wage. And—"

"That's enough!" Shar raised her hands. "They're Westwood, they're awesome. No one needs to know their life story."

"And they're black," I concluded. "So it suits me, being a *vampire* and all."

The dig wasn't lost on her.

"Meg," she said, coming over to my bed and sitting

down next to me. "I'm sorry about Alana. Things are different. But I couldn't…"

I pictured Shar trying to tell the abandoned trio about the subtle change in their and our relationships: *Meg may be a little on the strange side, but she's really cool when you get to know her…* No. Not happening.

I nodded. "I know. Come on, finish up and let's get out of here."

An hour later, we were browsing the top floor of Century 21.

"Tell me again why we're here?" I asked. Shar was digging through a rack stuffed with jeans, not listening to me. I touched her arm. "Haven't you bought enough clothes?"

She looked up from her search. "I really thought there was some hope for you, rocking those shoes," she sighed, shooting a glance at my feet. "But you still don't get the whole shopping experience. You're still in mourning colors. And"—she leaned in closer to me—"don't you want to get something that doesn't remind you of… *him?*"

I shrugged. I hadn't bought as much as she had; she'd been practically delirious when we had the no-limit credit card and a walk-in closet large enough to house a taxi. I just didn't attach the same sentiment to clothes—Shar acted as if every pair of jeans had a personality.

I looked at my watch again. We didn't want to set out too early; it would be better if Jeremy and Ian were waiting for us, rather than the other way around. I followed Shar over to a rack of dresses, and then I heard her gasp and click her tongue.

"What's the matter?" I asked. She looked really angry.

"I can't believe this!" She clutched a hanger furiously. An iridescent, turquoise-colored halter sheath hung crookedly off its plastic arms. One of them was broken. Shar shook the dress violently, the silk rippling like water. "I bought this at that boutique when we were shopping for the show at the Met," she growled. "The sales person said it was a limited edition and that I'd gotten the last one. Now it's here for $99.97? Do you realize that someone who buys fake Gucci off the street for ten dollars can walk around in my $5,000 Alexander McQueen dress for a hundred dollars?!"

My forehead wrinkled in pity for her, but not that much. "Shar?"

"What?!"

"What does a yellow dot on the tag mean?"

"That's an extra twenty percent off."

"Well, then your dress will only cost around $80, or something like that, with tax of course."

Her hand started to shake, and she stared at me in a way that reminded me uncomfortably of Persephone. She jammed the dress back onto the rack and stormed off. Resigned, I followed in her wake.

About an hour later, after a visit to the shoe department and some serious toe curling language from Shar about more bargains that had migrated here, we left and started making our way across town.

"When did you say we were meeting them?" she asked, looking at the sky, which had clouded over.

"In less than an hour."

She grinned hugely at me, then wrinkled her nose as a fat raindrop hit her.

"Hail a cab!" she cried, shielding her face with her hand.

"Don't want to smear your mascara?" I teased. "I think I have an umbrella." I started to dig in my bag.

"I'm always prepared," she said, reaching a hand into her purse. I got to my umbrella first; it was one of the accessories hurled at me by the Siren-dazed guys during that first shopping trip to Henri Bendel. Black and lacy, it was one of those Goth-loli confections from Japan, daintily Victorian and intensely feminine. I popped it open and held it over both of us while Shar continued to search in her bag.

Suddenly her face registered confusion.

"What's wrong?" I asked.

She stopped moving forward and shuffled close to the building. I followed, holding the umbrella. From the depths of her purse, she pulled out a light blue box.

She opened it and sucked in a breath. It was the mega-sized, crystal-clear blue diamond ring from Tiffany's, the one Hades had gifted to her but she'd never worn.

SHAR

Not You Again!

"What do I do with it?" I mused. The diamond sparkled on its snowy cushion; a few people pushing by stared and gaped. "I didn't know it was still there." In fact, the last time I'd seen it was months ago, after Hades slipped it in.

"What do you mean, 'what do I do with it?'" Meg replied. "Wear it. Enjoy it."

"I can't keep it. It's the one from *him*." I gave Meg a *duh* look. Didn't she get it?

She put a hand on her hip, annoyed. "So? Isn't most of your wardrobe?"

"I don't want it."

"What's the big deal?"

Was she really serious? I wondered if I had completely corrupted Ms. Save-The-World-from-Capitalist-Exploitation-and-Sing-We-Are-The-World.

"I don't want it anymore," I said.

"You? Not want a five carat, flawless, emerald-cut diamond? From Tiffany's?" Meg's mouth hung open.

"Guess I'm not the selfish, greedy, materialistic girl I used to be. You take it." I thrust the box at her.

"I don't want it." Meg clutched her umbrella with both hands so she couldn't touch it. "Besides being pretentious, unnecessary, and not my style, it's dangerous—baubles that big attract muggers."

"I'll donate it to charity," I said.

"Good idea. But before you do, try it on. Just once, to get it out of your system."

I gazed at the ring. "I don't know." Anything connected with Greek gods, I'd learned too late, meant trouble I wasn't prepared for. Besides, Persephone had the *exact* same ring, although that kind of thing was only a problem when you showed up at a soirée in a one-of-a-kind couture dress and found out three other people had the same one on.

"If you don't, I'll never hear the end of it," Meg muttered. "'Oh, I should've at least tried it!'" She raised her voice to a squeak, no doubt in imitation of me—though poorly done—and tilted her head from side to side.

Like I really did that! It was too stereotypical dumb blonde, which I am NOT.

"One quick twirl on the finger, then pop it back in the box and we can drop it off, or send it to whatever charity you want," she pressed. "You get to have your pink frosted cake and eat it too. You can say you owned a massive Tiffany ring and, knowing there are people out there who could use the money, you donated it to charity. Miss Benevolence with style. And I'll never have to hear, 'I should have!'"

That time, she did sound like me. I grinned. "Okay. But I'm really not keeping it." I opened the box, pulled the ring out, and slid the cool platinum circle onto my finger. Holding my hand out, I waved it back and forth, eyeing the sparkle.

I felt nothing. No smugness, no joy, nothing. The ring was beautiful, but it came from *him*. I didn't want anything from *him* or any other god.

"I'm done." I pulled the ring to take it off.

It wouldn't budge.

Okay, you're just a little emotional remembering the whole Sirens ordeal, I told myself. *Greek gods coming to life, contracts signed in blood, an ancient man sent to the Underworld, you and Meg almost turning into birds.*

I tugged and tugged. Panic started to choke me. *Get it off! Get it off!*

"Having a hard time?" Meg teased.

"It won't come off!" She had to see the fear on my face or hear it in my voice.

An arm—warm, muscular, and not Meg's—slid around my shoulders. The breath of temptation slid into my ears.

"I believe I can assist you with that."

Hades, Lord of the Underworld, personal nemesis, and all-around studly hunk. His hands, sleek and bronzed and gentle, twirled the huge diamond ring around my trembling finger. Holding my hand up to the light so that the ring sparkled like a star, he asked, "Stunning, isn't it? Even though it pales in comparison to you. Are you sure you want to take it off?"

Goose bumps raced down my skin. *Please, please, please, let me be hallucinating.*

"What. Are. You. Doing. Here?" Meg could barely get the words past her clenched jaw. I remained too dumb-founded to speak. On the busy city street, people passed by, oblivious to the scene of desperation occurring in their midst. Horns blared, cyclists zipped past, a nippy breeze fluttered scarves and coats; it was surreal.

He's blocking the sight of our little drama from human eyes. It was our own little piece of the Twilight Zone.

"I'm delighted you've decided to renew our agreement! After our last meeting, I thought you were actually tiring of me. I'm so glad I was mistaken." Hades leaned forward so his head was between us. First he smiled at Meg, then turned a suggestive leer on me. "So many delights I have planned for you two."

I shuddered and leaned away.

Meg threw off his arm. I followed her example. At least someone's brain was working today.

"Renew our agreement?" she croaked.

I cringed at the thought of our previous encounter with Hades. In his sultry, sexy, too-good-to-be-true-and-we-should-have-known-better manner, he'd promised to get us out of a dilemma that *he'd* set up, the snake. In exchange we agreed to become his one-time Sirens and send an old guy—a creepy, nasty sort—down to Tartarus. I still cringed at the fact that Hades had managed to fool us into the deal, but he was smooth. And here he was again, with his brooding looks of dark forbidden promises, his wavy auburn hair, and his chiseled abs.

"What do you mean?" Meg continued. "We finished our deal. Hera said so."

"And she's the queen of all of you," I added. *Tough talk!* But it was all I could think of at the moment, with his Calvin Klein *Eternity* cologne teasing my nose.

Then I whirled around and slapped a hand against his classically cut silver-sheen suit, so perfectly accessorized with a purple tie and lighter-shade shirt. With thick silver cuff links, of course. He knew how to dress to muddle a girl's brain. I shook my head to clear it of the enticing god in front of me. Meg and I weren't going to go without a fight.

"Save the charm, it won't work!" I yelled. "We don't care how nice you act, or how many perks you throw in—nothing's changed! We are NOT getting sucked in again!"

"Never." Meg gave him a steely blast of her icy blues. If anyone could resist Hades, it was her. For all her 5'3" stature, she was a dynamo. Very few people got past her if she didn't wish it. At half a foot taller and minus the dangerous curves, I, Sharisse Johnson, was a wuss. Well, unless it involved a pair of sexy red stilettos with little gold embellishments. That's what started this whole mess—not knowing when to walk away from the perfect shoe.

"Go away, Hades. Shar, let's get a little soap to slide that ring off, then we can return it to Tiffany's. Or drop it in the collection basket at the Salvation Army." Meg grabbed my arm and hauled me down the street, never looking back.

Neither of us had to. Suddenly, lounging carelessly against the shiny glass of the Victoria's Secret in front of us and buffing his blood-red ruby ring was Hades. Mannequins in pink polka-dot bikinis smiled down at him from the window display. Meg swung us both around—and we promptly slammed into his hard, sculpted, only-in-my-wildest-dreams body. The breath whooshed right out of me.

"It's not so simple, ladies. I truly had no intention of interfering with your insignificant mortal lives again, but you summoned me back."

I gasped. Meg growled.

"We did no such thing!" she argued.

"Not on your life!" I added.

His smile was slow, seductive, and really scaring the life out of me. Ooh, this was so not going to be good; I just knew it all the way down to my You-Can-Never-Be-Too-Pink toenail polish.

"You put the diamond ring on," he said to me, showing his supermodel teeth, then turned to Meg. "And *you* persuaded her to do it."

"Our contract never specified that we couldn't use the things we bought," Meg said. "Or that we had to give them up once we finished our task."

She was right. After we'd been duped by Hades and his divine cronies for the umpteenth time, she'd reviewed the details of the contract and committed them to memory. *It paid to be paranoid.*

"But Sharisse didn't buy the diamond," Hades replied smoothly. "It was a gift. From me."

Meg opened her mouth to speak, but Hades held up a slim index finger and waggled it.

"Some gifts, like *rings*, come with conditions. If you accept the ring, you accept the conditions."

This was one of those moments of clarity that pop into your head so suddenly it almost hurts. His gifts were tainted.

"Like an engagement ring?" I squeaked.

He nodded slowly, a saturnine smile making its leisurely way across his face. I couldn't breathe.

"And because I convinced her—" started Meg.

"You are just as liable," he concluded with a smirk.

And we were indentured. Again.

"We give everything back!" Not caring about the skin I would forfeit, I yanked off the ring and threw it, all five horrifying, evil carats, right at him. Bye bye, Tiffany's best. I tried to reach for Meg's hand and make a run for it, but as if in slow motion, Hades stepped back and caught the ring in midair. How *Matrix*.

He shook his head sadly. "It doesn't work that way, my darling. You accepted a gift, and so you are beholden to me once more."

"Hera!" Meg shouted.

Yes! Call the queen! She'll hand Hades his posterior.

Nothing happened.

Or not.

"She won't come," he chuckled. "You are the ones who initiated a continuation of the contract. She can't, and won't, interfere. Nice try, though." His gaze turned ominous. "This time, however, things are going to be a little different."

It suddenly got dark. But only where I was standing. I could see Meg and Hades clearly, like the sun shone only on them. In an instant, I felt like I'd dropped over the biggest hill on that vomit-inducing roller coaster at Six Flags I was dumb enough to ride on last summer. I felt weightless, yet was hurtling through space.

The sensation of falling stopped almost as soon as it started. Meg and Hades were still in front of me, but there seemed to be a glass barrier between us.

I banged on the pane with my fist; it was thick and unmoving. I swung around. There was nothing but gloom behind me. I stretched out a hand into it, touching a cold nothingness. Quickly, all the air around me chilled. A whorl of steamy breath curled from my lips before dissipating. When I wrapped my arms around my waist to stop the shivering, my hands touched bare skin; he'd dressed me in a pink polka-dot bikini, just like the mannequins! And in those infernal red stilettos!

My Life Ruined By Shoes, as told by Sharisse Johnson. Oh, I was going to give him the shoes—right in the privates!

Whipping back around, I threw myself against the glass barrier. My hands were pressed against it, and my breath, drawn in panic, created a fog on the glass in front of me, making it hard to see Meg's face clearly. I swiped it clean. Her eyes grew huge when she saw me. She banged on her side of the glass. I pounded back, but it made no sound or vibration. All I could do was cry. She put one hand over her mouth and paled. Was there no getting out? Frantic, I screamed for her. As the pane darkened, my last vision was of Meg kicking the glass, tears streaming down her face.

I don't know how long I stood there.

Alone.

In the dark.

Shaking with dread and cold, I wobbled a few steps away from the glass to see how far back my crystal prison extended. The gloom of a cavelike space yawned behind me. Searching around slowly, I saw pinpoints of light, which allowed me brief glances into the dimness beyond. Shadows moved, but I couldn't make out what they were. I got goose bumps on my goose bumps.

I want my cashmere sweater!

"Hello?" I called. A faint echo bounced back. This place was huge. I'd been in Howe Caverns in upstate New York, but not for long. The winding and twisting passageways were too claustrophobic. This place was too big, too dark. I trembled. *Where was I?*

Whenever Hades whisked me off someplace, like a privately owned tropical island or Ferragamo's in Milan, it was to tempt me. But there was absolutely nothing in this scenario that was the least bit beguiling. I couldn't figure out where he dumped me. I sniffed. It was dark. And moldy. And icky. I could be anywhere—a sewer, a subway tunnel, a mine.

First lesson about mortal females, Hades, is NOT to send them to a skanky dark place. And dressed in the wrong outfit!

M∃G
Fleeced!

I ran up to the window and banged violently on the glass. Shar stood on the other side of it, her low-slung jeans and bright green top gone, replaced by a neon-pink bikini identical to the ones worn by the mannequins—and the red shoes.

"Shar!" I yelled. "Shar!"

She hammered away from her side, but I couldn't feel or hear the beat. Suddenly she gave up and just stood there, crying. I pummeled the glass, harder if possible, then backed away, looking frantically for the entrance door. People swarmed around me, interfering with my view. Maybe if I could get inside, I could make my way into the window displays; but then I stopped dead.

Shar's hands pressed against the glass, ghostly halos of

moisture forming around her palms and fingers. With every breath she took, shallow and quick from the looks of it, a little cloud formed on the window, obscuring my view of her. Behind her, a black background brightened, becoming three dimensional and shadowy like the mouth of a gaping cave.

"Shar!" I screamed again. The glass started to darken and I backed away in horror, putting my hand over my mouth to stifle my scream. "No! Oh God, Shar..." I ran up to the window and kicked it again and again. The pane suddenly went black.

I felt my voice catch in my throat and whirled around to face Hades. "What did you do with her?"

I wasn't completely surprised by him slithering back into our lives. Somehow I knew we weren't that easily rid of him; I never allowed myself to let my guard down, and I looked for him in dark corners and in crowds.

"Really, Margaret, you're making a spectacle of yourself. Don't worry about Sharisse. I assure you, she's fine."

"No she's not! She's scared and crying. Where is she?" Turning back to the window, I felt cold fingers of terror creep across my neck. Shar was gone. The mannequins, plastic grins and all, stood in their places as if nothing had happened. "Where is she?" I demanded again.

"She's perfectly safe," Hades said, waving a hand. In an instant he'd moved us several blocks uptown, and we were seated at a round table under an umbrella at the vegetarian cafe where Shar and I were supposed to meet Jeremy and Ian. The lone omnivore, Shar agreed to this place only because they served pesto-soaked pasta, one of the few non-meat dishes she would condescend to eat. Remembering the double date we'd never have because she'd been whisked away, my anxious stomach constricted painfully. I clenched and unclenched my hands, my nails digging into my palms.

"Relax," Hades drawled. "She's alive and well. In my keeping, in Tartarus."

"Tartarus!" I closed my eyes then rubbed the spot between them and the bridge of my nose in worry. "She's all alone down there," I said, more to myself than him. "Does she even know where she is?"

"I'm sure she'll figure it out, Margaret. I promise you, no harm will come to her and she won't be alone." He held up a hand as if he were swearing a scout's oath. My instincts told me that he was probably telling the truth; for now, Shar might be safe, but I knew she had to be terrified. And did he mean she wouldn't be alone because *he'd* be with her, or someone—or *something*—else would?

An aproned waiter brought us tall glasses of iced water with thin slices of lemon floating on top. Hades barely nodded at him and he scurried away. "I ordered you the hummus plate."

"I'm really not hungry at the moment." I glared at him. "And I really don't want to talk about this here." The tables positioned closely around us were tightly packed; I could hear the woman next to me slurping up noodles.

"Surely you know by now that all our conversations are private and unseen—at least by human ears and eyes."

I shook my head, trying to make sense of it. Shar was gone, to Tartarus if I took Hades' word for it. But if that was true, why was *I* still here?

"Anyway," he continued, "as I stated before Sharisse left

us, the two of you are again in my service. I have another mission for you."

"Pffft! Of course you do!" I sneered.

Hades sipped his mineral water, looking bored.

"I'm going to take the fact that you haven't seen me for a while as an excuse. You've forgotten to whom you are speaking," he said slowly and evenly. "Unless you want your immediate future to be even more difficult, I suggest you moderate your tone. I am well within my rights to renew your services—"

"But Shar isn't here." I ignored his threatening tone.

The waiter came and plunked a plate on the table; it was artistically arranged with hummus and vegetables in a swirling shape, like a whirlpool. I pushed it away, not wanting to be reminded that I was being sucked into something awful yet again.

"The contract was signed by *both* of us, Shar *and* me," I added. "Like you said, I convinced her to put the ring on, so I should be down there with her."

He gave a humorless laugh. "I appreciate your facilitation of the whole process and your eagerness to join Sharisse in Tartarus, but with her there, I need you for an assignment up here. *Divide et impera.*"

I raised my eyebrows at him, confused.

"It's Latin for 'divide and conquer.' Those Romans did have a way with words, I'll give them that."

"I can't work alone," I insisted, narrowing my eyes at him. "You know that. The Siren powers work better when we were together."

"They're *stronger* when you're together, but very much

26

usable individually," Hades answered smoothly. "You still have the voice, Margaret. All you need to do is focus your intent. As a Siren, males will naturally be drawn to you."

"And I'll sprout a few more feathers." The acidic tone of my voice wasn't lost on him. He gave me a weary look.

"Not this time. Adding in that kind of motivation is only amusing once. And don't think I'm such a Kracken— I sympathize that you'll be doing this assignment on your own, so take your time. There's no deadline."

"I guess that makes Shar's time in Tartarus unlimited as well." I leaned closer, scared but not showing it. "I know what your game is. I have until the end of the summer, *when your wife comes back*, right?"

He eyed me coldly for an instant, but then his features quickly smoothed. "I'm sure you won't need that long to finish, Margaret, but I don't want you to feel any pressure. Of course, if you should fail"—he licked his lips—"Sharisse will have to stay in Tartarus and you'll be joining her. You'll be roommates for eternity. At my *every* beck and call."

I slammed my hands on the table, and the glasses, dishes, and silverware jumped. "This is completely, totally, and absolutely unfair!"

"Spare me the dramatics, Margaret. I have it in writing." An unfurled scroll hovered over the table, our signatures at the bottom. Hades sighed heavily. *"Where and How Sirens Are Placed is at My Discretion; Section One, Paragraph Six.* Now, you can continue your tantrum about this, or we can go over the particulars and I can send you on your merry way. We shouldn't keep Jeremy waiting."

Instantly, all was silent. The tinkle of silverware on plates and the constant chatter of people around us ceased. The woman at the next table, who was sitting almost at my shoulder, sat as still as a statue, the fork she'd twirled with pasta stuck midway between her plate and her mouth.

I turned back to Hades. There was no way out of this; I had no other choice but to comply.

"What do I need to do?" I said, closing my eyes and letting out a long breath.

"That's more like it," he said, snapping his fingers. Sound returned to the world. I had to remember not to push him too far; Shar and I were caught in his nasty little web. I sympathized with the fly, doomed just because it was in the wrong place at the wrong time.

"Your next assignment is to deliver Paulina Swanson to me."

"As Shar would say, *Hello?* Paulina sounds female—the Siren powers won't work on her. I won't be able to do it."

Hades tsked-tsked. "There you go with that negative attitude. You *can.* You *must.*" He ran a hand through his auburn locks. "Besides, you're not going to need your powers anyway. I have something else in mind."

He rose and picked up his linen napkin from the table. After a delicate dab on his lips, he shook it out, then snapped it in a fluid motion, and a marble statue—minus arms— appeared on the sidewalk next to our table. Draped around its shoulders was a short and shimmering coat of golden fur. It was fluffy and made the statue look broad and puffy.

"Fur is murder, no matter what color it is," I said, disgusted.

"It's not fur," Hades huffed. "Show a little respect. Few

mortals get to lay their eyes on this. Behold, the legendary Golden Fleece!"

"Fur or fleece, that has got to be the ugliest thing I've ever seen."

"How dare you criticize one of the most revered objects in ancient myth!"

"Would *you* wear that?" I asked, pointing to it.

"My taste leans more to the modern classics," he snapped. "But that's irrelevant. You'll need the fleece to complete your mission."

"The ram you got it from was sacrificed, wasn't it?" I asked, trying to remember the story. "That pelt probably has eons of bad karma attached to it."

He picked an imaginary speck off the sleeve of his suit jacket. "Yes, the fleece has a long history. The ram was the son of Poseidon, and so the fleece has divine powers. It was the price of Jason's kingdom; he had to brave many dangers to retrieve it and regain his throne. But don't worry about the ram—Zeus turned him into a constellation." He grinned mischievously. "Now he's a star!"

"I don't want to touch it." I crossed my arms over my chest, emphasizing my defiance.

"You'd better get over your aversion, Margaret. The fleece is the only way you can send Paulina to Tartarus, thus freeing Sharisse."

I looked at him like he was insane. "What do you want me to do, smother her with it?"

He stared at me with dark, piercing eyes. "Anyone who dares to wear the Golden Fleece is immediately dispatched to Tartarus. All you need to do is get Paulina to put on the fleece—"

"Which she won't do, if she has any sense of style or ethics," I interrupted.

"Get her to wear the fleece, Margaret, and your job is done. Sharisse returns home."

"Sorry, Hades," I retorted sharply, "but you don't truly expect me to believe this, do you? I have barely any time constraints on this assignment, no worries about turning into a bird, and all I have to do is get Paulina whoever-she-is to wear ... this?" I waved a hand at the statue and a ripple of vibrations danced over my open palm. I jerked my arm back.

"You can feel the power, can't you?" Hades said softly, menacingly. "But yes, Margaret, that's correct. And it won't take you long to find Paulina. I think you'll find she's the type you won't mind sending to me."

"I have reservations about sending anyone to you," I snapped. "And no matter what you say, I still don't trust you."

He gave me a mock pout and stirred a finger in his glass. "You're getting to be as maddening as Sharisse," he said. "She doesn't trust me either, and I never harmed a hair on her beautiful blond head. But that may change ... "

I'd forgotten about Shar for a few moments; now my fears for her came rushing back.

"What are you going to do to—"

"You have enough to worry about," Hades replied crisply, looking at a chunky gold watch on his wrist. "Don't you have a lunch date soon? I wouldn't want to delay you." He winked at me and vanished, leaving me alone at the table. The statue was gone, but a thick, black dry-cleaning bag was draped over the back of my chair.

When I could stop myself from staring at it, I remembered Jeremy. With a shaking hand, I unbuttoned the breast pocket of my jacket and pulled out my watch. Shar and I were supposed to meet him and Ian ... *now*. But Shar wasn't here. How was I going to explain that? Sudden illness? Family emergency? Eventually they'd want to reschedule, but there was no way I'd be able to produce Shar in the foreseeable future.

Wearily, I rested my elbows on the table and buried my face in my hands.

"Hey, gorgeous." I heard Jeremy's voice behind me.

I'd settled on "family emergency" as an excuse for no Shar—that would account for at least several days. I took a deep breath; tried to put on a face that registered concern, disappointment, and apology; and turned around.

Jeremy smiled down at me. He was alone.

SHAR

A River Runs Through It

I swiped my tears away. Crying like a spoiled toddler wouldn't change my situation. I kept hearing voices, babbling and moaning, but I couldn't see anything. Then the heavy darkness slowly dissipated, as though an unfelt breeze blew it away. All around me was a rocky gray landscape, and not more than five feet from where I stood, a river flowed, dark and rippling. I sniffed: no scent of urine or garbage. Okay, that ruled out sewer and subway.

My instincts told me I was supposed to cross it, but I couldn't—it was too broad, and I had not one inclination to put so much as a piggy toe into the black depths. Icky things could be living in there, like in the lake where my family vacationed when I was a little kid. It looked like such fun, swinging on the rope over the water and letting go. Only I found out that lake bottoms are mucky and suck your feet down to the ankles. It was chlorinated pools only for me after that.

"Now what?" I sniffled.

I took a few steps, stumbling on the gravel-strewn ground. The outfit was too much. *Leave it to Hades to put me in a swimsuit and heels to go cave exploring,* I fumed. And red stilettos with a pink bikini? The bathing suit, at least, was in keeping with the whole water theme. All that was missing was the stupid First Mate's hat. What I wouldn't give for sweats and sneaks right now.

Be careful what you wish for… my inner voice warned. Did I really need to learn that lesson again? At least he allowed me to keep my purse.

Dim shapes started to weave their way toward me. Little by little, I could distinguish features—of people.

Maybe they could help! *"When you're lost,"* my mom always said, *"don't be an idiot like your father; stop and ask for directions!"*

"Hello! Over here!" I hurried as fast as I could, trying not to break an ankle on the uneven terrain. As I drew closer, the shadowy people started moving toward me, and faster.

"Hi, um, do you know where I'm supposed to go? I'm new here." I gave them my sunniest smile. And lost it when I could really see them. One man had a wide, mud-caked tire imprint across his chest, and was that dried blood on his face? Two teenagers in medieval dress had arrows sticking out of them—one in the body, the other in the head, execution style. A woman, dressed in a bathrobe with only half her makeup on, tried to shove them aside. All had an ashen pallor and dark circles under their empty eyes. I'd seen enough horror movies to know the situation.

They're dead!

And the moment of death was captured in each one's appearance. An older gentleman, in ancient-warrior battle garb, might have died heroically given the big gash in his chest, but he was frowning and snarling. One of his hands reached for me, cold and clammy. I yelped and jumped, trying to back away, and broke out in a sweat as icy fingers clutched at my elbows, arms, and shoulders. *Zombie Hell!*

"Coin for Charon! Coin for Charon!" the gray shades beseeched, their faces slack. The motley crowd pushed closer, more insistent. I pulled farther away, cringing from contact.

Charon. Now where had I heard that weird name before?

Epiphany: *Doom. Gloom. Dead People. He put me in a bikini. Persephone's at a dude ranch…*

Hades sent me to Tartarus!

"Ewww! Don't touch me! Don't have any coins! Back up, personal space violations!" Steeling myself, I shoved my way through them; they felt cold like snow, yet strangely dry. I hurried down the shoreline to an empty place. They didn't follow, so I guessed they got the message. That's when I noticed all the bones. Chairs made from arm bones. A miniature temple of interwoven thigh bones. A table crafted of skulls and ribs. Even a diminutive Eiffel Tower, which I think was made of finger bones … Bleached eerily white, they were everywhere! Hoping my stomach wouldn't lose that morning's breakfast, I ran farther down the river.

When I was a safe distance away, I considered what my next action would be while hyperventilating.

Scream? *Who would care?*

Cry? *Who would care?*

Run? *Who would care?*

The infinite no-one-cares-about-me loop.

"Thanks, Hades!" I hiccuped. I didn't have a coin for Charon, so what was I going to do when the ferryman showed up? Maybe I could sweet-talk my way across the river. I wasn't in a hurry to get to the other side, but I sure didn't want to stay here with the moaners and grabbers.

WWMD? What Would Meg Do? That Death card! Some change this was!

And where was she? I'd been so caught up in myself I hadn't given a thought to her. I dreaded the idea of where Hades might send her. He was obsessed with me, and I got sent *here*. To what god-awful place would he send her? A mall? A meatpacking plant? A Barry Manilow concert? Poor Meg!

I plopped down ungracefully, not bothering to cross my legs like a lady should, for a good long pity party for both of us.

"Johnson! Sharisse Johnson!" someone called.

I perked up. *Someone* was looking for me! I didn't recognize the voice, so it wasn't Hades. Retribution would have to wait. I jumped up on top of a rock and cupped my hands around my mouth.

"Over here! I'm over here!" I waved my hands violently, although I doubted anyone could see me through the gloom.

Gradually a figure emerged. It was a man. Tall, mean, and lean. His face was uber-taut, like those athletic types on the cover of *Runner's World* magazine. They never ate carbs, drank soda, wore any shoe not ergonomically designed, or talked about anything but exercise.

Bet he's gonna be fun to deal with.

He was carrying a handwritten sign that said *Johnson, Sharisse*, just like the limo drivers at the airport.

Hey, it worked for me. I was out of here, going somewhere, and where it was, I didn't care. I hopped off my rock and tottered toward him.

"Hi!" I called as cheerily as I could.

He tucked the sign under his arm and gave me the once-over, then quirked an eyebrow.

"Don't give me that look!" I huffed. Thrusting my hands on my hips, I gave him the same critical examination. Running shorts and tee, sandals and a metal hat—with wings on them? All in gold! *And he thinks I'm dressed funny?*

He stiffened. "I'm Hermes, Messenger of the Gods. I'm here to see that you get over the Styx." He cleared his throat. "These are the rules—"

"There are rules to cross a stupid river?" I mean, talk about anal, but I guess people were dying—ha ha!—to get in. I stifled a laugh. *I must be going into shock if I'm making jokes about this.*

He compressed his lips. "If you want to stay here, fine with me. I'm only the *messenger*." Abruptly, he turned to leave.

"Wait!" I grabbed his arm. Not my sandbox, so I had to play the game his way. Whatever it took not to stay here. "I'm sorry. What are the rules? And what's with all the bones?"

Hermes sniffed. "The bones belong to them." He jerked his head toward a clutch of gray shades skulking near a candle stand made of skulls and spines. "Bodies and souls don't always stay together."

I wrapped my arms around myself. *This* body and soul were going to remain intact.

"Who makes furniture out of them?"

He gave me a withering look. "Those who can't cross have a lot of time on their hands. That's what happens when you don't have the fare. Which brings me to rule number one." He held up a finger. "Don't give coins to the souls who beg. They can't cross the River Styx to the Elysian Fields because they don't have the fare to pay Charon. And it's not up to you to give it to them. They are condemned to wander between the afterlife and the world of the living forever."

"I don't have any money to give away." *Unless my bikini has a secret pocket with a coin inside, which it doesn't, that won't be a problem.*

"Wait." He removed his helmet and checked his teeth in the reflection.

I gestured for him to continue. This mortal had uncomfortable physical needs that a powder room could address.

"Where was I?" He tapped his right foot, and the little wings on his sandals fluttered madly. "Sorry!" he whispered to them. They quieted and gracefully flicked like butterflies.

Okay. It's not like I don't talk to my darling shoes, but he gets a reaction!

"The rules?" I prompted, forcing my attention back to the conversation about me getting out of here.

"Don't interrupt and we'll get through these quickly. Hades' protocols must be followed." Hermes cleared his throat. "Don't give coins to the lost souls, no singing, no animals, please observe a moment of silence, children must be accompanied by an adult, tipping is allowed, and cash only. And proper payment is to be tendered after boarding but before commencement of service." He smiled at me like I was a simpleton.

And I was supposed to do...what? I didn't see any children. Why no singing—would it ruin the mood of despair? Animals?? And a moment of silence for...? How could I tip with no money? I'd spent the last of my money at Century 21 for a blouse I really didn't need. I rubbed my temples. A major migraine was starting to devour my brain.

Mommy! Or better yet, Meg! She'd make sense of this guy. God. Greek mutant. What*ever*.

"I think that's all of them." He smoothed his shirt, watching his biceps flex.

How could there be more? I wanted to bang my head against a brick wall, but I inhaled deeply, trying to calm my rising irritation. "Thank you for telling me the rules, Hermes, but I don't have any money to give to Charon. Hades zipped me off without giving me time to make sure I had the fare."

Because a girl should always carry around gold pieces for a sudden excursion to the Underworld.

"Haven't you been listening?" he shouted, startling me. "That's why I'm here!" He puffed up his chest.

"Of course I've been listening! You told me the rules— no giving dead souls money, no animals, no singing, and all the rest of the rules that don't apply to me because I DON'T HAVE ANY MONEY!" I shouted back.

Geez, the service in this place was seriously lacking.

"I think I should add another ten reps to my abdominal routine," he murmured, tapping his waistline, which had less fat than a piece of iceberg lettuce.

"Can we just go? I think I hear the boat." A soft slapping sound was growing steadily louder. A long, wide rowboat, sleekly black and outlined with gold coins, glided up smoothly, stopping at a large flat rock in front of me. A ghostly figure draped in torn, moldy linen stood in the back, holding a long pole in hands covered by rags. The figure didn't move or make a sound.

We stared at each other. Guess I had to be the adult here, although I was positive Charon was my senior by, oh, several millennia at minimum.

"Hello, Charon. I'm Sharisse. Nice to meet you." I held out my hand. Good manners are proper in any situation, after all.

A thumb, looking pretty pink for a guy who was supposed to be dead, jerked to the back of the skiff where a huge mound of gold coins lay, gleaming dully in the dusk. Several cascaded down as the boat bumped against the rock.

"Save the hello for someone who cares. Get your lazy carcass into the boat and throw the fare on top of the pile. Stupid coins are rolling all over the place."

If being down here made one eternally PMSing, no thank you! I looked pointedly at Hermes, then gestured to Charon with a jerk of my head. Hermes could worry about the fare.

"Oh! Here." He held out a golden branch, as long as my arm and slightly heavy.

"Uh, I believe it costs a gold coin to cross, unless you two have a deal worked out?" I asked. Was this a taste of what my undead life was going to be like? Hades was wrong—this *was* hell—and everyone was an idiot. I'd shortly be insane, wandering around giving the rocks names and drooling.

Hermes squared his sculpted shoulders. "You aren't dead, so Charon can't take a gold coin. A bough from the Tree of Life is the fare for living souls. Here."

He thrust the branch at me, and with a flutter of his cutesy sandals, flew up, up, and away. At least he didn't pop, flash, or poof out. I turned back to Charon.

"Here you go." I offered the branch. I couldn't quite reach him, since he was almost all the way in the back of the boat.

The dark hood turned my way. An arm raised, with only the fingertips showing. They wiggled, demanding I put the branch in them. I couldn't reach over the boat, and I thought the rule was not to give the fare to Charon until I was in the boat; would he take off with it once he had it and stiff me for the ride?

"Get in!" he growled.

What choice did I have? Standing in the gloom all by myself didn't appeal to me. And I was hungry. Maybe I could raid the fridge at Hades' place. He used food in his seductions—hopefully he'd stocked up just for me. Oh, the price of gluttony! Gingerly, I stepped into the boat, trying not to tip it.

Oooh, water, rocking motion, full bladder!

"Aren't you going to help me?" I demanded as I struggled to keep my balance.

Charon cocked his head to the side, implying the *duh* look. "I'm here to pilot the boat, not play ship's purser."

"But I'm not—"

He showed me the hand and turned away.

That's it!

I showed him my secret fast pitch, smacking him on the side of the head with the branch.

"Oh!" I breathed, à la Marilyn Monroe. "I'm soooooo sorry!"

The figure whipped around, the gray tatters swirling around his body. Rags didn't look good on mummies, and it wasn't working here.

"You did that on purpose!" Charon whipped off the hood—and then *she* glared at me.

My mouth dropped open.

"No, I'm *not* Charon. He's on vacation. I'm filling in while he gets some R&R."

"So who are you?" I asked.

She flipped her long, silky black hair over her shoulder. "I'm Aglaia."

Hmmm. If I admitted I didn't know her, she was probably going to act all pissy, like all the gods did when you didn't know their names, histories, where their temples were, what they did, who they hated, and whatever. What should I say?

She let out a long suffering sigh. "Can't you tell?"

Pop quiz!

"Uh, give me a sec—"

She jammed the pole into the muddy bottom and snarled, "Fires of Olympus! You mortals are so stupid! I'm one of the Graces, but I guess you don't hear much about us. It's not like we're one of the big gods, like Zeus, oh no"—

her face took on a really scary sneer—"gods forbid!" She snorted, then tossed her head. "*Some* people are jealous of our talents and make sure we don't get our fair share of time on Olympus."

I smiled back at her, a sympathetic look on my face.

Her hands fisted and she ripped off the rags. Her dress, made entirely of gold coins, clinked. That had to weigh a ton. Literally.

"We sing. And dance." She held out her hands, palms up. Another agonizing second of silence. "For the *gods*."

"So Agla, do you entertain only on Mount Olympus?" *It always helps to show interest in other peoples' lives.*

"It's Ag-lee-ay-a," she huffed.

"Sure thing, Aggie," I replied. I couldn't bring myself to call her Ag-whatever.

She gritted her teeth. "Just call me Splendor. And no, no singing and dancing on Olympus or anywhere lately."

Uh oh, another Greek tragedy. I put on my best tell-me-your-poor-wretched-tale face, even though inside I was thinking, *here we go again with the sob story.*

"I entertained all the gods, on Olympus or wherever they requested my talents. Then *she* got mad at me"— Splendor snapped her fingers—"and now I have to hide out here until she gets over it." She glanced around, grimacing. "Luckily, Charon is a friend. He let me take over here for a song while he's away."

Let's see . . . a ticked-off goddess making threats. I could think of three: Persephone, of course, but she'd never allow another good-looking goddess, or female anything, near Hades; Demeter, her mother, but she wouldn't want Persephone mad at her for sending pretty Splendor into her territory—she'd almost made that mistake already with me; and that left the queen bee.

"Hera?" I whispered.

"Shhhhhh!" Splendor hissed. "Don't say her name! She hasn't figured out where I am, and I'd like to keep it that way, thank you! She has spies."

Well, this was getting interesting, but it would have to wait for another time. "You'll have to tell me the whole story," I whispered conspiratorially, "but, ah, first I've got to get to wherever it is I'm going. Girly things to take care of." I promptly sat down on a bench and jiggled my legs.

She merely grunted, pulling the pole out of the mud. A desperate soul who had been hovering in the background—and who looked suspiciously like a recently dead senator—made a frantic leap for the boat. Splendor whacked him with the pole.

"You want on the boat, you either hand over the coin, or you go through *me*!" The poor shade fell into knee-deep water and was promptly sucked under, black bubbles furiously rising where he used to be.

"That's what happens when you spend all your retirement money!"

With that, Splendor pushed the boat away from the shore and resumed rowing. I shuddered, glad I'd never even dipped a finger in the river.

She didn't spare a glance for me.

Guessing she wasn't interested in becoming acquainted, I opened my purse. All the yakking had worn off my new fave gloss, Tangerine Tantrum. I pulled it and my gold monogrammed compact out, reapplied, and smacked my lips. Much better! A girl could face almost any dire situation when she looked fabulous. Perfect makeup was a courage booster. Maybe I'd die fighting, but I'd look good doing it.

"What is that?!" demanded Splendor.

I jumped. "What?"

She pointed to the lip-gloss.

"This?" I waved it at her.

"I smell oranges." She squinted at me, sniffed, then widened her large aqua eyes. "And it makes your lips shine!"

I shifted, snagging my bikini bottom on the rough-hewn seat. With all the gold he had, you'd think Charon would have parted with a few coins to have the boat refurbished for his passengers. We did pay, after all. Pulling free, I nodded at Splendor.

"Yeah, it is amazing! It's the newest line by Shiseido. It's called 'Fruits of Temptation.' I got this at the salon when I worked for Ark—never mind. But it lasts for a long time."

Splendor's eyes bugged out. "When I get out of here, I'm going to get some."

Hmmm. Forced to wear a raggy uniform in a skanky damp cave, ferrying irritable dead souls—except me, I didn't count because I wasn't dead—and hiding from a powerful goddess with a grudge. Could this lip-gloss get me out of here?

Splendor hungrily eyed the tube.

Oh yeah, she wants it.

She resumed poling across in silence, although she kept glancing at me covertly with a speculative but guarded gaze.

When I opened my mouth to speak, she turned away and hummed a tune. A clear indication to shut up.

Well! Ever since that night in the subway, it had been one person after another giving me the cold shoulder or a hard time. Jeremy was the first. Then Persephone, Demeter, and now Splendor and Hermes. The anti-Shar fan club was rapidly expanding. Why was there animosity everywhere I went? Had Hades hexed me for his own purposes? Maybe a little, but I had to be honest with myself and admit that maybe I wasn't overly likable. I'd begun to perceive that being friends with Alana, Kate, and Caroline was like being part of a plague; people respected the damage you could do, but they never welcomed you.

I was shallow. Or at least, I used to be. I'd learned a lot about myself during the past couple of months. It wasn't all about looking the best—it was about *being* the best; the best friend, the best person.

I missed Meg.

The boat thumped gently on a dock of black stone. Swallowing a few gulps, I gathered my purse and looked around. A long, shiny black marble pathway lead off to the—surprise! Black marble palace in the black distance. Not a single living thing in sight. With a mother-in-law like Demeter, whom he abhorred, I guess it was understandable that Hades wouldn't want any reminders of her in the Underworld. But it sure made for dismal surroundings.

I stood carefully, not wanting to end up in the hungry water and risk being sucked under like the dead senator by who-knows-what, or experience bladder leak. Rivers don't have rest stops. Hades better have a bathroom or I was in a tight spot—no trees! Open view!

My feet on solid ground, I turned to Splendor.

"Before you leave, here." I held out the lip-gloss.

She looked at me suspiciously.

"Take it," I said.

Her eyes narrowed to two slits. If I did that, I'd definitely have wrinkles in a year or two.

"What do you want in exchange?"

"Nothing. It's yours."

She didn't believe it. "You don't want *anything* from me."

"Can you get me out of here?" I asked.

"No."

I slapped the gloss into her hand. "So there's nothing you have that I want. See ya!" I gently stepped off the black stone dock. After a few moments, I heard the slow slap of the water as Splendor maneuvered the boat away. I gave her a tentative wave that she didn't return. She only stared at me from her spot on the water. I turned to go.

"Sharisse!" she called.

I whirled around.

"If you're ever, you know, down by the water … " She trailed off.

Poor Splendor. How long had she been stuck down here? I waved again. "I'll call you!"

She nodded, then lifted her pole. A second later the boat was swallowed by mist.

I made a friend! I thought, smiling to myself, and started down the path.

I hadn't gotten far when a figure slowly wobbled toward

me. Being on this side, I knew that at least he wasn't going to beg me for money. I squinted, trying to see better in the gloom. White hair pulled into a ponytail. A Humpty Dumpty figure. Buckled shoes. I recognized that pasty-looking face.

With a huge smile, he held out his hand, which matched the tissue-paper-thin skin on his face. Gingerly, I shook it.

"My dear! Such a pleasure to meet you! Benjamin Franklin, at your service." He made a courtly bow over my hand.

I was right! I was shaking hands with Benjamin Franklin!

Wait. What could *he* have done to end up *here*? Did this mean the only "here" in the hereafter was in Tartarus? I shivered at the thought. Eternity with Hades. All that time wasted in Sunday School when I could have slept in.

"You know who I am?" I asked.

"Of course, Miss Johnson. Hades informed me of your arrival and insisted I meet you personally. I would have been here sooner, but Charon and I always end up arguing." He leaned closer, whispering conspiratorially, "A penny saved is a penny earned, but he takes it a bit too far. No charity in him, that one."

"Uh huh." If he didn't know that Charon was on vacation and Splendor was filling in, I wasn't going to say anything. Or start any trouble. And what did someone say to an iconic figure in American history?

"Do you know that you're on the hundred dollar bill?" I asked. *Brilliant as usual, Sharisse.*

He preened. "Yes, Hades allows me to hear a few things from the mortal plane. But come." He took my elbow and led me toward the castle. "His lordship's prepared a special suite just for you!"

"I'll bet he has," I mumbled.

His eyes darted nervously over my indecent attire. "I'm sure you'd like to, um, freshen up."

No, I'd like to get dressed and use proper facilities, but I was not going to discuss that with a founding father. We walked along, old Ben humming a tune slightly off-key. Apparently musical ability wasn't one of his many talents.

I turned to look at him, frowning. "And why are *you* here? Weren't you a good man? Church-going, charitable and everything?" He stopped and I followed suit.

Ben smiled serenely. "Even saints have been known to falter, Miss Johnson. But I'm not here because of an indiscretion. Hades and I have a gentleman's agreement. I wanted to meet the great people of history, and in return, I keep order in his realm. I shall only be here a thousand years, and then I'm off to other places and things, which I'm afraid I'm not at liberty to discuss."

"Yes, I know all about the nondisclosure clause and his work-for-hire programs."

We started walking again to the palace/castle/mansion/temple/outrageous abode of Hades. Everything was over-the-top with this guy. And here was one of the greatest people in history, acting as his estate manager. Only Hades.

"Who else is here?" I asked as we reached the—what else—massive black doors.

"Many people. Some just pass through, others stay for a while. You'll meet many of them." Stopping at the morbid-looking doors in front of us, Ben laid his right palm on one and it swung open on silent hinges. "The domicile will recognize you once you meet with Hades." He ushered me in. "You are free to roam about, but I must warn you to beware of two things. First, the Pit." He gave me a chilling look over his wire-rimmed glasses. "It is to be avoided at all costs. The Titans are imprisoned down there and with good reason. They are wily, deceptive, and self-serving, and have surrounded themselves with the scum of both Olympus and Earth. While they are bound and cannot get out, anyone can venture in. If you do, you are on your own." Ben gave me a stern, fatherly look. "Do not expect anyone to rescue you."

I threw up my hands in surrender. "Got it. Not going in to see bad boys. What's the other warning?"

"Lastly, beware of those who talk of escape routes. Do not heed these wild tales. This is Hades' realm and I assure you, if there was a way out, he would have found and eliminated it. He is no man's fool."

But would he be a fool for a woman ... like me?

M∈G
Half Full

Under normal circumstances I wouldn't have minded an afternoon alone with Jeremy, but things were far from normal. He stood there, the sun behind him highlighting his tight, low-riding black jeans and worn leather jacket; the same outfit he'd had on when we first met in that pizza shop.

"You seem ... distracted," he said, tucking a dark lock behind his ear. He pulled a chair over to mine and sat, draping his arm around me. "Is everything all right?"

I leaned my head onto his shoulder, looking up into his sky-blue eyes and hoping they would take me to some place far away. It didn't work. I closed my eyes and pressed my cheek into his shoulder, breathing deep. Old leather, patchouli, *Jeremy*. And here I was again—watching my words and keeping secrets.

"Yeah. Just school and things, you know. Too much going on to keep track of."

Besides everything that had just gone down with Hades, I was bothered that Jeremy showed up alone and didn't ask about Shar. While the omission made me uneasy, I didn't bring her up; if the subject wasn't discussed, I wouldn't have to lie about why she wasn't here. Instead, I asked him about his fall schedule at NYU and what classes we might have together. He ordered a salad and finished my hummus plate; I couldn't eat.

To my relief, he had plans for the night, and sadly, I was glad when we parted ways at my subway stop an hour later.

"If everything goes well tonight, I'll have some good news to text you later." He smiled mischievously and ran his fingers through my hair, pulling me close for a kiss before allowing me to get off the train. It took every ounce of self control I had to smile and wave goodbye until the train entered the tunnel.

On the way back to the dorm, I rewound Shar's disappearance in my head, and then started walking faster. I wanted to be back in our room. Not that there would be any answers to our problem amongst Shar's things, but I had a desperate desire to get back and just feel her presence.

The dormitory was pretty empty when I got there; a lot of students went home on the weekends, then returned Sunday night for classes on Monday. Praying I wouldn't have to meet any eyes or make any small talk, I strode down the hall and rode the thankfully empty elevator to the third floor.

The institutional, cream-colored walls were punctuated every few feet with solid-looking green doors, and every now and again music blared out of some of them as I passed. A bulletin board overflowed with numbers for tutoring, jobs, books for sale, and summer-abroad programs. I got to our door having seen no one, and with a sigh of relief I unlocked it and pushed inside.

I'd left my laptop on; the screen saver, a slide show of the band Elysian Fields, renewed itself over and over. Posters lined the walls on my side of the room, so that not even a hairline of the standard-issue paint could be seen.

Shar's side of the room was empty.

I started hyperventilating.

Calm down! This won't help either of you! I scolded myself.

When I was in control, I nudged the door shut with my hip, threw my purse and the fleece—still in its garment bag—on my bed, and stumbled into the emptiness that used to be Shar's space. I opened every drawer in her desk, in her dresser.

Nothing.

Nothing hung in the closet.

Nothing tucked beneath the naked mattress.

Nothing hidden under the bed—not even dust.

An infinite circle of nothing.

I wandered over to my densely packed side, which contrasted harshly with the starkness of hers. Shoving the stack of textbooks on my desk to one side, I sifted through the papers underneath, hoping to catch a glimpse of one of Shar's powder-puff pink Post-it notes, but once again, nothing.

Continuing the frantic search, I tackled my dresser, going

through every stuffed drawer and every bottle and trinket on top, searching for something, *anything,* that was hers. All I found were my own clothes, black and purple nail polish that Shar would die before wearing, perfume she said smelled like a funeral parlor, and a tangle of Lucite necklaces.

I felt chilled. I'd reached that numbing sense of acceptance you get when something has gone horribly wrong; a kind of autopilot. All I could do was stare at Shar's half of the room.

She was ... gone.

At some point, it got dark outside, and I must've crawled into bed and fallen asleep, but I couldn't remember when. All I knew was that when I opened my eyes, pale sunlight was streaming in through the window. When I managed to squint at the clock, 7:04 blinked out in insistent digital lines. Horrified, I jumped up.

School!

I was still in my clothes from yesterday, and while I'd kicked off my Westwoods, I hadn't bothered to take off my makeup. I shoved on Converse sneakers and grabbed books, notebooks, and pens, stuffing them into my messenger bag. I dropped it over my shoulder, pulled my purse off the floor, and headed out. Catching sight of myself in the full-length mirror screwed to the door, I made a disgusted noise at my reflection. Black liner was smeared under my eyes, and my hair was sticking up in all directions. I found a fedora and smashed it over my dark mop, then left before I could start thinking about trying to fix anything. Shar always said I looked like the walking dead—now she was right.

Out in the street, I shambled over to the academic

building. The cool, fresh air woke me up a bit and I tried to look at everything logically. Maybe Jeremy not asking about Shar had nothing to do with Shar's disappearance. Maybe Ian had canceled and he was embarrassed, so when he saw that I was alone too, he didn't bother to bring it up. But what about that empty room? Would she need *all* her stuff in Tartarus? How long was Hades planning on keeping her?

What would I say if anyone asked me where she was? Shar was in my Calc and Lit classes and had other friends besides me. I decided to go with yesterday's plan—Shar had a family emergency and left, I assumed, for her parent's house in Bronxville. Hopefully no one would want me to elaborate. Thus armed, in I went.

The first bell rang just as I got to the second floor. Kids in the hallway started moving left and right, into the empty classrooms. Girls and guys turned to me as they passed. The girls smirked; I was a walking wreck. The guys stared a moment, some of them smiling slightly, before moving on. I wanted to demand that someone—anyone—say they'd seen Shar.

I slipped into the room past Mr. Lazarus, who was sitting at his desk taking attendance, checking off names in his grade book as people came in. A few people looked my way but said nothing. Once I was settled, I kept my eyes glued to Shar's desk and tried not to swallow my tongue when Maddie Harris plopped herself down into it; she usually sat behind Shar. My eyes shot to Laz, who was particular about people keeping their seats, but he made no move to correct anything.

Don't freak out. It's just a seat.

Then he got up from his desk and started babbling an

intro to the day's Calc lesson. I bent my head to my notebook and scribbled something, anything, to look busy. It was bad enough that Maddie was sitting in Shar's seat and that Laz said nothing about it, but without lifting my head, I felt sure the dozen or so guys in the class, in between taking notes, were glancing my way.

With a shiver I remembered the rules of the Siren game. *Males will be drawn to you*, Hades said. And they had been, even before our deal was renewed. Thanks to Shar and the mini-makeover she gave me—a sharp, sleek haircut coupled with an acceptable dose of color—I felt a new confidence. Whatever the reason, Siren superpower or revamped look, I'd been handling the attention I was getting. But now I had to be on guard; my powers were back, and even though they weren't as strong without Shar around, I'd have to be careful and use them only for the assignment.

The assignment! I was so consumed with Shar that I hadn't given a thought to Paulina Swan-whatever. I'd have to deal with that later. Right now I had to get through Calculus and avoid entrancing any of the males that crossed my path: classmates, teachers, janitors. Unless I engaged them with my voice, they'd leave me alone and I'd have no reason to bother with them.

Laz droned on and on, writing problems and page numbers on the board. Dutifully I jotted them down, gripping my pencil hard and digging it into the page. The point snapped under the pressure and I let out a small but exasperated sigh.

Laz turned around, caught sight of me, and smiled for a second before going back to his blackboard. I dropped my gaze quickly and carefully folded the flap of my messenger bag back to get another pencil. My hand was deep in one of the pockets when I heard a soft *plip*. As I straightened up, a neatly folded note was resting on top of my open Calc book.

I slowly slipped it off the desk, flicking my glance between it and Laz. Unfolding the paper as quietly as I could, I read:

Me, Jordan & Sarah r going 2 Starbucks @ 3:15, can u come?

Jordan. Sarah. There was only one other person in that trio—Trey Addington-North. Cautiously, I lifted up my head and turned to the right, only to see him staring at me from the next desk, a hopeful expression on his face. I raised the note a little, and he grinned and raised his eyebrows as if to ask, *Well?*

I stifled a laugh behind my hand. Blond, perpetually Bahama-tanned, and status-conscious Trey of the hyphen-ated last name was asking *me* if I would join him and his pals for their daily latte slurp at Starbucks? I wondered how Jordan and Sarah would feel about *that?* My guess was not too happy, since they'd never liked me. As for Trey, we'd sat next to each other in this class since September and I was lucky if he would pass worksheets to me.

Before I could stop myself, I looked over at him again, expecting to see the superior expression he usually wore when speaking to the unwashed masses. Maybe he'd be laughing that I actually believed he was serious. Instead, I found him grinning expectantly.

The bell rang.

Grabbing my bag and shoving books, papers, pencils and whatever into it, I wrangled my way to the front of the room, a clutch of guys straggling around like shy groupies after a rock star. They kept their distance, although they hung in the doorway. Was this Hades' idea of diminished powers? Either that or I was totally working the neurotic mental patient look.

"Gentlemen, don't you have somewhere to go?" Laz said to them—they were blocking the entrance, preventing the next class from coming in. When they didn't budge, he went over to shoo them away and I seized my chance.

I glided over to the desk where Laz kept his grade book and discreetly scanned the roster of names, written neatly in his block printing in alphabetical order. *Harris, Hernandez, Jackson ... Kwan?* No Johnson, Sharisse. An uncomfortable tingling raced up my spine. I read it again. And again. She simply wasn't there. We'd had two tests, five quizzes, and God knew how many homeworks so far for this quarter. I knew she'd done them—we studied for the last test together and she beat my score by three points, but now there was no record of it.

"Margaret?" I jumped when Mr. Lazarus said my name.

I looked up from the grade book and found him standing on the opposite side of the desk, smiling as he had when I broke my pencil during class. Hades and I would definitely have to have a chat.

"Do you need something?"

I mashed my lips together, somehow turned them into a smile, and shook my head. "Nope, I'm good." Then before he could say anything further, I spun on my heel and headed out the door. Thankfully, my fan club had dispersed and gone to whatever class they had next. But I hadn't escaped completely.

"Meg!" a male voice shouted. Trey jogged up to me. "So, can you come?" he asked.

This is ridiculous! Last week you wouldn't give me the time of day! I put my face in my bag as if I were looking for something.

"It's my treat," he added.

"I can't," I mumbled. "I'm meeting my boyfriend after school … and if I don't leave now I'll be late for French!" I ran for the stairwell, not looking back.

Classes proved uneventful. In French I sat in the back of the room off Madame Cratier's radar, fielded a question in Social Studies without consequences, and survived a lab— with two guys on my team—by not making any requests or issuing any orders. At lunch I sat alone, burying my face in my notes to discourage any conversation. In Lit, again, Shar's seat was occupied by someone else, and she was MIA from Miss Winning's grade book.

When the final bell rang, I made my way down to Shar's locker—there was one last thing I wanted to check. No one had asked me about her, and I hadn't brought her up—yet. I wove my way through the milling students who chatted as they walked to their lockers, all the while search- ing for Alana Dean.

I spotted her at her locker, Caroline and Kate close by. I approached the group with trepidation. They were talk- ing and giggling, and when I heard Alana's voice, it dredged up the memory of that last text, the one that Shar read to me before she was taken away: *Going out with your vampire roomie again?*

They ignored me as I sidled up to them, and I stood there for several seconds, apparently invisible.

"Alana," I began. She didn't turn around right away, but I could tell she heard me—or at least her friends did, because they stole glances at me, whispered, and snickered.

When she finally did face me, she regarded me like I was something stuck to the bottom of her shoe.

"Alana, um, can I talk to you for a second?" I asked.

"Why?" she snapped, a sneer on her face. I wanted this to be quick, but she was determined to turn it into a sideshow. Months of Shar's waning interest must've really taken its toll. Caroline and Kate looked down their noses at me, covering their mouths to unsuccessfully mute hasty giggles.

"Just for a second."

"I don't have time for you—"

"It's about Shar," I cut her off.

She looked confused.

"Have you … heard from her?" It was a good place to start.

She shook her head and narrowed her muddy eyes at me. "Who?"

"Shar. Sharisse Johnson."

"I don't know any Sharisse." Alana tossed her long brown hair back.

"Look, I know things haven't been the same between you two," I said, choosing my words carefully, "but it's really not her fault—"

"You look," she said, annoyed. "I don't know what you're

59

talking about. I don't know any Sharisse Johnson. None of us knows any Sharisse Johnson." She inclined her head toward the girls, who shook their heads and laughed. "It's bad enough to know Meg Wiley!"

It was too rude.

"Yes you do," I insisted, stepping up to her and putting my hand on the locker next to hers. "She's your friend, my roommate, God help me. And this"—I banged on the locker door—"is her locker. She … "

The trio had backed up a step. Alana cracked a smile and then howled with laughter, her friends quick to join her.

"OMG, you are *insane*!" she tittered. "This"—and she banged the locker just like I did—"is Caroline's locker." She pulled Caroline to her side, and said, "Prove it to her. Open it." Caroline dutifully twirled the combination and the locker popped open. Pictures of Caroline, Alana, Kate, and some guys were plastered in neat rows. Nothing of Shar's resided there.

"See," Alana went on, "I guess being in a room all by yourself for so long has affected your mind. Better go to the nurse and see if she can give you something for that."

The three of them laughed again. Caroline slammed her locker shut and they walked off, leaving me standing there, horrified. The skin on the back of my neck prickled and stung.

He erased her! Is it permanent? Is this what'll happen to me?

I didn't want to think about anything the future might hold in store. I figured that thanks to Alana's networking, the female population of the school would soon think I was a loon and Hades' wonderful gift would have the male segment panting at my heels. Together, those things would be a lethal combination.

Eventually, I made my weary way back to my half-empty dorm room; there was nowhere else to go. Inside, I was once again confronted by Shar's complete absence.

Suddenly I heard a loud buzz coming from the direction of my desk. In the space I'd made last night by swiping my books aside rested an iPhone—the newest generation of the one Hades had given to us for our first assignment. It buzzed and buzzed, and the screen blinked with a red light. I snatched it up and a text flashed on the screen.

> Margaret, I thought this would be of use. And just in case,
> I took the liberty of blocking some of the features
> so there won't be any awkward calls to anyone who
> shouldn't be involved in our business, like last time.
> H.

My hand started to shake and the thing buzzed again. A new text popped up.

> That's no way to treat the fleece! Hang it up!

"Hang it up?!" I squawked, throwing the iPhone on my bed and snatching up the fleece. "Here's what I think of your nephew *von pelt*!" I lifted the thing above my head, not bothering to take it out of its garment bag, and hurled it toward the center of the room.

One second it was hurtling through space, the next it was ... gone!

I felt ... strange. Light. Not a lightening of the heart, but a physical kind of light that made me dizzy. My vision blurred and the room started to get dark. I stumbled toward the dresser, hoping to hold onto it, but I never made it. A surge, like a quick drop in an elevator, overtook me. I blinked, and the dorm room, like the fleece, was gone.

Where was I?

The first thing I became aware of was the presence of two people. I strained to hear their muffled voices. One of them, definitely a girl, was crying. Hard. I couldn't make out what she was saying. Suddenly, the dimness was swept away and I saw them.

Hades … and Shar!

SHAR

You've Been Hired!

As I walked down hallways lit with torches, I discovered that Hades' palace was surprisingly light. Almost warm. The black marble was only on the outside; the inside was a pure, dazzling white. Who knew?

"And here you are," said Ben congenially, leading me through double doors into an immense room. "Your rooms are to the left of the throne. Like I said, wander and explore to your heart's content. I highly recommend the Elysian Fields. You can either take a door right from the palace, or use the pedestrian walkway leading from the dock."

"The fields are kind of like heaven, right?" I asked.

He nodded with a beaming smile. "Yes! I'm often found there. That's where the most fascinating people are."

"Like who?" This was getting interesting.

He clapped his hands. "Let's see. So many I can't name them all. Marilyn Monroe is appearing on the stage, Caruso is, of course, at the opera house, Van Gogh won't talk to anyone, so forget him." A soft chiming sound escaped from his pocket. He withdrew a pocket watch that sparked a painful reminder of Meg.

"Dear me! Would you look at the time? I'm supposed to be teaching Miss Cleopatra chess. I've got to run!" He tucked the watch into its pocket. I grabbed his arm before he could run off.

"*The* Cleopatra?" I choked. Talk about an original fashion icon.

"Yes, yes, I mustn't tarry. She gets ever so temperamental when I'm late. I shall see you later, my dear."

"Wait! One last question!" I pressed. "If you're dead, how come you're not…you know, a pile of bones or a shade?"

Ben paused and took off his glasses. Withdrawing a snowy hankie, he cleaned them while he spoke. "I guess it can't hurt to tell you how things work down here, as long as I don't go into any personal details. Tartarus is the land of the dead. If a soul does not possess the requisite coin to cross the river, it is doomed to remain on the far side, away from the Elysian Fields. Its mortal coil slowly rots until it becomes a shade. Hence the bones."

He straightened his waistcoat with its shiny brass buttons. "Once a soul crosses, it is rewarded by retaining its vessel. You might say I've been preserved, like strawberry jam." His eyes twinkled. "Still as sweet—at least for a time. Those still living, like you, can only cross with a branch from the

Tree of Life, which protects your body. An added bonus is that time has no meaning here, so you won't age."

Time might not pass here, but my life on the mortal plane was still ticking away—without me!

"And now I must go." Ben gallantly raised my hand in his. His skin held no warmth nor pulsing blue veins. It was a bit on the creepy side, but I smiled as he left a chaste, dry kiss on the back of my hand. The doors closed behind him and I was alone.

The room was humongous. Large fireplaces threw off gaily dancing flames but somehow the temperature was perfect—no hot or cold spots. At the far end was a huge white marble throne, just like you'd see in a Hollywood movie version of a Greek god's temple. Hades was a god, so I guess a throne wasn't out of character. But it wasn't solid gold, or the black marble he seemed to favor for everything else; it was so *typical*. I thought he'd be more original.

Then my eye caught sight of a young man lounging on the throne. He sat crossways, as if he couldn't be bothered to sit up straight in this seat of power. I cautiously moved closer.

"Hades isn't here right now." He barely glanced at me.

"I can see that." The words almost stuck in my throat. This guy was a breath-stealer. Whoever he was, he could be the poster boy for sex and sin with that bod. Low-slung jeans, bare chest, messy blond hair. He looked up and I almost expired. His gray eyes were magical. I stepped closer.

Ooooh.

With a raised eyebrow, he gave my outfit a critical look. If there were curtains or drapes, I would have torn them down and wrapped them around myself. Feeling uncomfortable reminded me of another pressing problem.

"Um, I'll be right back." I scuttled off to the left of the throne, as Ben had instructed, and through the doors. I couldn't have skidded to a stop any harder if I'd been wearing Goodyears on my feet: a sumptuous suite in a rainbow of pink—yeah, yeah—and all *my stuff* artfully arranged around the room. The photo of Meg and me when we'd gotten out of the apartment Hades set us up in. The crystal dragon my dad bought for me when I was ten. Everything.

First things first. I flung off the heels and ran to a door. Bathroom. Good.

Business taken care of—*where did he get towels that thick and fluffy?*—I yanked open another door. Closet. Filled with all my shoes, purses, scarves, and belts, but *no clothes*. At least, none that were mine. Instead there were bikinis, Grecian gowns with one naked shoulder, and other filmy, flimsy things I doubted I'd ever have the courage—or, when it came to Hades, the desire—to wear.

The pig!

I pulled out the most discreet gown I could find—white with gold trim, just above the knee, one-shouldered—and donned it. I looked like a virginal sacrifice. Huh. I guess if Persephone was always in black, he'd want to look at something different. I slid open a drawer.

My underwear??? Now I was going to hurt him. *NO ONE* touched my underwear. It was sacrosanct, it was personal, it was *MINE*! I threw on the most conservative pair, plain white bikinis, and stormed into the throne room where

Mr. Yummy was eating grapes, à la a mythology scene from a Renaissance painting.

"Like your little love nest?" he asked sardonically.

"Excuse me?" I fisted my hands. "Where is that soul-sucking, sleazy, conniving snake?" Whipping my head around, I hollered, "Oh, just you wait, Hades! No one touches my underwear! And where are my clothes?!" I stomped and growled at the empty room. Mr. Yummy sat up straight.

"You're not Hades' new girlfriend?" he asked, both eyebrows raised.

"Does it *sound* like I'm his girlfriend?"

He shrugged. "Down here, anything's possible."

I narrowed my eyes. "Never."

His smile was stunning. "Great! Hi, I'm Cas—"

"Hi Caz. I'm Shar. When does the despot return? It's time for a take-down."

Caz laughed. "I think maybe you could do it, too." His face sobered. "I don't know when he's coming—"

"I'm already back," purred Hades, gliding into the room. "Oh, *mon amour*, my love slave. I see you found your room. Do you like it?"

I took a deep breath to tell him exactly what I thought about the situation, but he held up a finger and I was frozen. He turned to Caz.

"Leave. And do not let me hear that you are filling my little sunshine's ears with nonsense."

Caz rose leisurely and strolled his gorgeous, half-naked self out the doors, which boomed shut behind him.

"Now you may continue." Hades took his throne and smiled down like some beneficent prince.

"You slug!"

"I thought you called me a snake." His eyes danced.

Now I was really mad. *You touch my personal things, eavesdrop on conversations, and make me shut up?* How did Persephone put up with him, six-pack abs and drop-dead looks notwithstanding?

Frigid antipathy settled in. "I've changed my mind. I don't want to insult the snake, and I can't think of anything lower than a slug at the moment."

So there.

His response? A deep, throaty laugh that echoed off the walls. "*Mi amore*, I am going to enjoy your visit tremendously. You are such a spitfire."

I'd like to burn your a—

"I just finished up with Margaret. Let's talk about your part of the assignment. You will be my companion for however long you are here."

"Companion?" I gasped. "How will you explain that to Persephone when she returns? And what do you mean, assignment?"

He sighed dramatically and made little circles with his hand. "Mere formalities." He rose from his throne and moved closer, circling around me. I stepped away, not trusting him. He only chuckled. "Don't worry about Margaret. She knows what she has to do. Allowances have been made for your absence. You"—he returned to his throne—"will act as my hostess, and be pleasant and courteous to my guests. I'll let you know when you are expected to be available. And since I'm blessed with your feminine company, I think a party is in order. This will be more fun than that juvenile affair at your school. Now, we need a theme. Any thoughts?"

The Spring Fling is not juvenile! It's the last dance before the prom!

I snorted. "Call it the W'Underworld Ball and make people dress up in funny costumes."

"A masquerade. Ah, yes!" A slow, devious smile spread across his smooth golden skin.

That doesn't bode well.

"Forget I said anything," I mumbled.

"*Chérie*! You're not getting into the spirit of the thing!" Hades spread his arms. "Think of the fun we'll have, picking out our costumes. Who would you like to be? Marie Antoinette? Anne Boleyn? Mata Hari? Hmm, I see you as the Scarlett O'Hara type."

He was being playful, and while he was devastatingly luscious, I was neither stupid nor gullible. I picked at a rough nail, showing my disinterest, although I imagined any fête thrown by Hades was bound to be on the monumental scale even for an Olympian god.

"I need a manicure," I said to myself.

Instantly a nail technician pulled my cold hand into her warm ones.

What?

There stood Hades, elegant in a turquoise Lagerfeld silk shirt, dark chocolate-brown pants, and black Manolos with no socks. We were in the most posh salon I'd ever seen, even more so than the one Arkady sent Meg and me to when we were getting ready for his designer show at the Met. Everything was a mélange of cool blues and clean whites. Very Pacific California. A quick glance down relieved my panic; I was dressed in a coral linen sheath by Chloe that I'd seen in Saks only days before. A little wiggle on the seat—yes! Thong included.

"Oh, what have you done to your beautiful hands? It's a good thing you came right in," cooed the woman. She was petite and dark-haired, reminding me of Meg. "I am Mala." She smiled briefly and went to work on my wretched nails.

"I'm Tiffany," said the young woman I'd just noticed pampering my feet.

"When you're finished with your manicure and pedicure, we'll take a stroll down Rodeo Drive while we discuss your costume. I have a personal couturier who'll make whatever you desire." His smile was warm, inviting, and oh so lustful. All the females, and a number of males, eyed him hungrily. If only ... *don't go there!*

But Rodeo Drive! A custom-made outfit for a fantasy costume ball! It was more temptation than a girl should have to bear.

Think about Meg. Think about starving children. Think about vicious goddesses threatening your life.

"I never agreed to go to a ball." I had some fortitude left. *Oh Mala, your hands are bliss!* She was rubbing my hands with a soothing cucumber and melon moisturizer.

"Remember, it's not just your pretty, delectable little neck, it's Margaret's too." Hades' look darkened. "You both have obligations to fulfill, and this is yours."

When I opened my mouth to argue, he leaned over me, placing a finger over my lips.

"Enjoy the moment. It harms no one to be pampered."

"Won't Persephone get mad when you throw a party and she isn't invited?" I persisted.

He scowled and pulled back to resume his seat on an overstuffed chair.

"You can be so provincial sometimes, Sharisse. You need to loosen up."

All I could do at first was sputter. *Loosen up?* "I'm parading around the Underworld in skimpy clothes, talking to people who've been dead hundreds of years, having strangers touch my intimate apparel, and being made a hostage hostess! Is there anything else? Oh yes, you forgot to bring on the hell hounds!" I shrieked. He might have winced. Every dog for ten blocks might have cringed.

"My little drama queen," he teased.

I glared. "You still haven't answered my question. What about Persephone? First thing she'll do as soon as she can is come after me. Somehow, I think she'll find a way to blame me for the party, for her not being invited, and for who knows what else." I could feel my control starting to slip away. If not for the nail technician, my hands would have been balled into fists. *Meltdown imminent.*

Hades rubbed his chin thoughtfully. "If I'm lucky enough to still be enjoying the bounty of your presence when Persephone rejoins me, I'll make other arrangements for you. How you comport yourself determines whether I send you to the Pit"—he made a worried face—"which I emphatically encourage you to avoid, or to a pleasant, tropical island until Margaret either finishes or fails at her task. If the second option is what comes to pass, Margaret will join you and I will find a suitable job for her. *N'est-ce pas?*"

I seethed. "Oh, so it's into the golden cage for us until you can play?"

His eyes gleamed with dark delight and he slowly licked his top lip. With a panther's lethal grace, he rose and glided over to me. Not a good sign. And I was trapped in the pedicure chair.

"It's your duty to make me happy." He was a breath away and leaned in for the kiss.

The weight of being alone in Tartarus, not knowing what was happening with Meg, having no control even over my wardrobe, was too much. I cracked under the strain.

I wailed. Great heaving, loud, wet sobs.

Hades jumped back as though I had swung a knife at him.

"I want Meg! I can't do this!" I cried.

Hades actually looked shocked that instead of making a flip remark, I was bawling loud enough for the denizens on Mt. Olympus to hear.

"Sharisse! *Mon coeur*! Don't cry!" He seemed at a loss for anything other than insipid platitudes.

I cried harder, until I was hiccupping and in danger of hyperventilating.

All the people around us were frozen. Hades grabbed my hand from the inanimate technician and held it gently in his.

"You have to fulfill the contract. It's written and even I can't undo it!"

"I d-d-don't c-c-care about the c-c-contract! I wanna see

Meg!" I could barely catch my breath. My head began to swim and my sight grew fuzzy.

"Don't faint! Breathe!"

Not wanting to be vulnerable to Hades-knew-what, I gulped in air as fast as I could.

"Slow down, easy!" he whispered. It almost sounded like he cared.

He has a motive for everything he does. Don't make him out to be compassionate! Even so, I followed his soft instructions and got my breathing, heart rate, and pulse to gradually calm down a bit, even though my emotions were as turbulent as a hurricane.

"Rest just a moment."

I nodded weakly and closed my eyes. As I was wondering what would happen next, I heard a whistling sound. Opening one eye, I saw dark, looming cliffs. The imported marble floor was gone, and I stood on crumbling black rock. Swiveling my head around, I thought I could make out white furniture ... a little round table and three chairs.

Made of bones.

We were back across the River Styx, and a black missile was heading for me.

It smacked me right in the face.

Stumbling, I managed to catch it, and myself. It was a garment bag.

"What the—"

That's when I saw Meg standing there.

MƐG

To Hell and Back

We screamed in unison.

"Shar!"

"Meg!"

Shar was holding the fleece, but dropped it on the ground and ran into my waiting arms. I hugged her tightly.

"Are you okay?" I whispered into her shoulder.

She nodded vigorously and swiped at her face. She *had* been crying hard; her eyes were puffy and her cheeks were streaked with tears. "Yes. Are you?"

I tried to find my voice but couldn't speak. Breathing took a great effort, and my chest heaved like it was filled with rocks. The whisper of a shriek came out and I choked.

"He...he...took you away!" I babbled, the tears starting to flow. "He took all your stuff … n-n-no one remembers you! It's like you don't exist!"

"I'm here, I'm here!" Shar stroked my hair, trying to calm me down, but I could see what I'd said disturbed her. She led me a few paces away, toward a small table and chairs that stood nearby. Together we staggered over the uneven, gravelly ground.

"He's such a creep!" she continued in a whisper. "Even though I'm glad I have it, my *underwear* is here! He touched them! Now I'll have to buy all new ones!"

I knew she was trying to make light of all this, and I felt my sobs lessen just a bit. I wasn't insane. Shar hadn't been erased—we were here, together. I ran a finger over the surface of the table; it was weird, ridgey. I stared at it and the matching chairs, trying to focus and calm myself. The legs were slender, elegant, and white, like … *bones!*

I jerked my hand back, and through my tears, I saw Hades off to the side. His eyes crinkled. *This whole situation amuses him*, I thought. *We're just his puppets.* That made me start bawling again, even harder this time.

"Meg, Meg," Shar soothed gently, but I heard her voice cracking. She grabbed both my hands in hers and bowed her head over our intertwined fingers. Then she cried too.

"Margaret! Sharisse! Stop!" Hades said sternly after a few minutes.

I didn't want to hear his voice; it only made everything worse. I laid my head on the table next to Shar's and together we howled.

"Sharisse! *Mon amour*, come now, don't start crying

again," he pleaded, stepping up to her and putting a hand on her bare arm.

Violently she shook him off, shot him an evil albeit wet glance, then turned back to me and cried some more.

Hades paced around us, his expression quickly morphing from annoyed to alarmed. He had to know there was no end in sight; once started, the hysterics had to run their course.

Finally he threw up his hands, pulled over one of the bony chairs, and threw himself into it, tapping his foot while leaning his elbows on his knees.

"All right, all right," he groused. "What if there was a way for you two to talk on a regular basis?"

We looked up, mistrustful, but it brought the wailing to a halt. Seeing that he'd made an impression, he rushed on.

"Being the magnanimous god that I am, I will allow you to communicate. Once a week. For five minutes."

"Once a week? Five minutes!" Shar whined, "Is that all?"

"It's something," I said, feeling a tiny tad like myself again and pathetically grateful for even this small concession. Just the thought of being able to talk to Shar made me feel better. She let go of me to wipe her face with the back of her hand.

I did the same. "Where exactly are we?" I asked.

"You are on the brink, Margaret." Hades flashed his perfect smile at me and pointed into the darkness, where I could now make out some body of water. "That is the Styx. Cross that and you'll enter my realm."

"No thanks." I shook my head.

"Well, if you fail ..." He raised his hands in an open-palmed shrug. "Then this will be permanent. But then, you'll both be in Tartarus, and I'm sure Sharisse will tell you that it's not all that bad."

"I beg to differ," Shar sniffed.

Hades wiped a tear from her mutinous face. "*Cara mia*, always playing devil's advocate! It makes you so … alluring."

He glanced at her with a lascivious look and we both shivered. There was no way either of us was going to stay here permanently; we had enough incentive to get our jobs done.

"How will Shar be able to talk to me?" I asked.

A bejeweled box, about the size of a milk crate and bound with iron clasps and hinges, appeared on the bone table. Hades eyed Shar intently. "Sharisse, this will be waiting for you in my throne room, but be careful. Pandora will have a fit if you damage it."

"Pandora?" Shar interrupted. "You mean this is …?"

"Pandora's Box—exactly, *mon amour*!"

Shar cocked her head. "Can you please stop calling me that?"

"If that's Pandora's Box, don't open it, Shar," I warned. "All the troubles of the world are in there!"

Hades yawned. "The box is empty." He lifted the lid and we both flinched as the hinges squealed. Nothing happened. No monsters, disasters, or plagues descended upon us.

"See?" Hades said. "I told you the truth."

"But then why would Pandora keep it?" I asked.

"Souvenir?" Hades shrugged. "Because of its history, it has become a window on the world. Open the lid, and if Margaret is at the designated place at the appointed time, you'll be able to see and talk to each other."

"But how will I know when she's going to be there?"

Shar asked. "Couldn't we just use our cell phones? You can do that, right?"

"Questions! Questions!" Hades tutted, handing Shar a delicate gold-link bracelet with a watch face. "This will help you keep mortal time in my domain. It will chime three times: once as a five-minute warning to get to the throne room, once when the five minutes commences, and lastly when the five minutes are up. Ben Franklin designed and created it. Useful man to have around. I must see if I can renew his contract." Hades gave us a wicked smile.

"Ben Franklin?" I asked. "As in *Benjamin Franklin?*"

Shar nodded.

"But—" I started.

"I'll explain later," she said, taking the watch and fastening it around her wrist. "Let's just say he's the Underworld's major-domo."

"Got it." I turned to Hades. "Do I get a box too?"

"Of course not!" he scoffed. "There's only one Pandora's Box, and it's not going back to the mortal plane even if it *is* empty. Every Tuesday, between, say, 6:55 and 7:00 p.m., go here." He flicked his wrist and a thick, cream-colored business card appeared between his buffed fingernails. When he handed it to me, I could see that it was shaped like a tiny cake covered in curlicue writing.

Pandora's Box
1118 57th Street

"Pandora's Box, the *store?*" I eyed him warily. "What do they sell there?"

A dry chuckle escaped his lips. "Take your mind out of

the gutter. It's a gourmet confectioner. To die for." He bit his bottom lip. "And some have. Just be in front of Pandora's by 6:55 tomorrow evening and you'll be able to talk to Sharisse to your heart's content."

"For five minutes," I snapped.

He pointed at me and I felt a pinch on my arm. There was a popping sound and a feather floated to the floor.

"You said—"

"Don't push me, Margaret. Go to the window at the designated day and time and if Sharisse is inclined to speak with you, you'll see her in the window of Pandora's. Now, this little reunion has gone on long enough. *Mi corazón*." He nodded at Shar and she vanished. He and I were standing in my dorm room, the fleece hovering at his elbow.

"Where's Shar?" I demanded. "There were things I wanted to say. Things I had to ask..." I looked around helplessly.

"You'll have an opportunity to talk to Sharisse tomorrow. Hopefully my generosity will be an incentive for you to perform. And by the way"—he glared at me—"never, NEVER do that to the fleece again."

I watched as the closet door slid open by itself. The crowded hangers parted, making a more-than-ample space for the fleece. The garment bag floated in and settled gently on the rod.

"It needs quiet time," Hades said, walking over to the closet and smoothing out the bag before closing the door by hand and vanishing.

I flung myself onto my bed and curled up, staring at Shar's half of the room. It looked as barren, desolate, and

empty as I felt. At least I'd be able to talk to her tomorrow—
if Hades kept his promise, which I wasn't about to bank on.

There was a bang on the door.

"Go away," I said, more to the pillow than to whomever
was out there—probably Alana and company come to torment me about imaginary roommates. Then the door handle
shook, as if someone was putting a key into the lock. I pushed
myself up on the bed and watched the knob quickly turn.

The door was thrust open and two men in dark suits,
black shades, and earpieces came in, carting several Louis
Vuitton trunks on wheeled carriers.

"In here?" one of them said to someone out in the hall.

"My paper says Room 29. Doesn't it say Room 29? Just
move so I can get out of this hallway!" a voice grated from
just outside.

The men quickly pushed the luggage farther into the
room and stepped aside, letting in a tall, solid-looking girl
dressed in a loose, spangled navy top; beat-up, leathery looking pants; and pansy-yellow flats. A gray scarf with little
silver horses embroidered into it was tied around her neck,
and feathery sable hair stuck out the back of the trucker hat
perched on her head.

She surveyed the room quickly, not bothering to take off
the huge, dark bug-eye glasses perched on her nose. When
she caught sight of me, sitting on my bed and clutching my
pillow, she stared for a moment, then let out a breathy sigh
that seemed to catch in her throat. Was she disappointed to
find me here?

"Derek!" she grunted at one of the men. He rushed over

to her and the two of them conversed in hushed voices, she growling and he apologetic.

"I guess this will have to do for now!" She waved a hand, dismissing them. Hopping to her command, they scurried out the door, closing it behind them.

The girl paced up and down, her heels clicking against the smooth linoleum tiles on the floor. She went over to the window and looked out, then rushed back to the door, opened it a crack, and peered out before slamming it shut again.

"Why isn't there a deadbolt on this?" she said, looking the door up and down. "Or at least a slide lock with a chain?"

"Dunno," I said, getting up and finally realizing what had just happened—I'd gotten a new roommate.

The girl leaned back against the door and slumped. "Not exactly what I expected."

"You mean having to room with someone?" I offered, not kindly. I didn't know if she didn't like the idea of me as a roomie, or roomies in general, but I wasn't too keen on her. Too pushy, obviously too high maintenance, and I didn't want anyone taking Shar's place.

She didn't answer, but threw up her large hands before tucking them in her front pockets. She looked around the room over the top of her glasses, her glance resting on the posters on the walls. She tilted her head. "This is promising."

Excuse me?

"I'm Meg," I said, planting myself defensively in my half of the room.

"Nice taste in tunes, Meg," said the gangly girl. Her eyes, still hidden behind her shades, seemed to be fixed on the wall, her head moving up and down in a fluid motion as if she was keeping time to unheard music. She was checking out the photo of Matt Davey, the lead guitarist for Elysian Fields. "I'm Paulina."

"Oh," I replied, keeping my voice even. Of course my new roommate was Paulina Swanson. Like last time, Hades had given us—or rather, me—an in.

There was another pounding on the door. For the next four hours, Paulina's suited, secret-service-type goons moved her in à la *Design Star*—when they were done, it looked like she, not Shar, had been my roommate for the last seven months. The room had morphed from goth/Barbie to half empty to EMO-den, although it didn't take Paulina long to turn Derek's OCD for organization into a whirlwind of disarray. He would unpack a case only for her to go sifting through a drawer or bin, leaving clothes hanging over edges and scattering CDs like birdseed. Shar had complained that I was a walking havoc-wreaker; was I this bad? Well, even if Paulina's posters, semi-slovenliness, and sartorial expression seemed to match mine, it didn't matter—she just pushed in and took over. Only Shar had license to be that way with me, and while Hades may have put Poo-lina in Shar's place, I wanted none of it.

At least, until Derek started unloading her sound system—an industrial mosh of equipment that looked like it belonged to a professional DJ. Floor-to-ceiling speakers, CD changer for I don't know how many CDs, laptop, iHome, surround sound; if she set the volume to two, it would probably knock down the walls. I fought to put this into perspective as the entire Elysian Fields catalog—

including rare, live, and early performances—were loaded and started playing en circuit.

Think of Shar, think of Shar, think of Shar! A silent mantra played in my head like a loop until I felt like I could hear Shar's voice speaking, like a little angel on my shoulder: *Think of the kind of deal Paulina must have made with Hades for all this!*

As if on cue, the voice of my own conscience joined in. *Paulina's awful! But look at her. How old could she be? 17? 18? 19 at most? Kids don't make deals with the Lord of the Underworld.*

But even as I thought this, I remembered why I was here in the first place—me, kid, deal with Hades. And of course there was the very real possibility that Paulina wasn't a kid at all. Maybe she was a million years old like Arkady, but wily enough to not overlook any details like not getting stuck in an aging body. If that was the case, she could be really dangerous.

I stayed on my side of the room and watched her shuffle around, hoping to get a clue about who and what she was. All I learned was that she had dark ghetto fashion sense, a wicked music collection, and was paranoid and difficult. Why else would she keep opening the door a crack to see if anyone was outside, then start blasting music—practically inviting everyone on the floor to drop by and visit?

Resolutely, I approached the closet and slid my door open. Nothing tumbled out this time. Assaulted by my belongings when they'd opened it to put Paulina's clothes away, Derek and friends had taken it upon themselves to reorganize my stuff, too, whether I wanted it or not. At that point I'd been too shell-shocked to stop them.

I lifted out the garment bag, laid it on my bed, and began to unzip it, noticing that as I did so, the stereo volume went down.

"What's that?" Paulina's gravelly voice was in my ear and I nearly jumped out of my skin. She'd slid silently up and had waited to speak until she was right behind me. When I whirled around to face her, she was looking at me from behind her glasses; it was dark outside and she hadn't taken them off yet. I didn't like the idea that she was watching me at such close range; it made me uncomfortable, but I kept my cool.

"I'm getting ready for tomorrow," I said, casually pulling open the garment bag so that the fleece spilled out. "It's supposed to be chilly, so I thought I might wear this."

I drew the fleece out and held it up. Without its master present, it wasn't giving off vibes of power, but it had changed. Free of its plastic sheath, it was as light as a fluffy wad of spun sugar, with an odor to match. With any luck this would ramp up the temptation factor. The fleece needed all the help it could get.

Paulina's mouth hung open and she slid the glasses down the bridge of her strong nose. She didn't take them off completely, but it was enough for me to see her eyes under the shadow of her hat and her choppy bangs. They were steely gray. What was that expression … that the eyes are the window of the soul? Hers weren't giving any secrets up. What would mine tell her?

"Where … did … you … get … that?" Paulina's voice reverberated with quiet awe.

She wants it! Could I really be this lucky? Will she just push me aside and put it on? I worked hard to control the expression on my face, keeping my features nonchalant, free-and-easy. Normal.

I shrugged. "It's vintage." Not a total lie—the fleece *was* old. I wanted to add, *do you want to try it on?* But I never got a chance. Paulina's star-struck, slack-jawed expression twisted into a disgusted sneer.

"Hope you didn't dump too much cash on it," she snorted. "How many little creatures gave their lives to make that nasty coat?"

She spat out the "nasty coat" bit and I felt my stomach twist in frustration and defeat. A lump formed in my throat. I should have known—there was no way this would be that simple. Nothing with Hades was.

"It's actually fleece, not fur," I managed. I couldn't give up; even if I couldn't get her to wear it now, I had to get her to wear it eventually.

"Whatever it's made of, it's whack," said Paulina, shoving her shades flat against her face and turning her back on me. "I'd hide that thing away where no one will ever find it, if I were you."

Believe me, I would if I could, but you have to wear it so Shar can come back.

On went the music again, even louder than before. Resigning myself to the fact that there was nothing I could do at that moment, I started pulling together an outfit for tomorrow: black boots, black leggings, and a green top, much like the one that Shar was wearing when Hades took her. No one else might know or care that she was in Tartarus, but I did. As I smoothed out the sleeve of my top, I realized that I was humming and bopping along to the music.

"That's way better." Paulina loomed over me again, smiling like a vulture. I could smell her breath, peanuts and chocolate. She'd been chomping on a Snickers bar; the empty wrapper was squashed in her paw. She flicked her head in the direction of the fleece, which was now lying in a crumpled heap on the floor at the foot of my bed. How did it get there?

I was thinking that I'd better hang it up before Hades appeared, froze time, and reprimanded me for mistreating it again. He'd seemed pretty stressed about it, and I got it that since technically the fleece was once his nephew, he wanted it handled with a little respect. As I bent to pick it up, it seemed the bass thumped out of time with the music. I stopped and listened, and sure enough, it happened again—but it wasn't a problem with the download or the speakers. Someone was banging on the door.

I turned to Paulina and motioned for her to turn the volume down, but she stood frozen like a deer—no, moose—in the headlights. I glanced at the clock. It was 9:55 p.m. We had five minutes until quiet hour, but sometimes the RA was anal. Still, we had to answer the door, and Paulina wouldn't budge.

"Turn it down before we get in trouble!" I shouted.

Mechanically, she shuffled over to the stereo. When the volume was lowered to almost a whisper, but not totally off, I opened the door.

Alana, not the RA, was on the other side with Kate, her

shadow. She wore a self-satisfied smirk, as if her mere presence had caused the hallways to go suddenly silent.

"It's quiet hour," Alana snapped.

"Not for another four and a half minutes," I shot back. I wasn't tolerating any more disrespect, especially from Shar's former friends, even if they couldn't be blamed for not knowing what was going on.

She said, annoyed, "Some of us are trying to—" Then she stopped, craning her neck so she could see inside the room. Back came the smirk. "So... they finally found a roommate for you."

Kate snickered, and then she and Alana pushed their way in, uninvited and unwelcome guests. Together they gaped at Paulina's side of the room—the mess, the sound system.

They ignored Paulina, who glanced at them from the corner. I couldn't tell whether she was just watching or trying to blend into the wall like a chameleon.

"Overdone," Alana clucked, jerking her thumb at the speakers. "No wonder it was so loud!" Then her eyes caught something on my side, and she started moving toward my bed. She bent down and picked up the fleece.

A little sigh came out of Kate, and I heard Alana say, "Ooo!" in a tone very different from the derisive one she'd been using only a moment before.

Anyone who dares to wear the Golden Fleece is dispatched immediately to Tartarus.

Paulina, who hadn't moved or spoken, now walked over to Alana's side. "That really suits you. Maybe you should try it on. See how it looks."

An unholy light shone in Alana's eyes, and she quickly shook the fleece out so she could see its shape.

"No!" I said, pushing everyone aside and snatching the fleece away. "It's mine!" I shoved it into the garment bag, not bothering to put it on the hanger, and tossed it into the closet, slamming the door shut. For good measure, I leaned against it. Alana and Kate stared at me for a moment before Alana let out a huff and turned to go.

"Keep the music off—it's quiet hour now."

"Ya think?" I snapped, and slammed the door behind them, but not before I heard Kate snicker, "They're made for each other."

Not likely!

I stepped up to Paulina and stuck a finger in front of her nose. It was bad feng shui, but some people only responded to aggressive energy.

"What do you think you're doing, telling her to try it on?"

"What could it hurt?" She held up her broad palms.

"I don't care if you don't like that coat—it's *mine.* This is *my* side of the room, *my* closet. If I want a landslide when I open the door, so be it. Hands off my stuff!"

Paulina peered at me. She was still wearing her glasses. Her mouth twisted into a half sneer, half grin. "Whatever you say."

SHAR

Who Let the Dog Out?

I hadn't seen Hades since the reunion with Meg, nor had I seen Caz. I got bored sitting in my room, even with all my music, book, and DVD collections. So I decided to explore, killing time until I could talk to Meg again.

Contrary to myth, rumor, legend, and history books, Tartarus was not all doom and gloom. Yes, it was icky and dark and had that whole land-of-the-dead theme going for it on the banks of the river, but within the palace it was a whole different world. From the throne room, one door led to a huge ballroom with mirrors and glittering chandeliers and gleaming white marble floors. Another led to an arcade/video game room with more tech stuff than I could name. The next one opened onto a pool the size of a small lake, complete with slides, fountains, Jacuzzis, and floats. Other doors led to other hallways, down which I discovered a bowling alley, a horse arena, IMAX theaters, weight rooms, a stadium, and a paintball arena.

Boys and toys. I wondered where the salon was. Hades always had perfect hair and buffed nails. Did he ever need a dentist to maintain his stunning smile?

One large door led outside. What lay beyond was unexpected and truly amazing. Aqua sea waters lapped against a pristine, pink-sand beach; craggy, burgundy mountains with caves loomed in the distance. I wondered if any other gods had seen this stunning vista. While I preferred the beach to the game rooms, this great outdoorsy world still had a very "indoor" feel to it, like I was on a movie set.

Still, it was better than the dismal gray rock surrounding the river. Plunking down on the beach, I sighed with bliss as I buried my toes in the warm sand. A gentle surf rolled over my feet. No way could this be confused with hell.

Was that a bark?

Oh, damn. Hell hound! I jumped and whirled around to see Cerberus coming at me at great speed.

I miss my cat!

I froze, not knowing what to do. I couldn't outrun it. Maybe I could out-swim it? I dove into the surf and was paddling for all I was worth. When I was totally out of breath, I turned around.

And there he was, the water only up to the neck of his three heads, slimy drool dripping from all of them. He was eyeing me.

"Nice goggy. Don't eat Daddy's friend," I sing-songed. He tilted his heads.

Without making any sudden movements, I started swimming back to shore. The demon doggy followed, never letting me get too far ahead. When my feet touched shore, I could feel his hot, sticky breath on my back, letting me know that escape was impossible. He growled low in his throat.

I'm dead. Bye Mom, Dad, Meg, Kitty Chanel, and all my lovely shoes. Maybe Hades will donate them to charity. I turned around to face my fate.

A red rubber ball plunked me on the head.

"Ewww, it's covered in spit!"

He growled again.

"Okay, fine. Fetch!" I threw the ball as hard as I could, and it sailed a good distance down the beach. Shopping wasn't my only recreational activity—I had a mean throwing arm, as Splendor found out. Away flew Cerberus, bouncing like a puppy. Who knew? Easier to handle than his master.

We played for I don't know how long, since the light never seemed to change. Did it ever become night? I didn't see a sun—it was just a perfect blue sky, like an upturned bowl.

My arms tired, I toed the ball away. "That's enough. We'll play tomorrow." I turned away from the demon dog.

Grrrrr.

I whipped around. "Are you kidding me? I played with you! Tomorrow we'll do the fetch routine, but I'm hungry! My arm is tired! I've had enough!"

All three heads growled again, one dropping the ball at my feet.

I narrowed my eyes and shook my finger at him. "I *said*

tomorrow. If you don't stop whining, I won't play at all. Now be a good goggy—" Tongues lolling, tail wagging, he bounded off. Okaaay. That worked.

"Is he gone?" Out from behind a large pile of rocks popped Caz, still as devastating as the first time I saw him. My little heart went flippity flip.

"Yes."

"Good. He doesn't like me. And I don't like him."

I laughed and shrugged. "He's just an overgrown puppy. He wants to play. Throw the ball and he'll love you."

Caz shook his head. "I'm not willing to risk it. I like being in one piece and unswallowed. How are you? Settling in?"

I grumped. "I don't plan on being here long enough to settle in."

We started walking down the beach. Idly, I wondered if the light might gradually dim and stars would peek out. "It looks like a real sky." I pointed upwards.

"Hades creates illusions well. Sometimes you can almost forget you're down here; you'd swear you were on the mortal plane."

I looked down at the bright rainbow bikini I sported. "Maybe you can, but I can't. This isn't my home. There's no sun, no sense of time, and very few wardrobe options."

He smiled. "I'm sure Hades will give you whatever you want."

"Oh sure, for a price I'm not willing to pay. I have to play his silly games until I can get out of here."

He looked at me quizzically. "No one leaves Tartarus without his permission."

I gave him a determined look. "Where there's a will, there's a way."

"Why are you here anyway? You obviously aren't willing, and since you're not dead, there's an interesting tale to hear.

I narrowed my eyes. "How do you know I didn't die?"

He shrugged and bent over to chuck a stone across the gentle waves. "Did you notice anything different about old Ben?"

I didn't have to overanalyze Caz's question. Ben looked like the Ben Franklin I'd seen in paintings, and while he felt real when he'd kissed my hand, his appearance was ... off. He had no pulse, veins, or warmth. He was like one of those wax figures at Madame Tussauds. Close, but not totally right.

"He's kind of like a walking, talking statue," I said.

But Caz wasn't. He looked very ... healthy and oh so real. *Mmm ...*

He nodded. "When Creation was divided up, Zeus got the best part of everything under the sun—Mt. Olympus and mastery of humanity. Poseidon got everything under the sea, and its creatures, and Hades got what was left—everything under the earth. He felt slighted; he was the eldest and should have received the best, even though it was Zeus who'd led the way out of their father's prison. And who wants to look at dead people for eternity?"

Caz sat down on a large, smooth boulder of sparkling orange. He gave me a questioning look, patting the empty space next to him.

My face felt hot. He was nice and ... hot.

Don't go there. You're worlds apart. It can never be anything more than a short-lived friendship.

Ignoring my boring brain matter, I sat demurely next to him.

"So," Caz continued, as he tried not to be obvious about inching closer. "Hades, since he's absolute ruler here, makes his kingdom a sort of Olympus Down Under."

"That's why it's light and pretty and his throne isn't black!" I cried. Now it made sense. Hades was in a snit because Zeus won the big enchilada, cosmically speaking. This was his Olympus.

"And he allows souls who pass to keep their bodies, so that he doesn't have to look at shades. Except"—Caz sported a wry grimace—"he doesn't get it quite right."

I huffed. "And they have to do his bidding." I thought of Ben.

Caz laughed. "That too."

I frowned, thinking about how the shades by the river would be there forever. Poor miserable things.

Caz scanned the area. He was fidgety and nervous and I was sure he was looking for the sudden reappearance of Cerberus. Or maybe Hades.

"Some souls are doomed, either by one of the gods or by something they've done," he explained. "They're stuck on the other side of the river, or down in the Pit, or they're wandering in far worse places."

"Horrific way to spend eternity," I said softly.

His voice was almost bitter. "Yes it is. Remember that, when you anger Hades. None of the gods are to be trusted. They've proven fickle and heartless to both humanity and their own kind, uncountable times."

Caz looked sad, and I felt my heart constrict in response.

Even though I didn't know what his particular arrangement with Hades was, I didn't want to see anyone suffer. Hades might even be pitied too; while Poseidon and Zeus enjoyed their realms, there wasn't much in the Underworld to be cheery about. So he created his own happy place.

My fingers lightly touched Caz's and we smiled awkwardly at each other.

"So what's your story, Sharisse?"

Looking into his soft eyes, I wanted to tell him the whole sad tale, but I couldn't. A cute face wasn't worth an extra day in this place, and I'd suffer much worse than that if I dropped so much as a vowel. Nondisclosure was the binding rule. Shaking my head, I just said, "Call me Shar. And I can't talk about it. What about you?"

Caz looked across the twilight landscape; it seemed there was a nighttime here. "I can't tell you, either." His tone was distant.

"Then we're at an impasse, I guess." I wasn't really surprised. Probably everyone down here had secrets. I know I had mine.

Awkward silence.

"So, Hades is having this party," I began. "The W'Underworld Ball. Will you come?"

Caz turned to me. "He's throwing a ball without Persephone here?"

I grimaced. "Yeah, I'm the substitute hostess." I brightened. "And, as a good hostess, I'm inviting you."

Caz looked at me doubtfully. "I don't know. Persephone has an awful temper, and when she finds out you're here, first she'll scream at Hades, then feed you to Cerberus, and finish by making life miserable for the rest of us. I think I'll camp out in a cave until that war is over. It'll be quieter and safer."

I snuck a sideways glance at his strong jawline, pink lips, and patrician nose. Quite the package. If only ... but that wasn't possible. He was here, and if he wasn't dead, he had his own problems with Hades, so there was no taking him with me if I was freed or could escape.

"Well, please think about coming anyway. I won't know anyone but you and Ben."

Caz tried to smother a snicker. "Be careful of old Ben. Considers himself a ladies' man."

My face scrunched. "He's old enough to be my great-great—"

Caz shook his head, a huge grin on his face. "Don't let that fool you. And sure, I guess I could come to the ball."

I grinned back at him. "In costume, and don't tell me what it is—I want to see if I can pick you out of the crowd." *Like I wouldn't know that delish body no matter how it was wrapped!*

"I'll know you the moment I see you." He stared into my eyes. I let go a little sigh, wishing he would kiss me.

Ding! Ding! Ding! The bracelet watch was chiming the five-minute warning to see Meg.

"I've got to run! I'll see you back at the palace!" I ran down the beach, not slowing to see if he followed.

I skidded to a stop in the throne room in front of the table with Pandora's Box. Lifting the lid, I saw a swirl of colors, like paints running down a sink drain. Suddenly, Meg's face appeared.

"Meg!"

I was so glad to see her. For once, Hades kept his word about things happening the way he said they would.

"Shar!" she squealed, then narrowed her eyes at me. "What the hell are you wearing? I didn't know you owned something like that."

"I *don't*. This is *his* idea of everyday wear, apparently. At least I don't have to wear black leather." I shuddered delicately. "This is the most conservative swimsuit in my closet."

She made a disgruntled face. "Not exactly being subtle, is he? Didn't he leave you any of your own clothes? But look, we've got less than five minutes, so let's make this count." She looked over her shoulder, her eyes shifting nervously as if she was making sure she wasn't being watched. "What does he have you doing down there?"

"Meet the Martha Stewart of the Underworld," I said, throwing up both hands and waving them at her. "I get to co-host Hades' Spring Fling. It's a costume party. I think I'll go as a nun. Maybe a leper. Which would he hate more?"

"Oh. My. God." Meg tried not to giggle. I understood—this situation was too ludicrous to be credible.

"What about you?" I asked. "Are you okay?"

"I guess," she answered, looking away.

"Talk to me. What's wrong?" My stomach sank in horror. "What do you have to do?"

She tossed her head back. "Where do I start? Like I told you last time…Hades pretty much erased you. No one remembers you, not even Alana."

I tried not to look upset. Not that I missed Alana or anyone else yet, but being erased was unsettling, to say the least.

"So, all your stuff is gone and then, poof! I get a new roommate! She—"

"You have a new roommate?" I interrupted. My voice sounded very small and hurt.

Meg bobbed her head. "Guess who I have to send to Tartarus? My new roomie, Miss Paulina Swanson."

"Oh," I nodded sagely, a bit relieved. At least Hades was making it easy; my visit to the Underworld might be shorter than I'd thought. "Seems like Hades has been a busy little demon. But how will you get her to a portal? You can't Siren her."

"Ehh!" Meg made a buzzer sound. "Things are a little different this time, so sayeth the Lord of the Underworld. I don't have to find a portal or use my eerie powers." She held up her hands and wiggled her fingers. "I have to get her to wear the Golden Fleece, and let me tell you, no one in their right mind would even want to sit next to it, although Alana and Kate seemed to like it, go figure. But that's not the worst of it. You thought it was bad with Arkady being deaf and blind and never available? Well, Paulina saw the fleece—and she hates it, won't go near it. And if today's any indication, she's my freaking shadow. She trailed me everywhere I went." Meg looked over her shoulder again. "I'm lucky I was able to ditch her to come here. I'm going to need some help with this."

I thought for a minute, tapping my bottom lip. *How to get a roomie who's always around to wear something she despises? Hello? Opportunity!*

"Throw it over her while she's asleep," I suggested.

"Shar, you're brilliant!"

I beamed. *All this and brains too.* I heard the tinkling melody of the watch again.

"Is our time up already?" Meg said, putting her hand on the window.

The image of her face in the box flickered, went dim, and then went black.

Game over.

MΣG

BFF? NFW!

The room was dark and quiet. Paulina's team of unpackers/
movers/decorators/bodyguards had draped the window with
some heavy velvety material, so day or night, with the lights
out, the room was a cave.

I was awake, with Shar's genius idea echoing in my
brain: *Go and get the fleece and put it over Paulina. She's sleeping, and she'll never know what happened. She'll go to Tartarus
where she belongs, and Shar will be back here where she belongs.
Mission accomplished!*

Hades' voice seemed to intrude. *Simple, no?*

I'd set the iPhone alarm for 4 a.m., hours before anyone
would be up, and slid it under my pillow. And here I was,
ready to do the deed before the thing even went off.

The bed frame groaned as I sat up. My heart fluttering, I waited several seconds to see if silence returned. It did. As quickly as I could, I swung my feet onto the floor. Stifling the noise my voice wanted to make as my toes hit the icy tiles, I didn't give myself a chance to get used to it. Up I got, and I made a beeline for the closet.

"Good morning!"

"Ahh!" I started, partly from the surprise greeting and partly from stubbing my naked toe on one of the bed's iron wheels.

Paulina snapped on the lights. She was awake and completely dressed.

"Classes start at eight, right?" she asked, crouching down next to a huge and empty messenger bag, the kind professionals use. It still had price tags dangling off the strap.

"Yes," I grumbled, finding the clock and expecting it to read something like 3:51 a.m. It didn't; it was 7:35, giving me only fifteen minutes to get dressed. I cursed.

Stupid Hades. Of course the iPhone wouldn't work—another of his practical jokes.

"Scary!" Paulina took a visual survey of my purple sweatpants and ratty concert tee and grinned flippantly. "Don't worry. Take your time and get ready. I'll wait for you."

"Thanks," I said, not meaning it in the "you're such a good roomie" way, but in the "don't do me any favors and thanks for nothing" way. Hopefully it would ensure she'd be gone by the time I got back from the bathroom.

I shuffled out to the showers and spent a blissful five minutes under the hot water. I didn't have much time, but

I didn't want to rush; I figured P-girl had less time to wait than I was going to take.

She'd followed me around almost all day yesterday—except when she was dragged away by administrators to plan her schedule. After I'd sneaked off to talk to Shar, she'd found me again and told me she had an appointment with Ms. Newton, our principal, first thing this morning. I was hoping to have relieved both myself and Ms. Newton of the burden of Paulina's presence by this point, but it was not to be.

And she wasn't gone when I returned from the bathroom. As promised, she was waiting for me, perched on the edge of her bed, long legs outstretched and encased in big black biker boots, one hand deep in a jumbo-sized bag of granola. I stepped behind the Japanese folding screen I'd set up in one corner of the room as a decoration and got dressed. I felt strangely self-conscious around her, though I couldn't say why. Sure, we were both girls, but this wasn't Shar, with whom I'd been to hell and back. I wanted to expose myself to Paulina as little as possible—my physical person included.

She waited for me while I put on my shoes and packed up my bag with deliberate slowness. As I fastened the last clip, I realized that I'd done none of my homework and hadn't looked over any problems for the Calc quiz I had to take first period. I dropped my bag, slapped my palm against my forehead, and cursed again.

"Something wrong?" Paulina's voice registered something that sounded like genuine concern. I didn't need that.

I shook my head. "Just another screw-up on my part. Bye-bye, A- Calc average. Let's go."

Paulina followed me to the academic building in silence. We arrived with just enough time for me to deposit her in the main office with Ms. Newton and get to Calculus without scoring a detention for being late.

As I was making my way to class, I felt a phone buzzing in my bag—not Hades' iPhone, but my own phone, with a text message. Flipping it open, I could see it was from Jeremy, along with another fifteen or so messages that I hadn't read since Sunday. Quickly I scrolled through:

> U doing anything 2nite? Must b busy miss u. Where r u?
> U OK? Meg?

Had I been so caught up in the assignment and Shar and Paulina that I hadn't responded at all? Quickly I typed in a reply:

> Sorry sorry sorry! School gave me a roomie. Chaos! xxx

Almost immediately he answered:

> Thought u'd 4gotten me :(Guess what?!

I texted back:

> Never forget u. 'sup?

I held the phone for a second or two, vowing that going forward I would check it regularly, hourly. Then it beeped a reply:

> Got tickets 4 Elysian Fields! You & me. ttyl xoxo J.

Jeremy and my favorite band; I should've been thrilled, but instead I felt sick—but I couldn't let him know that. I took my seat and texted back:

U made my day <3 u

The bell rang. Laz got up and shut the door, then returned to his desk and pulled a wad of papers out of his briefcase. I added my voice to the collective groan offered up to the math test gods.

Laz started passing papers out to the first row. I turned my head slightly. Trey winked at me, ignoring the incensed look on crony Sarah's face.

I faced forward so that I didn't have to look at him. The person in front of me handed back a stack of quizzes. I took one, passed the rest on, and then quickly scanned the problems. About half didn't look impossible.

As I reached down to my bag to get out some pencils, the intercom phone at the front of the room rang. Laz stopped handing out papers and picked it up.

He listened for a second or two, then said, "We're having a quiz at the moment, can it wait?" A pause. "Oh, I see. Yes, of course. I'll send her right down." He hung up the phone. "Margaret, you're wanted in Guidance. The rest of you"—he shot a warning glance at Trey and Sarah, who were whispering furtively—"begin."

Thankful for the momentary reprieve, I grabbed my messenger bag, got up, gave Laz his quiz back, and strolled down to Guidance, not caring what they wanted. I'd just won some time. No matter how long they had me there, trips to my locker, the bathroom, and maybe the nurse would be in order to gobble up the period, and I would have a cool twenty-four hours to prepare for a make-up quiz.

The minute I got to Guidance, however, I knew why I'd been called down. Paulina sat in the waiting area, grinning at me. Maybe it was my narrow escape in Calc, but I involuntarily smiled back and gave her a little wave. *What's wrong with me!?*

I put on a serious face, tried to convince myself that my counselor must want to talk to me about college applications, and approached the reception desk, head down. *No unnecessary contact with the dead girl walking!*

"Hi, they called me down. Meg Wiley?" I asked.

"Mr. Elwood wants to speak to you, dear," said Mrs. Roache, the Guidance secretary. "You can go right in."

Mr. Elwood, a small, bald turtle of a man whose obsession with schedules, charts, and time slots bordered on religious, sat at his desk looking around nervously. He jumped in his chair when I walked in.

"Margaret! Thanks for coming down, I'm sorry we had to interrupt your quiz."

"No worries, Mr. E." I sat down in one of the chairs opposite his desk.

"Well." He cleared his throat. "I want to apologize personally for not giving you a heads-up"—he made air quotes with his fingers—"about your new roommate. It must have been a shock for you. The whole situation was beyond my control, but apparently Miss Swanson met all our criteria, and I'm sure you can be sympathetic, her coming to a new school so late in the year and so close to graduation!" He rambled on, starting to sweat and eyeing me defensively, as if he expected me to launch an assault of objections at him.

Not your fault, Mr. E. But I can think of someone I'd like to register a complaint with.

I did a Hades-esque openhanded shrug. "Things like this happen. What're you gonna do?"

Mr. Elwood let out a long, dramatic, and obviously relieved sigh. "Oh, I was so worried! You've been on your own since September, and now getting a roommate at this point…"

My heart lurched. *No I wasn't! Shar was here, and she's coming back!*

His head moved like a clock's pendulum, as if the back and forth would balance things out so that it all made sense. Then he clapped his hands together once, loudly. "But now I have a big favor to ask of you."

I squirmed in my chair and swallowed hard; I had a bad feeling that whatever it was, it involved Paulina. "Uh, sure?"

"Wonderful!" he beamed. "Miss Swanson's father is abroad, and coming into an academically challenging school at so late a juncture, it would probably help if a student could, you know, show her around, introduce her to people. Her schedule's all set. She's tested very high, so she'll be an asset to the school, I'm sure."

Before I could suggest the names of the five most outgoing and popular students in the senior class, he sealed my fate, utterly.

"Since you've gotten off to such a good start, I'd like you to be Miss Swanson's go-to person, her buddy." He clasped his hands and held them together tightly to illustrate the perceived strong bond between us. "I've managed to schedule her classes so that she has some with you."

Then he handed me a sheet of paper. A quick glance told me that I was looking at what used to be Shar's class schedule—the same time blocks, teachers, everything. What next?

Giving Paulina, who couldn't stand or walk closer to me if she'd tried, the grand tour of the academic building took up all the periods until lunch. Then she had to go to Phys Ed alone, and I got to ponder my fate over a mozzarella and tomato caprese sandwich.

So Hades had seen to it that Paulina would be constantly in my presence. Shar and I had complained when assignment #1, Arkady Romanov, was inaccessible. This was going to be the opposite, but just as bad. Worse, actually. She'd trailed after me on her own at first, and now it was sanctioned by the school. She didn't get my hints that we were not simpatico. So what if we liked the same kind of music? That was all surface gloss. How could I like someone who usurped not only Shar's place but my space, even if it was unwittingly?

When it was time to move on to Lit, I hadn't taken so much as a bite of my lunch. I dumped it and headed to class, realizing with dread that Paulina would be my seat neighbor. Sure enough, she was there, already in her place when I walked in the door. Trey was there too, but unlike this morning, he kept his face in his book and acted like I wasn't there. At least I wouldn't have two leeches.

"Happy Ides of March, people," said Miss Winning, snapping her attendance book shut and plucking a thick book filled with sticky notes off her desk. "Let's talk about *Julius Caesar*."

Let's not. I never did catch up on my reading. I shrank into my seat.

"Thinking about the last act you read, how do you explain Brutus' actions? He's Caesar's friend, and yet he helps to murder him."

Winning's roving eye passed over me. Then I heard her call the name I least expected to hear.

"Paulina? You've read *Julius Caesar*?"

"And saw it a couple of times," Paulina said coolly. The titters around her died as she went on. "I felt sorry for Brutus. Caesar's his friend, but what he's facing is bigger than both of them."

Winning nodded, and I squirmed. "Can you elaborate?"

"Brutus believes he's acting on behalf of Rome. If he thought only of his own friendships, that'd be kind of selfish."

"Excellent, Paulina. Can anyone continue this? Laura. Tell us what you got out of Act III."

As Laura stumbled through her answer, I stole glances at Paulina, who sat flipping quietly through her copy of the text. It was as dog-eared as mine; I liked reading Shakespeare's plays—the bloody ones. I found myself impressed that there was some thinking going on behind those bug-eyed dark glasses.

There I went again. *Who cares if she can spout a good answer for Miss Winning? So she likes Shakespeare. Tonight she can addeth her story to his collection of tragedies when she meets him in the Underworld.*

Or not.

On Thursday, Paulina was up before me. Again.

And the day after that.

And the day after *that*.

On Sunday, I snuck over to her side of the room to find her bed empty, and on Monday, she caught me lurking behind our door when she sauntered in from the bathroom, all dressed and toting her monster shower caddy. It was all I could do to make up a lame story about chasing a stray pen that got away from me. So much for my plan to ambush her when she walked in.

When Tuesday dawned, I took little comfort in the thought that I'd get to talk to Shar. I wasn't too happy about the prospect of telling her I'd failed. Hopefully she'd understand that her easy solution had proven to be more difficult than we'd both anticipated. I could always try again. And by tonight she might have a few more ideas on how to extricate us from this situation.

I tried to ignore Paulina, plopped in Shar's place. At the end of the day, I didn't stop at my locker, or the bathroom, or anywhere. I wanted—no, needed—to get away. How was I going to do this? I couldn't totally alienate Paulina; avoiding her wasn't the way to get her to wear the fleece. But I was having a hard time seeing her everywhere that Shar was supposed to be.

Once outside, I was able to breathe easier. I quickly made my way over to the hole-in-the-wall coffee shop near the dorm. A huge latte and a cookie wouldn't solve my problems, but it would help me feel better.

Hustling to the door, I jerked it open, got on line, and ordered the biggest skim mocha latte they made, along with a chocolate chip macadamia nut cookie. I paid, got my treat, turned to go down to the barista to pick up my mega coffee—and almost slammed into Paulina.

How...?

"What are you doing here?" I asked, trying not to sound perturbed.

She shrugged. "I felt like...a latte."

"Well, the line starts there," I said, jerking my head toward the back of the shop.

"Oh." She looked away with an almost lost expression— if someone could look that way with those monster glasses on. I felt a tiny twinge of guilt.

"Look, I have a few places to go, so I'll see you later," I said. "Okay?"

She started a slow, sad shuffle toward the back of the line. The twinge turned into a nasty pinch.

Why me? Why me? Why me?

"Wait," I said, before I could stop myself.

Paulina turned around. By the way her eyebrows tilted up and her mouth opened a crack, I could see the hope registered on her face.

"I'll wait for you here," I sighed. "Go get your stuff."

She smiled hugely and loped off to the back of the line.

You're an idiot, Meg. You don't befriend someone you have to betray. I could just see my conscience wagging its finger at me.

Paulina kept looking back, as if she was checking to make sure I was still there. Every time her shrouded eyes met mine, she'd shoot me that weird half-smile that on a guy would have been cute.

Finally, a huge drink and bulging bag of treats in hand, she sidled up to me.

"So where are we going?"

Where were *we* going? I'd been trying to escape Paulina, and now I'd invited her along. "I was ... just going to do a little shopping. I guess."

She took a sip from her cup. "Okay."

Shopping with Paulina was nothing like shopping with Shar. For one thing, despite how far she'd come with music, Shar would never spend an hour perusing downloads; Paulina and I managed to blow away nearly two hours loading up several of her slick devices. But I turned her down when she offered to get Elysian Fields' newest songs for me. An outing was one thing—that could be considered research. Accepting gifts was another.

We wandered over to the colossal windows of ABC to admire the displays.

I spied a bracelet made of ebony beads, with a silvery charm of a running horse. Its mane was sculpted in such a way that it looked like it was captured mid-gallop. It looked happy, wild, and free. *Unlike me.*

"Oh, I really like that!" The gush escaped before I could stop it; it was the first thing I'd revealed about myself all afternoon.

"It's nice," Paulina agreed. "Want to go have a look?"

I nodded. What harm could looking at a bracelet do? Hades hadn't given me the no-limit Visa or apartment this time—all I'd gotten was the iPhone, which was turning out to be absolutely useless. In addition to blocking the call function so that I couldn't reach the one person I most wanted to talk to, or any helpful goddesses either, there were new apps he'd loaded apparently just for me: *Acropolis Cleaners*, specializing in fleece. *Archimediate Time Management Services*, legendary experts in delegation, scheduling, and prioritizing. *Harpy Assassinations*, for when you didn't want to get your hands dirty. *Fury Us Legal Services*, fair-deals-r-us. *Carnivoropolis*, a guide to NY's meateries. And the phone was a constant reminder and link to Hades; he could harass me whenever he wanted.

Paulina opened the store door for me, then followed me inside. The bare floors creaked as I moved from table to table, looking for my bauble, when I heard a clock chime. Once. I pulled out my watch: 6:30. I only had a half hour to get uptown to Shar!

"Paulina!" I called. She came right over.

I stood on one foot, feeling bad about ditching her like this. "I forgot I have to … meet someone. I'm really sorry."

There was that sad kicked puppy look again, but I didn't have time to think about it.

"I won't be long. See you back at the dorm, okay?"

She nodded.

"Later," I said.

Not waiting for the half-grin that seemed to have a mysterious softening effect on me, I turned and bolted out the door and over to the subway.

The Express Q landed me on 56th Street, but I had to race up the avenue to get to Pandora's Box. I arrived there, panting, at 6:54, and stood in front of the window waiting for the moment of change. People walked in front of me and behind me, blocking my view of the display: a life-size mannequin, posed in an elaborate red dress and made entirely of chocolate. The same as last week.

I kept glancing at my watch. When the minute hand hit 6:55, the window went black. I backed up a step, and a second later, Shar stood in front of me, wearing a filmy, one-shouldered white dress trimmed in gold. She looked like a goddess.

"Nice dress. I like it better than the bikini," I said, ignoring a banker type who gave me a quizzical look, then a wide berth as he strode by.

She pursed her lips. "Funny. I don't have a lot of choices—barely there, somewhat there, or not there at all. I'm working with what I've got. Give me a break!" Then she tilted her head. "I'm guessing you didn't get a chance to try the fleece. Since I'm still here."

I shook my head and dug in my purse for the iPhone, which I held up. "I've been trying all week. She's always awake first, dressed and sitting in the dark, waiting. Talk about creepy. I try to get up early; I even set the iPhone for 4 a.m., but it didn't go off. Probably you-know-who. Do you have any other ideas?"

"Sleeping pills in her water bottle?" Shar shrugged. "Tell me about her. What classes is she in?"

"She's in Calc with me. And Lit.

"Those are *my* classes!" Shar started.

"I know. By some *miracle* Elwood was able to plug her in all the right places," I said shrewdly. The implication wasn't lost on her.

"Whatever." She looked away. "Go on. What does she like?"

"Music," I said. "You should see the sound system she brought in—it takes up an entire wall of the room! She put on this Elysian Fields live album and I thought I was actually at a concert." At the last words I caught the sound of my voice—it seemed a bit too enthusiastic. Shar didn't look happy.

"Just music?" She slitted her eyes at me.

"It's only been a week. The crew that moved her in turned the room into a cave. Her bed's black, most of her clothes are black..." I trailed off.

"Sounds like you two have a lot in common." Shar crossed her arms over her chest—was she pouting?

Better not tell her about going out for coffee and then shopping—although I didn't initiate that.

"You have to know this is all Hades' doing," I said. "He's making things deliberately challenging on several levels—separating us, putting me with someone with the same interests, giving her your schedule; all of it to psyche us out."

She dragged her eyes to meet mine. "You really think so?"

"Absolutely. I'm sure he'd love a cat fight between you and me—one that distracts us from what's really going on. And I bet there's more to this, just like last time."

She nodded grimly and was about to say something when I heard her watch chime.

I put my hand up to the glass. "I'll try again!" I shouted quickly. "And I'll see what else—"

The glass went black, and then back to the chocolate mannequin. Our five minutes were gone, and we'd accomplished nothing. When I turned to go, a homeless man and an old lady with a shopping trolley were staring at me like *I* had problems.

"Excuse me," I said, but I didn't have to; they both backed away. As Shar would say, *Whatever*.

All the way home, I steeled myself for dealing with Paulina and justifying why I'd been nice to her. I'd have to be polite, but distant. No connections. With no other options, I had to try sneak-shanking her with the fleece again. Tonight I'd have to have it ready, perhaps tucked under my bed. Maybe I'd just not sleep at all—I'd pulled all-nighters before.

When I got back to the dorm, light slid out from under the crack of our door and music played softly on the other side. Taking a deep breath, I slid my key into the lock and went in. Paulina's messenger bag lay on the floor next to her bed, but she wasn't there.

"Must've gone to the bathroom or something," I muttered to myself. I was glad I had a few seconds alone. I had to get ready for tonight, and I really didn't want her to see me get the fleece out. In fact, maybe it would be better if all conversation was kept to a minimum.

I walked over to my bed and was about to toss my stuff onto it when I saw a little silk bag on my pillow. It was blue, the same color as my eyes. I picked it up; it felt weighty. Untying the knot on the bag, I gasped as I slipped out the horse bracelet. A little tag fluttered out:

For Meg, from me. P.

This was going to get seriously complicated.

$SHAR$

Not Telling!

Light filled that sumptuous yet foreign bedroom. Not sunlight, but the odd brightness that passed for daytime in Tartarus.

I was still here. Meg hadn't succeeded. Yet.

Groaning, I picked up the watch from my bedside table. It didn't tell real time—in this place, time was impossible to measure. There were no clocks or calendars, and sunrises were irregular. Even my body clock couldn't tell me when to sleep or eat. I only knew that when the hand on Ben's watch neared the twelve o'clock point, I might get to talk to Meg. Not that I ever noticed the hands moving until right before it chimed. The only thing I was somewhat certain of, based on our five-minute meetings, was that I'd been here a little over a week. Another call from Meg would mean it was two weeks.

I couldn't wait to talk to Meg. I wanted to be at the box for every precious second. With an exasperated sigh, I blew up my messy bangs, got dressed, and squandered away more time exploring the palace—the game rooms, the movie theaters, the indoor pool. I didn't want to go "outside." Somehow the beautiful settings seemed more lonely. I even missed Cerberus, who wasn't answering my whistles.

When the watch finally jingled that it was time to talk, I hurried to the throne room. Running across the floor, I skidded to a stop right in front of Pandora's Box and lifted the lid.

"Shar!" said Meg, her face beaming.

"Meg!" I replied with a facetious brightness. "I'm still here!"

She blushed. Something wasn't right.

"I know. I'm sorry. The morning trap's not gonna work. She's always up before me. I even set an alarm for two a.m."

"And?"

She looked away and in a lame voice said, "I fell asleep again."

"Meg!" *You can catch up on sleep another time! I'll even do your homework, your laundry for you!*

"I'm sorry."

"Throw it on her when she's in the shower!" I practically shouted. Really, how hard could it be to put a fleece on someone?

"I'm trying to figure things out up here," Meg said, sounding defensive. "I have to play nice for appearance's

117

sake. And school hasn't stopped just because of this assignment." She put a hand over her eyes. "I'm up to my ears in Calc. And I have a Social Studies paper."

It was a lot, I guessed. I tried to feel some sympathy for her. But seriously, I was in *Tartarus*! I looked at her, ready to launch a string of reasons why she needed to put everything—school included—aside to finish this, when she lowered her hand and I saw her face. She was miserable. Of course Hades wanted us to be at odds with each other.

I took a deep breath. "That girl has my dorm room, my schedule, my friend, my *LIFE!*" Oh, little purloining Paulina was sooooo lucky I wasn't there. She was the person I should be mad at. Her *and* Hades.

"I did a little research," Meg offered brightly. "There's something *you* can do."

"Like what?" I pressed my lips together.

"There's a way out of there," she said, lowering her voice.

"Definitely?" I perked up. Ben warned me not to "heed wild tales" of escape routes, but was he dense? His not-so-subtle warning had raised my suspicion that there probably *was* a way out. He'd have served his master better by keeping his mouth shut. "But how do you know?" I asked. "And why are you whispering?"

Meg glanced from side to side, shifting her eyes.

"I'm attracting an audience here. I thought our conversations would be private, but … " She rolled her eyes. "Thanks, Hades!"

I felt a stab of guilt for giving her a hard time. Without a doubt, Hades was toying with her, and she'd been thinking about getting me out while I just waited around.

"Well? What do I do?" I prompted, glancing desperately at the hands on the watch. "Hurry!"

"You need to find someone named Eurydice," Meg said. "I looked it up just to be sure. She's the only one who almost made it out."

"Almost?" I sputtered. "You're sending me to someone who had an epic fail?"

"It wasn't *her* fault," Meg replied defensively. "Her husband, Orpheus, was a musician. He was so broken up when she died from snake bites that his songs made even Hades and Persephone cry."

"No way!" I said. "That's hard to believe, although Hades did relent a bit when we went hysterical on him."

"So anyway," Meg rushed on, "Hades told Orpheus that he could take Eurydice back to the mortal world with him, and set them both on a passage back. Orpheus was supposed to walk ahead of her. The only condition was that he wasn't allowed to look back, but—"

"He looked back," I finished. "Which means she's still here."

"The story goes that she was sucked back down and never saw the mortal world again. But she would know where the way out is. She's seen it."

"I'm on it." I nodded.

The watch started chiming.

"Time's up!" I cried.

"Look for Eurydice!" she shouted just before the box went black.

I noticed she hadn't said anything about trying to get the fleece on Paulina again, but still, I felt better. There was something I could do instead of waiting around and trying to avoid Hades, who truth be told had been surprisingly absent. Since he apparently relished having me down here, I thought he'd be making a pest of himself, but it seemed he was up to no good somewhere else.

"What are you doing?"

I jumped. Caz strolled up to me in his lazy gait. He was dressed in casual khakis and a loose, barely blue cotton shirt. Very airy and light, and sexy on him.

"Talking to my ... friend. Up there," I pointed. A heavy sigh escaped. I hadn't told Meg about Caz; there hadn't been enough time. And really, there wasn't much to tell.

"Hades lets you? That's a first." Caz's sleek blond hair slipped over his eyes. Impatiently, he brushed it aside.

I nodded. "Yes. I'm allowed to talk to Meg once a week." *Don't say too much! Contract violation! More time for bad behavior!* "She's, uh, keeping me up-to-date on homework. And stuff. But don't go giving him too much credit. We only get five minutes." I wiped sweaty palms on my Grecian gown. My hands always perspired when I was lying. Only my mother knew this, and I was determined to keep it that way.

"He's never allowed *any*one, not even Persephone, to talk to anyone outside his kingdom while they're here. She sneaks to the mortal plane to do that." Caz's gaze was shrewd. "I'm stunned. I'd ask how you managed that, but I'm guessing you can't discuss it."

I looked away.

He glanced around. "I was hoping to run into you earlier today, but I guess he's been keeping you busy. Want to go explore, or are you waiting for ... "

"Him? Pffft. As if." I made a face. "I'd like to see the Elysian Fields. I wanted to ask—" I just managed to shut my mouth before blabbing about trying to find Eurydice. Cute as he was, Caz was still in the "need to know" category for giving out information.

He cocked his head, those blue gray eyes, the color of a stormy sea, so beguiling, mesmerized me. I stared at them, forgetting what I was saying.

"Ask what?"

"Huh?" I replied stupidly.

"What did you want to ask? Something in the Elysian Fields you wanted to see?" he prompted.

Oh. Right. My brain went to bubblegum with him around.

Sweat rolled down my palms. "I wanted to ask if people really liked it here. Hades says it's not all bad."

Caz smirked. "It's not all good, either, but I'll show you around. Come." Before he could grab my hand, I swiped them on my dress.

"Wow, you've got really warm hands." He tugged me along to one of the side doors. He opened it and we stepped into a desert. Great hills of pink sand rolled, with an oasis not far in the distance. "Before we hit the Elysian Fields, you really have to see this." He grinned mischievously. We ran to a cluster of golden palm trees and I gasped at the lavender lake in front of me.

"It's *purple*," I breathed. Beautiful, breathtaking.

"Yeah. Hades likes to add his own twist to everything. Poseidon favors blues and greens, so Hades went in a completely different direction. I think it's a kind of game, like—"

And he sang, "'Ifffff Iiiiii were the kinnnnng of the pan-theeeeeeon.'"

It was a fair imitation of the Cowardly Lion from *The Wizard of Oz*. I couldn't stop the giggle.

"Yep, that sounds like Hades. Has to do things his way." I moved slowly forward. Of course, if the lake was purple, the fish had to be different too. Even as a kid, I never would have dreamed of fish with fur. Or the patterns and shapes I saw now. It was like modern art gone sea crazy.

"Un. Be. Lieve. Able."

Again Caz reached for my hand, and I followed. We ran over a shimmering pink sand dune to a red mountain range.

"Before we climb to the top, you have to see the caves."

Climb to the top of Underworld Everest? In a dress and sandals? This boy was seriously misguided. A cave didn't sound too doable either. I really needed to be looking for Eurydice. We'd already wasted time doing nothing, but I wanted to be with him. It'd been a while since I'd felt this way about anyone. Staying a little longer wouldn't hurt.

The cave opening was around eight feet in both height and diameter. We entered, pausing to let our eyes adjust to the darkness. The floor was stone, no dust! I wouldn't have dirt between my toes if the rest of the cave was like this. Although it would be cool to rinse off in the lavender lake. Provided the furry fish didn't bite. One never knew with Hades.

Caz moved to stand in front of me. "Okay, close your eyes. Let me lead you, and when I say, then you can open."

I started to object, but he cupped my face with his hands, warm and so not sweaty.

"Trust me."

Should I?

He was a prisoner, like me, and knowing our petulant overlord and his penchant for creative punishments, Caz wasn't likely to hurt one of Hades' pets.

Plus his eyes were too soft, his hands too gentle for me to believe he would do me any harm.

And I *wanted* to go.

I closed my eyes.

He moved behind me and gently, slowly, guided me forward. No steps or rocks interfered with my walk. When we'd gone about a dozen steps, I could feel the coolness of the cave and that slightly musty odor of damp rocks. Water dripped in the background and it sounded musical, like drops falling on bells.

"Look," he whispered, his breath soft and warm in my ear, his body close to me. My heart beat a little faster. I opened my eyes. The cave had become a concert hall cast in stone, the ceiling studded with diamonds and giving the illusion of millions of tiny lights. The columns were a rainbow of gemstones: onyx at the bottom, followed by rubies, sapphires, emeralds, and topazes. The breath left my body in a whoosh. All I could do was stare.

"Hard to believe Hades created this, huh? He's a mystery, that one."

I nodded dumbly.

"Sing something."

Finally coming to my senses, my head snapped around. "What?"

"Sing. La la la." His voice echoed, but it sounded better—

richer and deeper—than when he'd sung the Cowardly Lion melody.

The only song that came to mind was the birthday song. "Happy Birthday..." My voice was sweet and full, and so much stronger than in real life. This place was better than the acoustic music room at school.

"Amazing! I could do concerts here. I'd be a *rock* star!"

Caz looked at me for a full second before he groaned and laughed.

Oh yeah, I still had the wit.

"All right, Lady Shar Shar. We still have a lot to see."

This time, I grabbed his hand. He gave me a huge smile and off we went. It seemed like only steps and we were enshrined in a secret garden.

"The only garden in Tartarus," said Caz.

"But I thought, given who his mother-in-law is, there wouldn't be any flowers or trees." An adorable bunny hopped close but Caz yanked me back. He stooped and picked up a rock, throwing it at Thumper.

"What are you doing?" I demanded. "How could you?"

He pointed. The rabbit hissed, showing enormous fangs. He picked up another, larger rock. The rabbit hissed again and I shrank back. Caz lifted his arm and the creature bounded off.

"That's Hades' snub at Demeter. Takes all her cute and fuzzy animals and turns them deadly." Caz dropped the stone and quickly grabbed my hand as I bent to stroke a velvety petal of an iridescent chartreuse flower. "Be careful," he warned. "Not everything is at it appears. Even the flowers. Avoid them, they're lethal."

I heard grumbling and tried to step under the shadow of a large tree, but Caz pulled me back again.

"What're you doing?" he whispered, his brow furrowed, "You have to be careful here! This place is dang—"

"Shhhh!" I hissed, pulling him close. "I thought I heard someone."

He looked around. "Don't worry. It's just the gardener." He pointed to a stooped and wizened figure burdened with a pair of enormous hedge clippers.

My heart jumped into my mouth.

Arkady Romanov!

He looked just as I remembered, old and frail, but he moved around the garden with ease, hauling the shears. He cautiously approached what looked like a perfect tree with pink and yellow flowers. He hesitated for a moment before reaching up with the clippers and snapping off a low-hanging branch. The tree shook, and one of the pink flowers morphed into something that looked like a mouth filled with rows and rows of jagged teeth.

Like a monster in a bad horror movie, it darted at Arkady and he quickly pulled out a spray bottle with some pukey-colored liquid in it. He spritzed the shark-flower's petals frantically, and, cursing at it, gave it a vicious glare before moving on to a towering bush with great, dripping, bulb-shaped blossoms.

I held up a hand in surrender. "I've seen enough. Let's go."

Caz waited until Arkady moved out of sight. "I brought you here because this is the one place Hades mostly avoids," he explained. "Demeter is all about plants and gardens and fields, so he rarely comes here. We can talk and shouldn't have to worry too much that he'll show up." He led me over to a stone bench built around an ugly tree; its trunk and limbs were twisted, gnarled, and half-dead looking.

I was leery of it and scooted next to Caz. "Is this one safe?"

He laughed. "Yeah, this one is. Generally, if it's ugly in here, it's safe. That's another one of his inside jokes." We sat down.

"How do you know all about every place and thing down here?"

"Experience," he mumbled, his glance skittering away.

I looked at him expectantly. He wanted to talk, right? That's what he'd said, and why he brought me to the secluded gothic garden. He seemed nervous, fidgeting in his seat, looking everywhere but at me. Here's where those early beauty pageant lessons came in handy: *Be a gracious conversationalist.*

"The person I was talking with in the throne room is Meg," I began. "She's my friend and roommate at school. I miss her. And my life. I wish I was back up there. Is there anyone you miss?" It was a clever ploy to entice him to reveal something about himself.

He turned to me, tapping his fingers on his thigh. "I have a twin. Up there. I'm hoping I'll get to see him. Soon."

Then the conversation lagged. Could I tell him about my former life as a Siren?

Um, that's a big NO. Not without incurring Hades' punishments and pissyness, because technically I am still under contract.

And what would Caz think? He'd probably never want to speak to me again.

"I'm worried about Meg," I continued. "She's all alone. Usually we're there for each other, but I'm stuck here. And who knows, if I'm gone too long, she might go back to wearing all black or cheap plastic shoes—after all the work I've done on her! I have to get out." I jumped up, now too agitated to sit still, even next to Mr. Supermodel. I paced around a bit, careful to give wide berth to the rainbow-striped flowers.

Caz remained silent, looking at me without so much as a raised eyebrow. I couldn't take it anymore.

"Is there a way out?" I blurted. No sense wasting time beating around poisonous bushes.

He ran a hand through his hair. "I haven't heard of a specific way out. There are always rumors, but I haven't noticed anyone suddenly missing. I'd have to say that Hades would know the Underworld better than anyone, and if there is a way out, it's probably full of very unpleasant surprises. He doesn't like to be bested. At anything."

I huffed. "Don't I know it. He's constantly chasing me, taking all my clothes away, and making me wear these silly outfits, thinking I'll succumb."

"He wants you."

"Not getting me. I'm not for sale or negotiation. I'm a free agent."

Caz laughed and came over to me. "I like you. You're the only female who's ever said no to him."

"For now," said the sinful voice of my captor.

I jumped, my heart leaping into my throat. In slithered Hades, showing off a white and gold tunic similar to mine. He turned cold eyes on Caz. "A little temptation scene in a garden? That's been done." He pivoted to face me, warmth and, yes, lechery in his expression.

"Sharisse, my favorite Siren. You are a fitting addition to my garden of delights. Beautiful to behold, yet you can be so deadly. Have you seen Arkady yet?" he teased.

He crowded next to me and pointed a finger at Caz. "I believe you have someplace else to be *quiet*. Shoo." He flicked his index finger. With a hurtful glance at me, Caz left.

Great. Now that Hades spilled the Siren info, the only friendly face I'd see would belong to the Pillsbury Patriot, Ben. I could count on him to be shuffling around the throne room, dusting, and bringing me fresh towels and banal chit-chat.

"Do not waste your time with the likes of him, *cara mia.* He is unworthy of you."

A little jealous, are we?

"I thought you didn't come here. Caz said—"

"Do not believe everything you hear. Or see. And I missed you. I wouldn't want you to think I'd forgotten you while my affairs took me elsewhere. If you're here, then I want to be here too."

I ignored his little seductive pout. "I miss Meg, and Caz has been friendly and sweet. Now I bet he won't talk to me. And if he tells the others I'm a Siren, especially people sent here by previous Sirens, only your minions will come near me. What about *your* nondisclosure clause? Can I go home?"

He chuckled. "So captivating with your defiance. Others have begged and pleaded and *bargained* for what they want." He let the words drift off.

I turned my head away and walked over to sit on the

bench. "You'll turn blue holding your breath. And what's with the toga? Did the party start without me?"

His eyes flared a moment. "It's a very good thing I find you so enchanting, to allow you such leeway. No one else would dare to speak to me that way."

Okay, so maybe that sharp tongue my mother always warned me about was not working here. The best way to get to Hades was to appeal to his ego. Vanity has its uses.

I rubbed my face. "I'm sorry. That was rude. Not that you don't look great in it, but why?"

He looked somewhat mollified. "This is what we are required to wear when visiting Mt. Olympus. Zeus has his petty rules." He sniffed.

"Dress code, huh?"

"Yes. Stupid, isn't it?" he grumbled.

"No, I think it's more like upholding tradition. Everyone's wearing baggy jeans with holes and grungy shirts—it's nice to see something a little more elegant." That was true; I didn't own a single pair of jeans with rips or worn spots. That was Meg's thing. I never understood the whole 'I want to look as poor as I can' fashion appeal. How could anyone think poverty was fun or glamorous?

"Ah, a true woman of taste." He checked me over from top to bottom to top again. "You look absolutely perfect in that gown."

"I'm glad you like it. It's the only thing from the closet I'll wear. You'll be seeing a lot of it."

"Not even the turquoise bikini, once?" he pouted, moving closer.

"Dream on," I replied airily, rising quickly and scooting over to a weeping gumball tree.

"We'll see." His voice was right behind me, I could feel his breath stealing over my shoulders.

"So, nice garden!" I stammered, turning and stepping back. I wanted to keep him in my sights. "Caz said you made everything here the way you wanted it."

"Caz talks too much," he mumbled, "but yes. Careful! That tree chews on anything in its grasp. You're safe now, but if you venture farther in without me, the precious Caz can't save you. Only *I* can."

Yes, Mr. Megalo-maniac. I think we all get the pic.

I faked a girly squeal and jumped away from both tree and him. I kept moving, trying to hold him at bay. Bad things happen to girls in gardens with snakes.

"I love your lavender lake," I said.

"Thank you!" He had such a happy look on his face that I felt bad thinking how no one appreciated his ingenuity, sick as it could be. Really, though, he'd created some wonderful, unique things. "It was one of my most inspired creations, I think."

"Can I swim in it?"

"If you want to swim in it, you may. I will immediately instruct the inhabitants to keep to the bottom while you enjoy yourself. Maybe I should accompany you?"

Oh he was smooth! Trapping me into an invitation. How to get out?

"Sure. After I finish practicing my Calculus. And catching up with Ben. And I want to see the Elysian Fields. So many fascinating people there! I could do my history paper with firsthand sources!" I couldn't stop rambling, but Hades only chuckled softly.

"Sometime, then. Maybe when you are more settled in and used to everything."

Settled in? Seriously?

I didn't reply. He ran two fingers down my cheek, my neck, and was probably about to keep going when I jerked back. A slight flush colored his face.

"You refuse my advances at every turn. You will be my greatest conquest when you finally capitulate."

Not while I'm breathing.

"So, what's happening on Olympus?" I asked. "Big meeting of the gods? I'd love to see the temple." My heart was hammering in my chest. This bad boy had that deadly charm, deadly being key.

Hades gave me a sexy half-grin. "No mortals allowed; not that you wouldn't be a breath of life on that rock pile. But even if I could bring you, Zeus would castrate me and then there would be Demeter and Persephone to contend with. After dealing with me, they would turn on you." He circled around me, trailing that questing finger along my shoulders, giving me chills. "Demeter would be bad enough. She carries a grudge from your last encounter…" His finger skirted around my neck to the pulse at my throat, then paused. He leaned in closer, his lips just tickling the outer edge of my ear. "But Persephone would be… *vicious.*"

"Okay! Cross Mt. Olympus off the vacation list!" I slid away, closer to the poisonous posies.

"And a word about Caz, *ma petite*. He's not to be trusted. Everyone is here for a reason. Remember that. I'm all that stands between you and a very unpleasant future. A little gratitude is in order." He gave me a dark look.

"Um, thank you?"

"Not enough." He pulled me toward him and stole a kiss, lingering and full of sinful promise, which left me quite breathless. He knew how to rattle a girl.

He broke away, backed up a step, then spun on his gold sandal and stalked away, only to halt at the edge of the garden. Over his shoulder he said, "And don't forget Cerberus. After you play with him on the beach, clean up the mess he leaves. I believe that's in your job description." He vanished.

My life so sucked right now.

MΣG

In the Bag

Somehow, I'd managed to keep the Elysian Fields concert a secret from Paulina ever since I'd heard about it—but I wasn't really thinking about it anyway. I'd spent the past few weeks trying to keep on top of school, be congenial with Paulina, and somehow plot her demise. Then she happened to mention that the band would be playing next week, and I spilled by accident.

"Where are your seats?" Paulina raised herself onto her elbows and quirked an eyebrow at me.

"Beacon Theater, Mezzanine, row A." They were the best seats I'd ever had to any show, although at this point I was more excited about seeing Jeremy than the band. I scrolled through the last few messages we'd exchanged. Between trying to survive at school, figuring out how to get Shar back, dealing with Paulina, and waiting for the right moment to strike, my replies were scanty one-word answers. But at least I was replying now.

"Nosebleed!" Paulina huffed dismissively. "When I saw them—"

"You had backstage passes and Matt Davy handed you his plaid hanky," I interrupted.

She smirked. "It was *almost* that good."

I started to laugh, and then caught myself and turned it into a cough. What right did I have to be looking forward to concerts and giggling with Paulina—the one I was supposed to be shepherding into the fleece? At first I might have had some legitimate excuses for my failures: the shock of it all, trying to fall into a routine of normalcy so that I actually could do it ... But the only thing I'd managed to accomplish was having an increasingly friendly ease with her. It just kind of ... happened.

"So, who're you going with?" she asked, sounding too interested. She swung her long legs over the edge of her bed and got up to fiddle with her sound system.

"My boyfriend got the tickets," I said, frowning as I scrolled through the texts again. I closed my eyes and saw his elfin face, straight dark hair, and blue impish eyes.

"Oh." *Did she sound disappointed? What—did she think I was going to ask her to come along?* "Does he go to school here? I've never ... seen you with anyone."

I shook my head. "No, he's out of high school. He's at NYU. I'll be going there in the fall." I turned to her. "Did you leave someone behind, or were you seeing anyone before you moved?"

"No," she said too quickly—which had to mean "yes." "Bathroom!" she snapped and left, slamming the door behind her.

I've touched a nerve. At last—after so many conversations about music and classes, and time spent making catty, nasty, and totally appropriate remarks about Alana, to whom Paulina took an instant dislike—here was a clue about what her deal with Hades might be. Maybe she sold her soul for love … and like Arkady, wasn't specific about details and things went wrong.

Should I delve? I shook my head. I didn't need to know anything about Paulina that would distract me from getting her under that fleece. But …

But what?

There was no excuse.

I couldn't go to the Pandora's Box window again without another plan of action. I shouldn't even have to go to the window—Shar should be back by now. The information about Eurydice was a nice save, albeit a desperate one. Shar had seemed excited about the idea when we'd parted, but I was guilt-ridden—yet another week had gone by and she was still in Tartarus. I'd failed to do anything on my end, and it was like I was putting the burden of resolving this completely on her. But even if she did get out, what about Paulina? Hades would still want her, and I was obliged to deliver. I had to try something, even if it didn't work.

I looked at the clock: 9:18 p.m. Whenever Paulina went to the bathroom she took forever, and she'd only been gone for a couple of minutes. If I couldn't fleece her tonight, maybe I could try something tomorrow during the day.

I went over to the closet, opened it, and unzipped the garment bag. As quickly as I could I yanked the fleece off the hanger, rolled it up, and stuffed it into the recesses of my messenger bag. I couldn't close it fast enough, and caught my skin more than once in the bag's plastic clips.

I couldn't say why I didn't want her to see me handling it. *You just don't want to hear her go on about it like last time,* I thought, but I knew I was lying to myself. It was true that I knew little about her other than what I'd so far observed, but she just didn't *feel* foul to me. My sixth sense always set off alarm bells when I was around someone creepy. I shivered in Arkady's presence, and when Hades appeared, my skin crawled. Yet even with her wacky sleeping habits, Paulina didn't make me want to watch my back.

I felt a pang of guilt when I saw the empty garment bag and hanger. Hastily I hid them away in the back of the closet and rolled the door shut, only to see my messenger bag staring up at me from the floor. I felt sick, like I was setting a trap. Trying unsuccessfully to dismiss that thought from my mind, I kicked the bag under my bed, turned the music down to lullaby level, lowered the lights, and settled into bed.

When Paulina eventually returned, I stiffened and clutched my blankets. She turned off the lights but left the music on; she usually kept it playing all night. But instead of going to sleep, she padded over to my side of the room, her long lean frame draped in shapeless sweats and tube socks. She stood next to my bed, looming over me like a specter. My eyes adjusted quickly to the dimness, the room illuminated only by the sound-system lights. Under the dark frame of her hair, I could see her eyes glittering in the dark. I sunk into my sheets, wishing the bed would swallow me up.

"Sorry about being so abrupt and stalking out before," she said awkwardly. She turned her head to look away.

"No big deal," I mumbled from under the blankets.

"I've just had a lot on my mind." She sounded incredibly sad.

I lowered my cotton-blend shield a bit. "I'd say so. Coming here, being new and all."

She shook her head. "I'm used to moving around. It's not that."

"Well then, what is it?" I asked, shifting so I could see her better. "Whatever it is, it can't be that bad, can it?"

She plopped down on the floor and sat cross-legged on the rug at the side of my bed. "It can," she replied, keeping her eyes on the floor. She rubbed her face. "I'm worried about my brother. I haven't seen or heard from him in a while. No one has. I'm hoping that he hasn't gotten himself into any kind of trouble. You know, the kind you can't get out of without help."

Whoa. So maybe it was for family, not love, that she'd made a deal. Was she waiting anxiously to see if her brother— possibly strung out by the sound of it—was safe, or had Hades duped her? That wouldn't be surprising, and it seemed more plausible to me than her having an evil alter-ego. I knew what making deals with Hades was like; there was always some hidden trick, agenda, or loophole, and always in his favor. And always made when people were desperate.

"I don't have any brothers or sisters," I faltered softly.

"But I have a friend ... Shar. I haven't seen her in a while. Sounds like it could be the same sort of situation."

Not really, but it felt good to say Shar's name aloud to someone and not have them look at me like I was crazy.

She laughed mirthlessly, darkly. "I doubt that."

"Maybe. But I know what it's like to have someone you care about just ... vanish." I chose my words carefully. "And I haven't talked to anyone about it. Until now."

In the dimness, I thought I could see her lips twisting into that half-grin.

"When was the last time you saw him?" I asked gently, hoping for more clues. Her face straightened.

"It's been a while. It seems like a century. What about your friend?"

"It's still kind of fresh. For me anyway," I said carefully, not wanting to reveal much more. Telling her I was still in touch with Shar would kind of defeat the purpose.

Paulina yawned. Then in an effortless, catlike movement, she got up and went over to her side of the room, got into bed, and turned to face the wall. A few seconds later, I heard the light sound of snoring.

Was she sleeping? I should try it now. Would it be the ultimate act of loyalty to Shar ... or a low-down dirty double cross? My hand crept toward my bag and my fingers found the first clip.

Click!

Shhhhh!

"Looking for something?" she mumbled.

Busted.

"Just making sure I had my Lit book."

"'Kay. Night."

Not only did she move like a cat, but she slept as lightly as one. I wasn't even going to try. I'd have to find another way. I closed my eyes and was asleep in seconds.

The next morning, Paulina was up and dressed, and I hit the showers and then skulked behind my screen; our usual routine.

We walked the block and a half to the academic building in silence, but something had changed. Paulina seemed more relaxed. She kept the glasses on, but she wasn't blatantly avoiding everyone that passed. Me? I was only slightly less wretched than the night before. Paulina and I had formed a kind of bond, but what about Shar?

We went directly to Calculus and took our seats. Laz looked bored, checking off names in his grade book, and Trey and company sat in a huddle chatting and whispering, taking no notice of anyone around them, me included. It was almost as if time had turned back to before the assignment, before I was ever a Siren. *I wish.*

I bent down to get my Calc book out of my bag. I unclipped one strap, and then another, then lifted the flap. Golden fleece frothed over the edge like the foaming head on a mug of beer.

I heard a little gasp behind me. Quickly I stuffed my hand deeper into the bag to retrieve my book, but as it slid out, so did more of the fleece.

"What is that?" I heard someone whisper.

I shoved the fleece back into the bag and snapped the clips shut.

"Is there a problem, Margaret?"

I lifted my head. Mr. Lazarus was staring me down from the front of the room. He looked annoyed; apparently I'd interrupted his intro to the day's lesson.

"Um, no, Mr. Lazarus." I opened my book and tried to look busy.

He huffed and turned back to the chalkboard.

Bringing the fleece to school was turning out to be a mistake, since people were drawn to the damn thing. There had to be some alternative way of doing this—something where either Paulina chose to put it on, or some other way to help Shar escape. But which, and how?

When time came to change classes, Paulina gave me a little wave and slipped out of the room ahead of everyone else. As I got up to leave, my phone buzzed in my purse. A message from Jeremy:

> Missing u. May B ur roommate will let u out 2 nite?
> XXX. J.

Before I could answer, Hades' iPhone went off:

> Am setting aside a cot in the closet for you—looks like you'll be staying with me soon. Just do it!
> H.

I closed my eyes in resignation and shoved the iPhone back into my bag. I tapped back to Jeremy:

> Sorry can't go out. But we r on 4 the concert!
> XXX. Me.

I couldn't in good conscience go out and have fun, not

with Shar still gone and Hades breathing down my neck. I added:

& the Spring Fling. Got dress, hope u will like!

That was good—I had two solid dates set up with him. My not being spontaneously available shouldn't bother him.

I ignored Hades' message.

Gathering up my things, I made for the door, only to find Trey waiting for me on the other side.

"Meg," he started, but I cut him off.

"Leave me alone," I said, and didn't stop walking. Something had to give—Paulina, Jeremy, Shar, Hades, window groupies, or the damned fleece. The fleece would have to go back to the closet, at least for now, so no one else would see it. I didn't like carrying it around—there were too many opportunities for something to go horribly wrong. I decided to ditch lunch and book it back to the dorm, where I would dump the fleece in the closet and run back for Lit.

The morning chugged by until the last few minutes of Physics, when I realized that I hadn't taken any notes in lab—not too smart—or gone to the bathroom—equally bad move. Once class was dismissed I slipped downstairs, past the cafeteria and into the ladies' room. I shut myself up in a stall and just stayed there. People came and went, chatting, joking, laughing, but in my 3 x 4 cube, I felt blissfully alone.

I left reluctantly, and only because I knew I had a limited window of time to get the fleece back to home base. When the main section of the bathroom was empty, I took the opportunity to reorganize my bag—books on the bottom, fleece on top so that when I got back to the room, I could stuff the thing in the closet and get out quickly.

A toilet flushed, a stall opened, and out stepped Kate. She curled her top lip at me but said nothing. Neither did I. I moved in front of my bag to block her view of the contents and tried to finish repacking when I heard another flush, and the bang of another stall door.

"Oooh, one half of the dark duo," Alana cooed sarcastically, then her tone softened. "Oh."

I'd managed to prevent Kate from seeing the fleece, but Alana got a full view. She stepped up quickly and plucked it from my bag before I could stop her.

"It's that *jacket!*" said Kate, pushing me aside.

Alana held up the fleece. A gentle shake and the matting and bunching from being cooped up in my bag disappeared. It almost looked alive.

Someone I didn't know came into the bathroom and immediately joined them. "Alana, where did you get that?"

"Hey, that's mine," I said, but everyone ignored me.

"I think it'll fit," said Alana, starting to swing it around her shoulders, but Kate grabbed hold of an end and pulled.

"I saw it first." Kate tried to tug it away.

"Can I try it after you?" asked the girl who'd just come in.

I heard voices outside; more girls were coming into the bathroom. Forcing my hand into their midst, I clutched the fleece and yanked, but to no avail. Six hands—not including mine—were latched clawlike onto it, and they weren't letting go. The only good thing was that no one could put it on.

A wicked idea came to me. I watched the tug of war for

a moment, and then with more glee than I should've taken, I stomped on Alana's foot. She howled and let go of the fleece.

"Why'd you do that?" She turned to Kate and poked her on the shoulder with a perfectly manicured finger.

Kate let go to slap Alana's hand away. "I didn't do anything!"

In shock, the other girl let go.

This was exactly what I needed—a catfight that made everyone in the bathroom forget the fleece. I grasped it with both hands and pulled it to me, only to stagger backwards with its sudden weight—it felt like one of those lead x-ray aprons they put over patients in the dentist's office. Stumbling toward the door with my prize, I rolled it up and tucked it under my jacket before grabbing my bag and bolting out the door.

That was close. Too close!

I ran down the hall, as far away from the cafeteria as I could, and kept moving until I got to a nook that was dark and silent. Stopping, I pulled out the fleece and popped it on top of my books, then slapped the flap of the bag over it. I clicked the straps and pulled them tight. Done. I wanted to kick myself. I'd lost my chance at getting the fleece back to the dorm—why hadn't I just gone straight there? As I hoisted the bag over my shoulder, it felt incredibly light. How could that be? I had my Calc and Social Studies books in there, and the fleece too.

The fleece.

I didn't want to open the bag to check, but I had the sinking feeling I just sent my textbooks to Tartarus. At least Shar could use them to catch up; I'd have to borrow

Paulina's and figure out how I was going to pay for replacements. Hades owed me.

Wearily I made my way to Lit—thank God I'd taken that book out to make room for the damned fleece—and finding my chair, sank down into it and put my head on my desk.

I didn't need to look to see if Paulina was sitting next to me; of course she was there. I felt her warm, heavy hand on my shoulder.

Without lifting my head, I rolled it on the desk so that I faced her. She'd taken her glasses off and was looking me square in the face, at close range—the first time she'd ever done that. Her steely gray eyes were wide with concern.

For me.

If she had something to hide I'd be able to see it, I thought. But Paulina's eyes were ... kind, yet shrewd.

"Are you okay?" she asked gently, squeezing my arm.

I wanted to cry.

No, I'm not okay. My best friend is stuck in the Underworld and the only I way I can get her back is to send you to take her place. At first you were really annoying and I was ready to do it, so long as I didn't think about it too much, but now ...

I shook my head. "I'm just having the world's crappiest day."

She flashed her lopsided grin. "You're stressed out. I know something that'll fix that."

I narrowed my eyes at her as she pulled her cell out of her back pocket and started tapping in a text. About a second later the phone blipped and a grin spread over her face as she read the reply.

"Yes!" she hissed, and slid the phone back into her jeans pocket. "We're going to see D'On as soon as school lets out."

We are?

"Who's D'On? He's not some sort of ... dealer, is he?" I whispered before I could stop myself. Not the best thing to say to someone who's brother is MIA and probably mixed up with the "wrong people." But Paulina just shook her head and laughed.

"Trust me."

Hadn't I heard that before?

"Who is he? *What* is he?" I demanded, intrigued in spite of myself. Her own private chef? Personal trainer?

"You'll see," she said mischievously as class started. She promptly opened her book and didn't take her eyes off it until the bell rang.

Paulina magically appeared outside the door of my last class of the day. She refused to answer any of my questions about where we were going. She pulled me through the halls, into the street, and down into the subway. Back up into the street and then across avenue after avenue, I followed like her shadow, almost like she'd followed me right after we first met. After about half an hour, we stood in front of a squat, dingy building on Avenue A. She stepped up to the door and pressed one of the six intercom buttons.

A cheerful voice crackled out, "Come on up, P!"

The door buzzed and she pushed inside. Putting her foot on the first step, she turned to me with a sly grin. "He's on the top floor," she said, and started bounding up steps two at a time.

Fantastic. A six-floor walk-up with no elevator. *I won't be stressed out when I get to the top, because I'll have passed out!* I clomped up the worn, seemingly endless steep steps. Paulina waited for me at each landing, where I stopped to pant.

"Nearly there," she encouraged. As I climbed, I wondered how Paulina—who wasn't a city native according to Mr. Elwood—knew about this obscure little place, whatever it was, and this D'On, whoever he was.

When I got to the last step, I doubled over.

"Mmm hhhmm."

I looked up, and startling violet eyes stared back at me.

"You weren't kiddin', P. This one needs to unhinge." A man with warm amber skin, a sinewy tall frame, and a mass of dreadlocks thrust out a strong-looking hand. "This way, baby. You spend some time here and you'll feel like a whole new person."

He pulled me into a brightly lit room. One wall was all windows, like our old Siren apartment. All the others were mirrored. Everywhere I looked, there I was. The tap of our shoes echoed on the pale wood of the highly polished floor.

"It's a dance studio," I said looking around, trying not to catch my reflection.

D'On threw his head back and laughed. "She is *smart!*"

I turned to Paulina. "You brought me to a dance studio? For what?"

"Whenever things get to be too much, I come here," she said, shrugging off her jacket. "A couple of hours with D and I'm good to go."

"You know it, P," D'On quipped, and handed me a bottle of water, which I nearly snatched out of his hand; I was hot, out of breath, and so thirsty.

"I don't dance," I protested, taking a swig. And then another. And another. It was cold and had a heady, fruity flavor, probably one of those vitamin-infused things.

"Everyone can dance—you just gotta let go," D'On crooned, taking the now-empty bottle from my hand and tossing it aside. He hadn't let go of me and he was drawing me farther into the room, walking backwards in sync to music that started from somewhere, or maybe had been playing when we first came in. I was too taken aback and busy trying to catch my breath to remember, but I suddenly realized I wasn't tired anymore, or huffing and puffing.

"See, you doin' it!" he cried.

I looked down at my feet, which were like D'On's, moving in time to the music. A look in the mirror showed that all of me was moving. My body jerked to a stop and I blushed, feeling incredibly silly, until I saw Paulina in the mirror.

She bumped and ground, her legs, arms, torso, and head jerking like badly connected train cars. I stifled a giggle, but as she kept dancing, the moves became smoother, more fluid. She twisted, writhed, and stomped in rhythm.

"That's the way, P!" D'On shouted, letting me go to clap his hands to a new song that started up.

I gasped. In the mirror I saw all three of us doing the same moves in tandem—D'On perfectly, Paulina slightly less so, and me, a bit better than I thought ever possible.

"Yeah, girlfriend, you got it, you got it!" D'On sang along with the music. "Let go!"

Let go let go let go…
  …of your inhibitions…
    …of Hades…
      …of your worries…
        …of the fleece…
          …of any guilt…

There was just the three of us and the music, the thump of bass, the sparkle of synth and chimes, and endless enticing melodies. Sweat dripped down my forehead as I stood in between D'On and Paulina, all of us stomping, waving arms, shaking.

Song after song played; we danced and danced. I shed most of what I was wearing until I was down to leggings, a tank top and my sneakers. Paulina wore a loose shirt and skinny jeans, her muscular arms and legs working it. As a song wound down and ended abruptly with the crash of cymbals, I lifted my head, ready to slide into the next move. I was facing the wall of windows—it was dark.

Shar!

"Oh my God, what time is it?" I screeched, skidding over to where my bag and clothes lay in a heap by the door. As if in slow motion, I found my pocket watch: it was 6:32.

I looked up, panic-stricken, and frantically gathered up my things. "Thanks so much for this, but I have to go—"

Paulina looked at me, puzzled, and started to move toward me, but D'On stopped her.

"Meet you back at the dorm!" I called, not looking back. I raced down the steps, nearly tripping and killing myself at least twice. Out in the street, the chill air slapped me as I glanced around helplessly; it'd taken us a half an hour to get here, so it would take close to that for me to get to Pandora's. I panted in frustration. Every second I stood there was a second wasted.

I bolted for the subway and practically tumbled down the steps—there was no time to find or buy a metro card. I hopped the stall, not bothering to be subtle, ignoring the indignant shouts behind me. A train pulled into the station and I got on it, not having the luxury of caring about where it was going. Refusing to meet the eyes of anyone in the car, I listened for the announcements. The train was going uptown. It was an express. *Luck! Luck! Luck!* I just might make it.

At 6:55, the car doors whooshed open at 56th, only one street away from Pandora's. Out and up the steps I bounded. *That dance class loosened me up if nothing else*, I thought, reaching the street and taking off down the block.

I got to the corner and started weaving through the people on the street, but stopped when I saw a group standing in front of the window, bigger than the one that had gathered around me last time.

Not waiting for them to move, I pressed on, pushing by people and walking right up to the glass. The display had changed; a gigantic chocolate frog squatting on a chocolate lily pad stared back at me. Chocolate bees buzzed around chocolate flowers.

"There she is!" I heard someone whisper, and then a snap and a flash reflected in the window. *Did someone take my picture?* The window darkened, and suddenly Shar was there in another of those barely there dresses, gazing out the window as if she couldn't see me.

"Here I am!" I yelled.

She started when she saw me. "Oh my God, what happened to you?" she asked, looking me over with concern. "Did you ... fight with her or something?"

I caught a fraction of a reflection of myself in the window. I was panting and my hair was damp with sweat. I was still wearing just my tank and leggings; I'd been carrying my coat and bag. I shivered, maybe because being outside with no coat on had finally caught up with me, maybe because along with my own face, there were about a dozen others behind me that I could see in the glass, watching me intently.

"No." I shook my head and, dropping my load to the ground, tugged out my jacket and wrapped it around myself. "I went ... "

"Where?" she demanded.

"It doesn't matter," I said.

"It matters to me," she snipped. "Were you ... working out?"

"No!" I said, shaking my head. I lifted my bulging bag up so she could see it and jerked my head at it, hoping she'd get the hint. "I tried to fix it at school, to get you out, but then—"

Shar crossed her arms over her chest. "Let me guess—*something* came up," she said coolly. "And it seems that whatever you were doing was far more important than getting me out of here. Or maybe you think I'll be here a while since you sent me some homework!" She brandished my Calc book.

"That was an accident!" I protested, but then I narrowed my eyes at her. What was she insinuating? She *was* right—I'd gotten distracted by Paulina and the dancing. I was angry at myself more than at her, but that didn't mean she could sit back and be a party girl. "Sorry if I'm not playing the knight in shining armor, Princess," I said, snidely. "I suppose you've been too busy getting ready for the Wonderland Ball or whatever to look into things from *your* end!"

Shar crossed her arms over her chest and looked away. Guiltily.

Had she even tried?

"I found the Eurydice stuff out for you," I said, forgetting my earlier regret, my tone slightly accusatory. "Why don't you find some info for me? It would be a lot easier to get this done if I—"

"Does that even matter?" Shar blurted. Her lip started to quiver and a tear tracked down her cheek. I unclenched my fists and took a step closer to the window. Hades strolled by in the background, wearing nothing but a very small towel. He gave me a boyish grin and waved.

"What the—" I started, but I heard her watch chime and the glass went black. A second later, I was staring at the frog again.

Taking a deep breath, I banged my head against it. A trickle of moisture ran down the glass.

I turned to go.

"Window girl!" someone from the crowd called. There were at least twenty people standing in a semi-circle around Pandora's. One of them, a middle-aged woman, smiled at me.

"Window girl! What did the frog say to you?"

"Why do you want to get him out?"

"What accident? What did it ask you to do?"

A few people tittered, but then another one called out in a serious voice, "Tell us, did it give you a message? Is the world going to end?"

"Leave me alone," I grumbled, gathering my things and pushing past them. Looking behind to make sure no one was following me, I saw the crowd disperse, some walking away, some going into Pandora's. I trudged back to the dorms four blocks away. I had too much to think about.

"Why did you leave?" Paulina asked as soon as I got in the door.

"I forgot I had to meet someone," I said wearily, shoving my bag under my desk. I didn't feel like answering questions or dealing with anything at the moment.

"The mysterious Jeremy?" she asked, her voice razor sharp. "What, does he have you running around after him every night?"

I snapped my head up to look at her. She was lounging on her bed, gazing intently at me.

Running around to see Jeremy?! No, I was late to see Shar because of you. And things are going badly with Jeremy because of YOU...

I looked at my bag with the fleece still tucked inside. I ripped it open and flung the woolly mass at her, but with her cat reflexes, she jumped aside.

"What was that for?" she demanded, her voice gruff.

"Jeremy."

And Shar. And me.

SHAR

Tick Tock, Time's Up

I trolled through my closet, trying to put together some kind of outfit that didn't require me to strut around half naked. I was not succeeding. And I was getting tired of the Grecian look.

"Why do you fight it? Fight me?" asked the lazy drawl.

I exhaled sharply, not turning around. "Because I have to. It's a matter of principle." Shoving hangers of skimpy bikinis and lingerie and other minuscule clothing aside, I spun around. "And why the obsession with the tropics? Haven't you heard the expression 'a cold day in hell'? Can't we have one of those?" I couldn't believe that I, Miss Summer Vacation, was asking for this. Truly I'd gone mad and the world had ended.

Lazing on my, no, *his* bed, as he liked to remind me,

in a sapphire blue silk shirt open to the waist, *the tease,* and sleek black pants, Hades brushed aside an errant wave of his auburn hair. He gave new meaning to the term "sexy messy."

"Because Persephone, stuck with her mother half the year, sees only spring and summer. So, when she returns to me, it becomes winter here and she can ski, snowboard, all that nonsense." He grimaced. "Me personally, I abhor the cold." He smiled that toothpaste grin. "I prefer to wear as little as possible, like this."

Quickly, I whipped my gaze away from him. I heard a rustle of sheets.

Not looking! Don't need that mental image! I had to divert the direction his mind was going, although I did wonder... *don't go there.* I steeled myself not to peek.

"What a good little hubby you are, giving up the warmth so the ice queen can have her palace."

Hades' voice whispered next to my ear and I tried not to jump. "Careful, mon pussycat." Next I felt his thumb and forefinger rub the back of my neck. "Now you've ruined the mood. I'll have to go torment someone else. Wonder what Margaret's up to?"

Without even a wisp of sound, he was gone.

"Yeah, go find out what she's up to," I muttered, "because she's not bringing me home anytime soon!"

After our last conversation, I was totally PO'd at Meg. She could deny it all she wanted—I knew what she was doing with Paulina. It was obvious they were hanging out, having a good time. She was exercising, or whatever, with the one person she should be sending away. Bad enough she always refused to go to the gym with me, but now she went places with Paulina, to get to know her before sending her off?

"How hard could it be to get someone to try on a jacket?" I asked Jack, my ratty stuffed toy squirrel. "All she has to do is play Makeover. Take something she owns, the fleece, and tell Paulina to try it on, and she'll wear whatever Paulina puts together. Really, didn't she ever play dress up as a kid?" I sulked. "They could even do a Halloween theme; it's what she wears anyway. She could give the new girl a goth makeover."

Okay, that was mean. True, but mean. I was just so frustrated! And after that crack about being a knight in shining armor and calling me Princess? I'd looked for the escape route.

Weeelll … that wasn't *exactly* true. I'd been exploring with Caz, roaming over so many wondrous sights: diamond quarries, underground falls of golden waters, too many marvels to catalog. But that *had* to count—I didn't know my way around, so I let Caz play tour guide. Eurydice just wasn't in the mountains. Or at the lake. Or in the caves. I still had to scour the Elysian Fields for her, but after Hades, the beast, deliberately blabbed about me being a Siren, Caz probably wouldn't be too keen on taking me anywhere else. At least I didn't have to keep my past a secret anymore.

I pushed Meg's Calc and Social Studies books off the bed in a huff. I'd been painting my toenails, then poof! There they were. Instead of sending Paulina, she sent books. I wouldn't get behind on homework, but if I knew I was going to be stuck down here for eternity, the *last* thing I'd do is Calc! A book on Greek mythology would have been sooo much more helpful for IDing people. And the gods. And the tedious details surrounding both.

I need a good run to clear my head. Oh wait, I only have little gold sandals, red stilettos, and black thigh-high boots. That made my choice . . . sandals and a walk. Forget the run.

I wandered over to the beach and threw the ball for Cerberus until my arm was tired. After petting him, cleaning up his monstrous poop pile—one would think he had three butts— and washing off the slobber in the aqua sea, I decided that if Caz didn't want to take me to the Elysian Fields, I'd go by myself. Someone there had to know where to find Eurydice.

Bypassing the door to the toxic garden where Arkady was, I headed toward the front doors of the palace. I'd been keeping an eye out for the inside route that Ben mentioned, but no luck yet. So out I went, stepping once again into the dismal, black stone world. Crossing a bridge that looked like something out of *Lord of the Rings* where Sauron resided, I came to another set of gates.

Black pearly gates.

Hades' humor was beginning to wear thin.

As I was about to knock, the gates swung open. Shrugging, I passed through and stood, shocked. To my left was a green meadow with cute little English-type cottages. More to the right was a perfect, TV-land suburban neighborhood. Down the center was a busy metropolis, where everything was shiny, clean, and sleek. On the far right were various ancient civilizations: Greek, of course; Egyptian; Mayan; Roman—the smallest because Hades hated them; and others. People walked around dressed appropriately for whichever world they belonged to.

Huh.

I spotted a group of rough-looking men, loaded with swords and cudgels and animal skins, over by an Irish pub called The End. I hurried over. This being the Elysian Fields and everybody already being dead, they wouldn't kill me, right?

"Excuse me!" No one heard me above the raucous song they were singing. My ears burned. Suddenly someone grabbed me around the waist and hoisted me onto their lap. I tried to fight but was severely overpowered.

"Now, Stoker, let the lass be," said a man with a strong Gaelic burr. He looked at me. "He dinna mean to harm ye, he jus' be havin' a bit o' fun." He bowed low. "I am Macbeth, King o' the Scots." He jerked a thumb at my captor. "And that be Stoker." The hulking Macbeth, wearing little more than plaid, a sword, and an eight-pack, nudged him, almost knocking Stoker and me off the stool.

I stopped struggling and turned to look up at him.

Stoker let go and I jumped away.

"Do I know you?" I asked. His black suit was English nineteenth century, maybe Victorian.

"It would be my pleasure if you did, but I cannot say as that I am familiar with you. Bram Stoker, at your service, miss."

OMG. *The* vampire creator. "I love your book!"

He blushed. Fancy that.

"You would *not* believe how much everyone adapts your storyline," I gushed. "Vampires are the ultimate. People just can't get enough of them."

"I am humbled, Miss. And you are?" He looked expectantly at me.

Somewhere behind me, I heard people shouting. I craned my head and caught just a glimpse of Caz coming out of a Parisian café.

I turned back to Bram. "I'm Sharisse. You should write a sequel! Gotta run!" I jumped up and started pushing through the crowd. When I got close enough, I caught the conversation around Caz. He was holding out both palms, like he was pleading.

"Why won't you tell me? I'm not like him!"

People shuffled away, shaking their heads.

"Hey, what's going on?" I asked.

Caz looked taken aback. "Shar. I didn't know you were here," he said smoothly. A little *too* smoothly. Something was afoot.

"How come they won't talk to you?" I pointed at the people backing away. "And who's 'him'?"

"It's a long, really boring story. Let's go to Italy. Would you like some cappuccino? A glass of wine?" he offered, taking my arm and leading me away.

Okay, like that wasn't an obvious "distract the blonde" move. *Hey, I got almost perfect SAT scores, bud. You're going to have to be a little smarter to just keep up.*

In what seemed like a few steps, we were settled at an outdoor café table.

"I'll take a hot chocolate with extra whipped cream and a dash of cinnamon," I said.

He looked at me, puzzled. "Don't people drink hot chocolate in the winter?"

"Don't people drink hot coffee and tea in the summer?" I shot back. Cute or not, he was starting to irritate me, and he was definitely trying to avoid something.

"Was Hades right?" I asked.

His head snapped up. "What?"

My hot chocolate, and his goblet of whatever, arrived. Without being ordered. Talk about service! If I could only find a Bloomie's, I'd be in business.

"Hades warned me not to trust you."

Caz stared down into his drink. "He would say that. He's my uncle. That's why no one will talk to me."

I choked on the whipped cream, grabbing a napkin to cover my mouth. "Your *uncle*?" I gasped. *So what does that make you, spy or good guy?*

He sipped his drink. Where had I smelled that delicious aroma? *Demeter.* She'd drunk the stuff when Meg and I worked for Arkady. Ambrosia, "nectar of the gods."

So. He really was one of *them.* Which explained a few things. He wasn't dead, and that was great—I didn't want to be attracted to a zombie-dead guy. But if he was Hades' nephew, there was no way I could trust him. "In league with the devil" crossed my mind.

On the other hand, Hades wasn't all warm and fuzzy with Caz as far as I could see. Caz was always jumpy, and didn't *I* know that feeling all too well. And, since Caz thought I was still a Siren, I knew he assumed he couldn't trust me. The question was, did I really want to get more involved with anything or anyone connected to the Underworld?

Sigh. A hot chocolate wasn't enough to soothe me

anymore. I wondered if I could order a real drink. Did dead bartenders in Old World Italy card people?

With meticulous care, I spooned the cream off my hot chocolate, giving Caz the time he needed to decide if he was going to spill his guts. I had a lot to ask, and I was sure he did too.

"He trapped me here," he said finally.

I laughed shortly. "Déjà vu all over again."

"My name's Castor, and my twin is Pollux. Our father is Zeus, although don't mention our names in front of Hera. She hates us."

"Do tell," I cracked, taking a tentative sip. The hot chocolate was now perfect. After a good slug, I set the cup down and gave Caz my best therapist look.

"She's not our mother. The other illegitimates and I are a painful reminder of Zeus' indiscretions" He blushed a bit. "There are a lot of us."

Men are dogs; that's what my aunt said when my uncle had his affair. *Hmmm.* Hades was a lech too. But then, so was Persephone, from what she'd admitted to Meg and me. Were any of the gods faithful?

It was my turn to blush. "I'm sorry, but I can't seem to keep all the gods in all the pantheons straight. There are just too many of you. What are you the god of?"

A small smile quirked up a corner of his adorable mouth. "Pollux and I are demi-gods; half breeds, you might say. When we're together, we can negate the powers of Hades' minions—the Furies, the Harpies, the *Sirens*." He raised an eyebrow.

I took a huge gulp to cover my embarrassment.

"Yes, um, about that. You see, Meg and I were shoe shopping and we argued over a pair of shoes." I wagged a dismissive hand. "You know how that happens. And then some cute guy, who turned out to be Jeremy, fell onto the subway tracks." I clapped my hands. "Then the train hit him. Well, we thought we killed him, and so we said—"

"That you'd do anything to undo it," Caz finished.

"Pretty much." I cringed. "That's how we were forced to be Sirens. But I'm not, now. Not here. I mean, I don't have to lure anyone to Tartarus," I babbled. God, I didn't want him to think I was still doing Hades' dirty work. "All I have to do is organize a ball."

"But your friend, Meg?"

I hesitated. "Without violating our previous contract, I don't think I can tell you. Hades told you I was a Siren, so that's old news. But if I tell you anything else, I'm afraid he'll use it as an excuse to keep me here longer."

As if eternity weren't long enough; I sure didn't seem to be going anywhere anyway.

Caz shifted uncomfortably in his chair, tugging at his collar.

"Hades wants to get my twin, too, who's hiding on the mortal plane somewhere. When we're separated, our powers are diminished."

I scratched my neck. "But if he has one of you, and your powers are weakened, then why would he need the other?"

"Good question. I'm guessing he wants to separate us permanently, or possibly try to ransom us to my father. Down here, Hades is supreme and not even Zeus can come in without permission. I can't leave to help Pollux, who in turn can't come here to rescue me. The only comfort I have is that Pollux isn't alone. There are friendly gods and demigods on the mortal plane."

Well, that was a conundrum I was also familiar with—although I had yet to meet a "friendly" god.

"So, how long have you been down here?" I asked.

He scrunched up his face. "I guess it's been about a hundred of your years."

My heart sank. "A hundred years! If there was a way out, you'd have found it by now," I said glumly.

"Not necessarily," he mused, tapping on his chin. "Are you familiar with Eurydice?"

I brightened. "Yes! Meg told me about her. Orpheus played to get her out, and he wasn't supposed to look back, but he did, so she's still here. Maybe she can help. You know where she is?"

Caz hesitated. We were both probably thinking the same thing—*can I trust you?* He might think I was using him, and how could I be sure he wasn't doing the same thing?

I'd have to take my chances—and make sure I didn't get left behind.

"No, I don't know," he finally answered. "And since no one will talk to me, I'll never find out." He finished his drink and leaned back in his chair. "Look, I think we should work together to get out of here. Join forces."

"Sign me up," I said, staring at him steadily. "I've been here too long, and Meg is having serious trouble if she can't get a girl to try on a fur coat."

Caz gave me a curious look, and was about to say something when my watch started chiming.

"Gotta go! I have to talk to Meg!" I rushed out, taking off my shoes to run faster. Luckily, the weird way Tartarus was set up, it seemed I was never far from the throne room; a few steps and I was back. I flipped up the box and waited. The watch chimed again. Our five minutes were running, but there was no Meg.

I waited.

And waited.

The watch chimed yet again.

Time's up.

MƐG

Between Rock and Hard Places

I didn't know where I was, but I liked it. It was outdoors, like a garden at night. The sky, a velvety black, was sprinkled with stars that twinkled and glittered. Flowers—roses, honeysuckle, jasmine—scented the sudden breeze that tickled my bare shoulders. I walked, my feet making little tapping sounds as if I were stepping on marble, not grass. Then I heard someone behind me and felt a warm hand on my bare arm. I turned and saw the outline of a tall person with broad shoulders and long, lean legs. I couldn't see his face.

Jeremy?

No, too tall.

Then who?

"Meg!" a voice whispered.

I strained to see the features, but the hand, at first so gentle, grasped my elbow.

"Wake up!" the whisper-voice grew louder. *Paulina's voice.* I was being shaken. "Time to wake up, Meg!"

"Stop!" I finally got the words out and opened my eyes. Paulina was bending over me, smiling, her glasses off.

"Time to wake up!" she sang in her low voice. At least she wasn't jostling me anymore.

"Back off!"

Paulina straightened and sauntered over to her side of the room. Annoyed, I kicked the blankets off.

"All I needed was five more minutes," I grumbled, trying to recapture the moment. I should have been dreaming about Jeremy; tonight was the concert and I'd finally see him. But I was sure that the person in the dream was someone else.

"Sorry," she said, but she didn't sound like she meant it.

"Bathroom," I replied, scooping up my robe and shower bucket.

A puff of steam greeted me as I walked into the shower; the place was hot and humid. And dark; several of the overhead lights were out. I found an acceptable stall and ensconced myself behind the plastic curtain and turned the water on. Gingerly I stood on one flip-flop and worked my pajama bottoms off with the skill of a circus acrobat. One leg and then the other, then peeled off my tee while I waited for the water to warm up.

I stood for several seconds under the comfort of the hot stream before reaching for my mesh scrubby. I squirted on a generous amount of vanilla sugar scrub, lathered it up, and started scrubbing arms, chest, stomach—ouch! Something pinched!

I examined the shower puff to see if the plastic tag-holder was still on it. I turned it around and around in my hands, but came up with nothing. That made no sense, anyway—I'd had the scrubby since before Shar went to the deep south. I started scrubbing again, and winced.

I looked down, only to see a mound of suds on my navel. I moved cautiously into the stream of water—and had to clutch the sides of the stall to stop from falling over. Around my belly button, in a swirling circle, were rings of flesh-colored, thumb-sized scales. They spread out to the edges of my waist and then up, ending at the swell of each breast. They covered the tops of my thighs and my bikini area... I reached around. More scales circled across my back. I grabbed a small round mirror out of my bucket, and after several attempts at twisting and wiping away suds, I could see that there were rows upon rows of scales, covering my behind in a weird, Daisy Duke micro-mini.

There was only one explanation for this overnight transformation.

Hades!

I was more mad than scared. This was *not* part of the deal—he even said so. What other sneaky, nefarious tricks was he going to pull? Could this be a natural consequence of accidentally using my diluted Siren powers? But I'd been pretty prudent about giving orders... hadn't I? I tried to remember the details of the last few weeks, but couldn't think of anything significant said to anyone other than that one incident with Trey.

I rinsed off and carefully patted myself dry. I found out the hard way that rubbing the scales in the wrong direction hurt. Immensely. I donned my bathrobe and, tying it loosely, scuttled back to the room.

Paulina barely looked up when I slipped around the door. Digging Hades' iPhone out of my bag, I tapped out a blistering and badly spelled message:

Scals! WFT?

Then, grabbing the outfit I'd laid out on my chair, I stormed behind the screen. As I tried to dress, I realized with dismay that the clothes I'd carefully chosen to transit from school to concert wouldn't work. Undies, bra, tights—problem; the elastic banding squished the scales together in places and made them dig into my skin like tiny razors. Blushing furiously I tried to come to terms with the fact that I'd have to go ... *free*.

"Paulina," I called, peeking my head around the screen and smiling, with teeth, "Can you hand me the dress on my bed and go in my drawer and get me my long socks? Please?"

She tossed over the dress first, then I heard her pull open a drawer.

"They should be on the top," I said, craning my neck to see, but all I caught was a glimpse of her hunched over my dresser. A second later she strolled over to the screen and draped the socks over the top.

"Thanks!" I said, shaking them out and praying that they didn't prove uncomfortably warm. I pulled the first sock over my foot and slid it up my thigh. The top didn't reach the scales; they'd be doable. I pulled on the other thigh-high, then popped the dress over my head.

"Cute," said Paulina when I stepped from behind the screen.

A buzzing sound came from my bag—a text message.

"It's probably Jerm." She made a face, then turned her back to me so she could focus on the contents of her backpack, which she'd just dumped on her bed.

I frowned at her attitude as I got my phone. Sure enough, there was a text from Jeremy:

> Can we eat B 4 show? 6?
> XXX.

I needed comfort, not complications. I couldn't do six; I had to be at Pandora's at 6:55 to talk to Shar. *Of course* my big concert date with Jeremy would be on a Tuesday, the designated window day—I was convinced that all coincidences, inconveniences, bad grades, cramps, and hangnails were Hades' fault. I couldn't screw up the window; our last conversation qualified as a disaster. I'd almost been late, I'd called her a princess, and I'd made her cry. Still, I wanted more time with Jeremy. I typed in a reply:

> Can't do 6 :(Can we meet @ 7:30 & grab something
> fast? XXX. Me.

A reply was not immediately forthcoming, so I toweled off my hair and smoothed it down with some gel.

"What's he doing?" I said aloud when he didn't get back to me right away. It was a simple question.

"Doesn't sound like he's worth your time if he can't reply to a message," said Paulina absently.

"He might be in class or involved with something," I snipped. "It's not an emergency. And besides, how do you know I'm talking about Jeremy?"

"I don't know if I should say … you might get mad and throw something at me again." She continued flipping through her stuff without looking up.

I slumped and sighed. "I thought I apologized for that," I said, "and you forgave me."

The half-grin made its appearance. "I did. I'm just being preemptive."

I narrowed my eyes at her.

"Don't worry, Meg. I still love you."

"Sure you do," I retorted, trying not to smile. "Just answer the question. How do you know the text was from him?"

She shrugged. "First, you said 'he.' Big clue. And he's the only one whose messages you get all girly over or talk about. And if someone hung on my texts that way, I'd be more attentive," she said disdainfully. "Just saying."

I wondered if I was really that obvious. Not that I cared what anyone thought; Jeremy was funny, sensitive, and beautiful. I was lucky to have him. "How do you know he isn't getting all emotional with my texts?" I challenged.

"He'd respond?"

"Funny, P."

My phone beeped just as we walked out the door.

> 7:30 cutting it close, may miss opening act.
> C u l8r.

Could a text *sound* angry? It was too easy to read into things, but I'd been putting him off, giving him short answers, and being unavailable for a month ... I'd fix all of this tonight.

> Thanks sweet! <3 u.

I used my free period to go to the library, determined to catch up on all the homework and reading I'd fallen behind on since Paulina arrived. It was a disturbing amount. I had to get it done today, as I needed to use my other free periods this week to make up three Phys Ed classes; I'd forgotten my gym uniform and had to miss them. Again, I blamed Hades. He saw to it that any time I might have to myself—any time that might give me the opportunity to finish with him—was occupied.

Even though I didn't officially invite her, Paulina came along to the library, carrying a full backpack. She found a comfy chair near the cramped desk I was working at and buried her face in a book. But I managed to finish my reading for Social Studies, as well as the three sheets of problems that Laz insisted I'd forgotten to hand in.

After school, we hit the coffee shop by the dorm. As we stepped in, the aroma of dark roast immediately comforted me; I could feel myself de-stressing.

Paulina stood in line next to me, and when it was our turn she ordered my usual and a super-size mocha latte/full fat/extra whip cream, three cookies, a sandwich, and a piece of cheesecake for herself. She pulled out a credit card.

I started to protest, but she waved me off. "I got this."

I didn't want her paying for me, but I didn't want to make a scene, so I stepped out of line and snagged a table. She joined me a few minutes later, settling herself in a low club chair.

"I think Jeremy should pay more attention to you and be a little less demanding," she said, taking off her glasses and tucking them into the knot of her scarf. No stalling, no subtlety; it was as if she'd been waiting all day to say it.

"What am I, then, if I'm always all gaga over him like you say?" I countered. "Maybe I'm too clingy."

"Good point." Paulina nodded. "Maybe you should step back."

"And maybe you should mind your own business," I snapped.

"Just saying what I see. I think you could do better."

"This conversation is over," I said, returning her gaze steadily.

Was I being unfair? Paulina wasn't aware of the pattern of my and Jeremy's relationship, that we texted each other every day because we couldn't see each other. How could she know that Hades' assignment and her arrival had thrown all that askew? It was sweet that she was being defensive of my feelings and welfare, like a good friend, but she had no idea what she was talking about—and she'd crossed the line.

And she *wasn't* my friend. I couldn't be that close to her.

"No more trash talking Jeremy," I said. "Got it?"

She nodded, picked up her cup, and took a long sip, all the while watching me closely. A sly smile crept over her lips.

"I know people at the Beacon," she said. "There are always tickets available ... "

I tried not to look horrified; I didn't want to introduce Jeremy to Paulina. Really, what good would come of that meeting when she was suddenly going to disappear—once I worked out how to wrap her in the fleece? There might be questions, unlike last time. Arkady was a recluse; all his employees probably still thought that he was enjoying an extended visit at an exclusive health spa. I shuddered, remembering the brochure that advertised the benefits of sheep placenta on the skin. Paulina, on the other hand, though antisocial, was young, wealthy, and apparently a globe-trotter, and so more easily missed.

Besides all that, I wanted to see Jeremy alone. Of course the concert would be mobbed, but I couldn't—no, wouldn't—have Paulina hovering around with that lopsided grin of hers.

"No," I said finally.

"Why not?" she asked matter-of-factly, pulling out her phone.

"C'mon P, it's a date."

"I won't be near you," she said, almost grudgingly. Then she teased, "I'll probably get better seats than what you have anyway, and backstage passes." She leaned in close and winked. "I'm sure I can get something for you, too."

"No thanks," I protested. "I mean, that's nice and all, but ... " I trailed off.

Paulina said nothing but slid open her phone as if she

was looking for a number. She hit the touchscreen with her thumb—she was going to do it!

I rose quickly from my place and leaned over the table, nearly knocking over both cups. I grabbed her wrist and lowered the phone from her ear.

"No, Paulina. Please. I mean, I can't stop you from going to see Elysian Fields, but you can't come with me." Guilt nipped at my conscience; I didn't want to hurt her feelings. "Don't take it personally, okay?" I said when I saw her jaw start to clench. "Look, Spring Fling is the weekend after next and you can come with me," I rushed on, before realizing— ouch—that Jeremy was taking me to that. They'd have to meet. But a lot could happen between now and then; she could be gone.

"Okay," she muttered, but seemed to brighten. The promise bought me some time, for that night at least.

When we parted, Paulina headed downtown—good, as I was going uptown. Maybe she was going to see D'On again to work off some of that extra energy she used to run both her life and mine, and all that food. Man, she could pack it away.

I walked the short distance back to the dorm. The room seemed strange … quiet and lonely with no Shar or Paulina. I didn't like it, and started getting ready for the concert and my five minutes at the window.

After trying on a bunch of outfits that either pinched, squished, or pulled at my scales, I ended up in the same ensemble I'd started out with in the morning, except with glittery thigh-highs this time and motorcycle boots. Not wanting to stay in the room alone, I set out at 6:15, which was more than ample time to get to Pandora's.

I headed uptown, then veered off to the subway. It was only ten blocks, a fifteen-minute walk and I'd still be early, but I was taking no chances. A train came quickly, and it looked, happily for me, empty. I stepped onto the car, and it was only when the doors whooshed closed and the train started moving that I discovered I wasn't alone. At one end of the car a couple sat, huddled over in conversation so that I couldn't see their faces. I only had one stop until I got off, so I settled down in a seat in the center and watched the blackness zip by.

"I told you we'd find her here," said a snide female voice.

I looked up. The pair in the corner had moved, by stealth it seemed, to the seats directly across from me. The woman was a statuesque blonde with stick-straight hair, clad head-to-toe in black leather and matte-black Wayfarers. She made an odd companion to the guy next to her, who was muscular but way shorter, and dressed like he was ready to run a marathon—except for the strange-looking gold winged hat, or helmet, or whatever it was he had on his head.

"Hello, Margaret," the woman said.

"Do I know yo—" I started to say, then stopped. I didn't have to ask; I did know her. "Persephone?" The air left my lungs.

She smiled, but it was shallow. "All alone?"

I looked around, as if doing that would ensure that I wasn't being eavesdropped upon, but then I remembered, her assigned jaunt at that rodeo camp in Texas, where Hera sent her for some R&R. She probably had a couple more days on the dude ranch, and then it would officially be time to go to momma's place. Till then, I knew, she couldn't see either Demeter or Hades. I was safe-ish.

"Yes, unfortunately," I replied, still keeping my voice low; one could never take too many precautions when it came to members of the pantheon appearing when you least expected it.

"So she *is* in Tartarus!" Persephone hissed, stomping a stiletto boot. Running Man tried to move over a seat but, without looking, she clamped a hand on his arm and he stayed put. She leaned toward me. "How long has she been down there?"

Avoiding her piercing stare, I bowed my head and counted the days ... had it been over a month already? I swallowed painfully. A hard lump formed in my throat: a paralyzing biscuit of fear, the realization that I'd wasted a lot of time, and a heavy dose of guilt.

"I'm getting her out," I blurted.

The train jerked to a stop. Three or four people got on, and I had to get off—this was my stop. I got up to leave, but so did Persephone. She reached over with a long arm and pushed me back into my seat. No one took any notice, and I didn't dare argue. *I have plenty of time; I'll still be able to talk to Shar,* I reasoned. *And now I can tell her that I ran into Persephone. That should make her understand how difficult my part of this whole thing has become.*

A warning bell rang. The doors smashed shut and the train lurched forward.

I couldn't tell, because of her dark glasses, but I had the

uncomfortable impression Persephone was glaring at me. She got right in my face so that we were almost nose to nose.

"How did this happen? Tell me."

I laced my fingers nervously then looked pleadingly at her. "I can't."

She jammed her fists on her hips. "You *will*."

"If I tell you," I said, desperately, "then I'm taking the risk of violating my contract, which means Shar and I could be down there permanently. You wouldn't want *that*."

Running man giggled, but then grunted as she elbowed him in the ribs.

"Shut up, Hermes!"

Hermes?!

She slashed a hand through the air. "You know that's *not* what I want. But this situation is unacceptable."

"It's not doing much for me, either."

"Save the glib tongue, Margaret. Do you have any contact with her?"

"Yes," I began, seeing a means of escape. "As a matter of fact, I was just on my way—"

"Good. Then the next time you talk to her"—she pulled her glasses down her nose to pin me with an icy gray stare—"you tell her to be extremely careful. Winter always comes. She and I will meet again."

"Really, I don't think you have anything to worry about. Shar's not interested in anything Hades has to offer. As wonderful as he may be," I added hastily, not wanting to insult her and thereby cause more problems for myself.

"That's not what I heard," she said, glancing at Hermes, who stared at the ceiling. "From what I've been told, she spends an awful lot of time wearing skimpy clothes and strolling the beach. Hades is forced to bear her company because of the contract. When he's not there, it wouldn't surprise me if she has a number of gullible men from the Elysian Fields dancing to her whims. That farm-fresh-virgin act is so predictably human. Isn't that right, Hermes?"

Hermes snuck a glance at me but said nothing. Beaches? In Tartarus? Yet I was sure I'd seen Hades walking around in a towel behind her. That explained a few things, like why my beach-loving roomie hadn't found an escape route and was always harping on me to get the job done. Persephone must have seen the doubt in my eyes.

"Not so confident about Sharisse's priorities, hmmm?" she mused.

The train pulled into the station at 115th Street, over sixty blocks away from Pandora's. Panicking, I pulled out my pocket watch; it was 7:03—I'd missed Shar completely. Couldn't anything go right?

"Please!" I said. Hermes looked at me like I was infected with something. I choked back tears. "I was supposed to talk to Shar, but—"

"Where do you need to go?" Persephone sighed, about to snap her fingers.

I shook my head. "I missed her because we were talking. We only have five minutes a week together and the time has past." I tried not to look accusatory, but it *was* her fault. I only hoped that I could guilt her into helping me let Shar know I was at least trying.

"If I fail, we'll both be down there for eternity," I said. "We're trying to work out the details of what has to be done.

I *need* to talk to her. If she thinks that I've given up, or betrayed her"—I lowered my voice to a suggestive tone— "she might turn to Hades for a shoulder to cry on. We know what *that* can lead to." I waggled my eyebrows.

The implication wasn't lost on Persephone. She pursed her lips. "Hermes is going back down with a message for my Hades." She licked her lips and Hermes rolled his eyes. "I suppose he can relay a few words for you, too."

Hermes nodded reluctantly; clearly that was an order, not a request.

"Thanks," I sniffed. "Things really haven't been going so well."

Persephone whipped out a diamond-studded compact and lipstick case, not looking at all interested in my problems, and Hermes seemed just as bored.

"Okay, tell her that … I'm so sorry I missed her. I was going to meet Jeremy for this concert but I knew we had to talk so I rearranged things to make sure that we did, but then I ran into you." I took a deep breath, trying to think of what else to say. "Just make her understand that I'm really trying to get this done and that I'll talk to her next week if it's not done. But it will be. I promise!"

"Work harder, Margaret," Persephone said, snapping the compact shut.

We all stepped off the train. I blinked, and they were gone.

At least Shar will know what happened, I thought, *and I won't have to deal with the Window Girl fan club. Maybe they'll be discouraged and won't show up next time—if I still have to talk to her there.*

I caught an express train that would land me close to the restaurant where Jeremy and I were grabbing a quick bite. Not bothering to check the time, I bounded up the station steps and quickly crossed the street, but I couldn't see him through the crush of people in front of the Sweet Pea Vegetarian Grille. So I texted him:

Where r u?

"Right behind you."

I jumped. I gave him a smile, but he said brusquely, without looking at me, "We lost our table. Let's get over to the Beacon. We might still be able to catch a bit of the opening."

"Jeremy—"

He walked, staring straight ahead, apparently ignoring me.

I tried not to whine. "I know it's been weird lately, but this is not how it's always going to be, Jeremy," I pleaded, not liking the way I sounded. He kept walking, but I grabbed his arm and pulled him to the side, making him stop. "Please, look at me. Don't be mad."

He glared down into my eyes.

"Please," I whispered.

His face softened and he cracked a wry smile.

"That's the problem. I can't stay mad at you." He unhooked himself from my grasp, put both arms around me, and hugged me tightly. "But it's because I want to see you." I could hear the frustration in his voice. He kissed the top of my head. "I miss you."

I wished we were alone and not on a crowded street. I

pulled away slightly and gazed up at him. "And I've missed you."

He bent his face toward mine. Not caring who was looking, I returned the kiss, putting my hands on his face and drawing him closer to me, but at the same time feeling strangely forlorn.

We did miss the opening act, but he didn't make a big deal about it. We found our seats—not exactly nosebleed—and watched as the floor and boxes filled to capacity; the concert was sold out and then some.

Light boxes that looked like skyscrapers erupted from the floor and there was a flurry of pyrotechnic sparks and strobe lights. Elysian Fields came on in a flash of fire, with cheering, yells, and squeals from all directions. I couldn't hear myself scream, but I know I did as they broke into their first song, the one Jeremy had used for Arkady's runway show. I felt myself swaying in time to the music.

About halfway through the song, someone shook my shoulder. I turned to find Jeremy staring at me, and liking what he was seeing, by the grin on his face. He raised his eyebrows briefly and went back to the music, but I caught him stealing glimpses at me, song after song. Elysian Fields played for an hour and a half before they broke for an intermission. As the lights came up, I realized that I was starving and had to go to the bathroom.

"Let's go out," said Jeremy, pulling me into the aisle and then into the crowded hallway. He handed me my ticket. "I'm grabbing a drink—do you want anything?"

I nodded. "A bottle of water and something to eat. Meet back at the seats?"

He gave me a quick kiss and squeezed my hand, not letting me go. "Where'd you learn to dance like that?"

With Paulina.

I blushed. "I went to this dance class with … "

"Your new roommate?" he finished for me, his face falling. I gave him a pleading look, and his lips puckered into a resigned sort of smile before he turned and pushed his way toward the concession stands.

I forged a path to the women's room, where, of course, there was a mega-line. I waited patiently as it crawled up, and I made it into a stall just before I thought I would burst. I took care of business, washed my hands, and pushed through the door back into the hall.

Except I wasn't in the hall.

I was standing next to a drum kit on a massive platform. About ten guys with band tee shirts passed in front of and behind me, carrying pieces of wood, wires, and extra guitars. I turned around and there was Matt Davy, standing right next to me, his tight shirt damp with perspiration and clinging to his skinny torso, his pinstriped rock star pants slashed at the knees.

I'm … backstage!

I started breathing quickly, thinking that it was a very good thing I'd already used the bathroom.

"Margaret!" Hades, sporting an inches-thick gold rope chain with a diamond-studded *H* dangling from it, walked up behind Matt and put an arm around him.

"Matt, I'd like you to meet an associate of mine. Margaret Wiley, meet Matt Davy."

Matt put his sinewy and callused hand into mine and

grinned at me with the charmingly gap-toothed smile that I knew so well from my collection of posters, CDs, and pirated jpeg images stored on my phone.

"Pleasure, Margaret," he said, his Brit-cool accent ringing in my ears. "Enjoying the show?"

All I could do was nod vigorously. I was turning into a gushy puddle and didn't care who saw me.

"Hold this for us, love," he said, handing me his guitar and taking his signature tartan handkerchief out of his pocket to wipe his face. He took the guitar out of my shaking hands and handed me the handkerchief in its place.

"Brilliant meeting you," he said, bending toward me and planting a kiss on my cheek. "H," he said, addressing Hades, "I've got to go check on my mates. Thanks for bringing her back—you know I love meeting the fans."

"H" for Hades gave a thumbs-up as Matt turned and slipped behind a curtain.

"We're going to have to do this more often, Margaret. It seems I've finally stumbled upon something that's rendered you speechless!"

"I'm backstage!" was all I could manage to get out.

He clapped his hands in front of my face to get my attention and I shook my head. I was still holding Matt's plaid hanky—a holy relic.

"You really don't deserve this little treat, Margaret, considering your lack of progress," he continued, stepping out of the way so one of the roadies could bring new cymbals onto the stage. "But I figured it was a way to get your attention."

Finally I came to myself. "My attention?! How about the scales? That got my attention!"

"That's the Margaret I know." A corner of his mouth quirked. "Do you like them?"

"What do you think? Not very Siren-ish, are they?"

"Well, most mortals think a siren is a mermaid." He shook his head. "Education these days."

"I don't care—this wasn't part of the deal." I poked my stomach where the scales were the most copious. "This wasn't supposed to happen."

"I said no turning into a *bird*," he chuckled. "But I decided to throw these in as a little motivator. You certainly are taking your sweet time with Paulina. I would have thought something this easy would be done by now. I've supplied everything you need. This isn't rocket science."

"You told me to take my time, you sneaking—"

"Am I so horrible?" he interrupted, looking dramatically pained.

"Yes, you are. And I've tried to do it, several times, and it…" My voice caught.

"It, what, Margaret?" He crossed his arms over his chest and looked truly bored.

"It just isn't working," I concluded lamely.

"Is it me, or are you a little hesitant about sending Paulina to Tartarus? Well, don't be," he said menacingly, not giving me a chance to answer.

"It would help if I understood her better. What was her deal with you?"

"The only thing you need to know is that her place is in Tartarus and it's your job to send her there. Put in a little more effort, show some initiative and creativity, but get it done. I might be inclined to add a time limit."

"You told us about Arkady—why not tell me about Paulina?"

"You don't need to know everything about Miss Swanson or what deal she's made. It's called nondisclosure. I don't discuss the particulars of your agreement with anyone. It could be ... embarrassing for you," he said with a condescending air.

I looked away, but he grabbed my arm and pulled me so that I had to face him. Beyond him, the lights on the stage dimmed and a roar went up from the crowd. I had to get back to the seats before Jeremy went to search for me. I'd never find him in this crowd.

"If you can't keep that in perspective, then think about this," he growled. "If you don't dispatch Paulina, then you and Sharisse will be in Tartarus with me forever. Sharisse won't mind, though," he said, stroking his chin and getting a faraway look in his eyes. Had he succeeded with her? No. No, he couldn't have, or he wouldn't be here bothering me. But beaches? Parties? Bikinis? It was all so Shar-esque. Then his attention snapped back to me. "She's seen that the Underworld has many attractions. While you certainly won't have my attention to the extent that she will, I'm sure I can keep you busy."

Nick Killian, the band's tall, curly-haired drummer, passed by, then stopped and stared, pale and wide-eyed, at Hades. He backed up a step.

"H. You're *here*."

Hades held me in place with a glare, then turned to shake his hand. "Amazing show, Nick! Tell everyone I said so."

Nick nodded, and ran onto the stage as if he couldn't get

away fast enough. He climbed a platform to get behind his drum kit.

"Please don't tell me you have a deal with Elysian Fields," I said, casting a worried glance out at the stage.

"Not all of them—just Nick there." His lips twisted wickedly. "And don't ask. Nondisclosure, remember?" He wagged a finger.

For some bizarre reason, I was relieved that Matt was untainted.

"Enough stalling, Margaret," Hades warned, his silky voice steely with an underlying threat. He steered me away from the stage to one of the doors that led out into the back alley. He opened it and nudged me through.

"I have to get back to my seat!" I cried, but instead of finding myself outside in the back alley, I was in the empty hallway that led to the mezzanine level.

A uniformed guard checked my ticket and let me in. I fumbled down the dimly lit stairs to the first row and stepped on the toes of a half a dozen people before landing in my seat next to Jeremy. A crumpled paper bag was wedged into my folded-up seat. Food.

"How long was that line at the bathroom?" he shouted.

I made a face and shrugged, lifting up my hands. I was still holding the tartan handkerchief.

Jeremy pinched a corner of it between his fingers. Like any self-respecting Elysian Fields fan, he knew exactly what it was. "Where did you get this?" he yelled just as a song ended.

I groped for an answer as Matt Davy wiped the sweat

from his brow with the back of his hand. He didn't have his handkerchief anymore.

"They ... were selling them at the concessions."

He stared at me for a long moment before nodding, then yelling and clapping his hands over his head as another familiar song started up. There was mistrust in his eyes.

SHAR

What a Tangled Web We Weave

Why did it seem that whenever a girl wanted a good long cry, someone had to interrupt it, and usually about something lame?

But there stood Hermes, buff and besotted with himself.

"What do you want?" I hiccupped. Meg not showing up for our daily talk had scared me at first, then angered me, and now I was hurt. How could she abandon me? After everything we'd been through, I thought we were best friends. Did she forget, or get sick, or did she simply have something better to do? And with the new roomie? Was Meg replacing me with her? Another sob escaped.

"I have a message for you. From—"

"Hermes, what are you doing here?" In strolled Hades. Lounging against the door, he displayed his broad shoulders in a stunning white tee, his hips snugged by faded, low-cut jeans, his crossed feet enveloped in butter-soft loafers. An epitome of the all-American hunk. Except that he was Greek. And a god. And a devil.

Hermes swung around. "I have a message from Margaret to Sharisse."

Hades' penetrating look was not lost on Hermes, who squirmed in his gold running shoes. The wings cringed, molding themselves to his feet. I swear if they could talk, they'd whimper.

"Then please, deliver it." Hades flung out a casual hand.

Hermes turned back toward me. "Um, hmm." He cleared his throat and adjusted the waistband of his running shorts. I rolled my eyes. Hades chuckled softly, and Hermes began.

"Margaret asked me to tell you that she's sorry she missed your meeting. She had to go to a concert, and she tried, but she missed you."

Well, I've been schooled! She really does have better things to do than save me.

My eyes filled, and I turned away so neither Hades nor Hermes would see. Taking a few deep breaths, I managed to squeak out, "Thank you."

Hades rushed over. "My little truffle! Don't cry!" He placed a firm hand on the small of my back.

"Message delivered. Goodbye." Hermes started to lift off, but Hades grabbed him around an ankle and yanked him back down.

"I don't believe I said you could leave."

Hermes landed with a thump. And a peeved look.

"*Chérie*, so she missed one chat." Hades approached me soothingly. "She has classes, and the assignment, and other things to do. Don't be so hard on her."

I whipped away from his touch. "Other things to do?! She *promised* she'd get me out. But I'm still here! What could be more important?"

Dragging Hermes over by his gold-trimmed tank, Hades ordered, "Tell Sharisse everything Margaret said."

Hermes pursed his lips and plucked Hades' fingers off his shirt. "*If* you don't mind?" After smoothing non-existent wrinkles, he gave me a bored look. "Like I told you, she said she was sorry, but she couldn't make your talk. She was meeting some Jeremy at a concert. She wanted you to understand that she's trying to get things done."

"That was all?" asked Hades.

"Yes, that was all," Hermes huffed, then rolled his eyes. "Oh, wait. One more thing. She promises she'll be there next time." He turned to Hades, hands on hips. "*Now* can I go?"

"No!" I yelled. Both of them turned in surprise. "You tell *her* that I won't be there next time because there shouldn't *be a next time.* And I have a ball to attend." I glared at Hades. "I need a costume."

And it won't be Mother Teresa!

Hades inclined his head. "For you, goddess in waiting, anything you wish." He flicked a finger and Hermes was gone.

And we were in Victoria's Secret!

I tilted my head toward the trademark pink script sign. "I'm not *that* mad."

"One can only hope," he sighed, peering at me from half-closed eyes. "But there is a beautiful aquamarine teddy..."

"Down, boy." I started to walk away.

He laughed and captured my hand. "So what character did you have in mind?"

"I'm thinking about it. Take me to a real costume store."

"I'll do even better than that." Hades closed his eyes and next thing I knew, we were in an elegant parlor room with delicate white French furniture, pale blue carpets, heavy striped silk drapes, and tall vanilla-scented candles everywhere. A small round podium, in a triptych of mirrors, reminded me of a bridal salon. Hades, in a sleek black suit, sat next to me on the couch. A furtive glance down, and I exhaled in relief. No bikini, no Grecian gown. Instead, I was clothed in a lavender silk dress; had to be Vera Wang. And crystal-encrusted shoes. Had to be Stuart Weitzman.

Oh, the bliss!

Straightening his flawless tie, Hades said, "This is the private studio of a good friend. She will create whatever you wish." He leaned in conspiratorially. "She designs for all my affairs."

Have that many? I wanted to ask, but instead said, "What if Persephone finds out?"

"My friend is very discreet."

I snorted. "Do you trust her that much?"

He nodded blithely. "Of course."

Girls are to gossip as Hades is to despot. Can't have one without the other.

I heard the whisper of silk. Turning around, I saw a tall, lithe woman, strawberry-blond hair piled high on her head, dressed in a flowing white gown. These Greeks seriously needed to add some color to their wardrobes.

When she reached us, I almost fainted.

Peeking from beneath her gown were six spider legs. *Where were the other two?*

"Arachne! So nice to see you! Sharisse needs a costume for a ball I'm giving. Whatever she wants. I know it'll be exquisite!" He gave Arachne a sly and secretive glance.

She smiled serenely, like a madonna, and gestured for me to approach the podium. Not wanting to betray the terror clawing at my insides about going near her, never mind having her *touch* me, I tried not to stumble forward. Hades was scrutinizing me. I would not show him fear. I swallowed, but it sounded more like a gulp.

Now I was having second thoughts about getting even with Meg by wearing something outrageously provocative. Not only would she go nuclear if she saw it, but it would provoke Hades' already overactive libido. Not a smart move.

I smiled tremulously at Arachne. *What to wear, what to wear.* Who thought I'd ever have trouble designing an outfit?

"I was thinking of—"

"Lady Godiva is one of my personal favorites," interrupted Hades, sipping a glass of red wine.

My smile was bland. "Too overdone. No subtlety."

He chuckled.

"How about Lucrezia Borgia?" I asked. She was beautiful, rich, opulently dressed—and poisoned a lot of pesky, irritating men. Perfect!

Hades shook his head. "I hope you don't believe the rumors about her; she didn't really poison anyone. Married three times, she had eight children. There were some boyfriends on the side, but overall, she is much maligned. You can talk to her over in the Elysian Fields."

I pouted. It seemed brilliant. I needed a strong character, one who didn't let anyone push her around. Cleopatra was already attending, so that was out.

I tapped my lips. "Maybe Eva Perón."

Hades' brows rose. "Interesting. She was strong, smart, and beautiful. She saw what she wanted and did whatever she had to to get it. And since I don't have a deal with her, she won't be at the party, unless you invite her."

With lowered lids, Hades' gaze raked over me. What was he thinking, planning?

"More importantly," he said, "I will be—"

My turn to dress him! I threw open my arms like a Hollywood diva. "Lord of Olympus!" I'm sure it's what he aspired to.

"That is blasphemy! Don't ever speak such things!" Hades stormed out, and I stood there next to Spider Woman, dumbfounded.

What'd I say?

"You shouldn't even joke about that," said Arachne, approaching me with a tape measure and frowning with disapproval. "Zeus does not tolerate that kind of talk anywhere. Blasphemy is severely punished." She circled around me, dragging those creepy hairy legs. "Is it to be Eva then, or will you allow me to create something unique for you?" she asked, her tone more pleasant.

Well, here I was, abandoned by everyone. It was high time I took charge of my life, not depend on Meg to get me out of here or let Hades order me around. Oh no, Sharisse Johnson—this is *your* life, save your own butt!

I gave her a saccharine smile. "No, not Eva. I know exactly who I want to be. I want to go as Estelle Eberhardt."

Arachne looked confused. "I know all the figures from human history, and I don't recall that name."

With a smug grin, I replied, "She's not famous, she's my great-grandmother, one hundred and four years old. I'm sure you can come up with something appropriate—drab, brown, serviceable, and sturdy? Won't Hades be surprised?"

Going over to my purse, I pulled out a thick stock card, shimmering black pearlescent with white, Greek-style lettering. A whole stack of invitations had appeared at my bedside before Hermes arrived, along with a note in elegant script:

Invite whomever you wish
xoxoxo and so much more, H.

"Here's your invitation," I said, handing her the card. "And don't forget, my costume's our secret!" If I could find a janitor, I'd invite him too.

"Oh, thank you!" Arachne gushed and squealed in delight, and her spider legs rippled under her dress. "I never get invited to his parties! I'll have to start immediately; I need a costume too! What should I go as?"

Miss Muffet? A black widow? Charlotte's Web? I had to say something. "A princess?" I suggested lamely.

With a swish, she pulled the skirt of her dress off,

revealing that she was a spider from the torso down. With a delight that sent shivers down my spine, she said softly, "I must start spinning now so we'll have our dresses ready in time." Her black, coarse-haired body and legs began twitching as she pulled a fine silken thread from her bobbing spinneret.

I couldn't run out of there fast enough. Luckily, one step out the door and I was back in the throne room. And back to filling time by playing with Cerberus, looking for Eurydice, and instructing Ben on the New Math and world events.

One morning, day, or whatever it was, I pulled on the usual one-shouldered dress, grabbed an apple out of the large, never-empty bowl on the graceful table in the corner of my room, and went to look for Caz. Any moment now—or later—Ben's watch might tell me it was time to talk to Meg. And I still wasn't sure *if* I was going to talk to her.

Caz wasn't at the aqua sea, the purple lake, the pink desert, or the garden of death. Nor the gemstone cave or any of the "natural" wonders. I decided to try the Elysian Fields. If he wasn't there, I'd ask around about Eurydice on my own. One way or another, I was getting the hell out of hell.

As I hurried over the bridge, I ran smack into Benjamin Franklin.

"Hello Ben!" I said cheerily.

"Ah, the lovely Miss Sharisse. And how are you?" he asked, falling in beside me.

I winced. "Not too well. I think Hades is mad at me, I'm missing a lot of classes, and I want to go home." I forced a smile. "Oh, that reminds me. Ben, here's your invitation to the ball." I withdrew another card and handed it to him. "I hope you'll save a dance for me."

He smiled widely. "I would love to, my dear!" He took my hand and kissed it, lingering a little too long in my estimation, especially with what I knew about him. Time to go!

"Great! I'll see you there! Bye!"

Wandering through the pearly gates into the Elysian Fields, I wondered where to start. *Ancient Greece,* I thought as I walked by the English pub I'd passed on my first visit. After a few steps, I was passing gleaming marble temples with soaring columns, elegant statuary, and the most stunningly chiseled male bodies. *Talk about a feast for the eyes!*

I finally knew how to travel in Tartarus. You thought about where you wanted to be, and you found yourself there. I wished I could do that back home; it'd save a lot of subway and cab fare. If only I could "think" myself back to the mortal world…but I tried that on several occasions and landed in the evil garden as punishment.

I was wandering around, past limpid mosaic pools and artfully designed gardens, when I spied Caz. There he was, dressed like a typical Greek god in the omnipresent white toga with gold piping, playing a lyre on the steps of a temple to I don't know which god, but which featured a pair of graceful swans instead of a man or woman. I was surprised that Hades allowed that in his domain, but hey, I guess it wouldn't be ancient Greece without all the deities.

"Hi!" I stood over him.

"Shar." He smiled and put the lyre aside.

Fearful of eavesdroppers, I pulled Caz into the temple. I didn't know whether Hades was listening and watching me no matter where I went; this was his world, after all, and I was nothing more than a minion. Finding a secluded stone bench in a side nook, I sat and Caz settled himself next to me.

I looked around. There were swans everywhere. Statues. Mosaics on the floor. Wall frescoes. A particular one caught my eye—two couples, in Greek attire of course. The men looked similar, and familiar … almost like Caz. Must be some relations. The faces of the two women also looked like I'd seen them before. One taller than the other, the tall one with a pert nose, the shorter with wide eyes. If I believed in reincarnation, I'd almost say Meg and I would look exactly like them in white marble.

Nah.

"What is this place?" I asked.

He smiled wistfully. "It's for my mother."

"She likes swans."

"You don't know the story?" Caz cocked his head. "Zeus fell in love with Leda, my mother, and came to her in the form of a swan."

"How romantic!" I said. "Swans mate for life!"

"Uh-huh." He raised an eyebrow at me. "Not this swan. But mom has nothing but fond memories, and he's looked out for us even though we aren't very close. He's not the 'daddy' type." He looked up and surveyed his surroundings. "But even as king of the pantheon, there's not much he can do to help us."

"That's what I wanted to talk to you about," I said.

"What's up?" he asked.

"Let's just say my partner is not getting me out of here anytime soon. She can't seem to do what she needs to. I

196

think she's now friends with the person she's supposed to send here and doesn't want to admit it, much less get her to put on the fleece so I can go home. And your twin Pollux hiding up in my world? I think those two things are connected." It had been in the back of my mind; Meg had to send someone to Tartarus, and Caz's twin was hunted on the mortal plane. Of course they had to be the same person. Hades wanted Caz's sister.

He looked away. "That's what I thought too."

"So what are we going to do about it?" I demanded.

His head snapped up. "What can we do about it? I've been trying to find Eurydice, but no one knows anything, or if they do, they're not telling me." He held his arms open, gesturing to the space. "We're stuck here, unless your friend does her job and you go home. But don't count on it. Even though Pollux can't free me or summon Zeus while he's alone, he knows all about the Golden Fleece. It's why your friend is having difficulty. There's no way a demi-god would put it on. Only humans can't resist the fleece. And from what you tell me, it sounds like she doesn't have the heart anyway."

I held up a hand. "Wait. Did you just say *he*?"

Confusion crept across his face. "Yes, Pollux. My twin brother."

I jumped up. "You never told me you had a brother!"

He rubbed the bridge of his nose. "I told you I had a twin."

I slapped my hand on my forehead. "You never said a twin *brother*. This Paulina has to be him. He's parading around as a girl? I have to warn Meg! Oh my God, I hope she hasn't been walking around in her panties!"

Caz grabbed my shoulders. "You can't! If she knows he's a guy, then as a Siren she could use her power to get him to put on the fleece. He'd have to do it—he's part human, and without me there, he's not strong enough to resist. He and I would be imprisoned here forever! Please, I'll beg—don't do this."

If I didn't tell Meg, she would fail and we'd both be here forever. If I did, and she succeeded, then Caz and Pollux were doomed. I didn't know what to do. Even if I found Eurydice and escaped, it was only a temporary solution at best, because sooner or later Hades would be breathing down my neck, waving the contract and singing about non-fulfillment. Then it would be back to the Land of the Dead for all of us. And he probably wouldn't be as lenient and smoochy as he was now.

With a heaviness in my heart, I said, "Even if we escape, the contract has to be enforced if Meg fails. Hades will come for both of us. Unless I can appeal to Hera to hide me. She helped us out last time. Either way, you're asking me to choose you and Pollux over Meg and myself."

Caz shook his head. "Let's not get Hera involved. We'll look for Eurydice. If we find her, we find the way out. Let's do it at the ball. It'll be chaos, and the perfect opportunity for us to sneak out of here. Once we escape I'll call my father. He'll be able to help us. But we have to get out of Tartarus first."

Glancing around the temple, I realized that Caz must be lonely. Even though there were a lot of people in the Underworld and he had relatives and friends here, he couldn't be with Pollux. Twin bonds were strong. Being an only child, I envied him that. Yet I knew what it was like to be separated from someone I cared for—I missed Meg. And now I understood how this whole situation had her confused.

But what about Caz's warning about not trusting any of the gods? Did that include his father? Or him? No matter what, I had to trust someone. Reaching for his hand, I marveled at the smooth strength in his fingers. There were calluses on his fingertips, no doubt from playing his lyre. He wasn't bad, although I wasn't going to rush out and order the CD.

"Let's try to find Eurydice again." I stood up and smoothed the hated dress. "Where do you think she could be?"

He looked up at me. "You really look beautiful in that. Better than most of the goddesses."

Well, maybe the dress wasn't that bad.

"Thank you." I preened demurely.

He reached a hand around the back of my neck and pulled me close. As we leaned together, our lips met and his mouth gently explored mine. I wrapped my arms around him and pressed against him, losing myself in the kiss and forgetting everything for a few moments except how hard my heart was beating.

"I wish we could stay like this forever," he said, reluctantly withdrawing his arms and stepping back.

"Just not here," I whispered. There was that adorable cocksure grin. Holding hands, we stepped out of the temple.

"I've searched all the ancient worlds," Caz said with a sigh. "Greek, even Roman. I still don't know where she is." He wiped the sweat from his brow, his hair clinging to his head in soft, loose waves. What I wouldn't give to have a few of those curls, I thought as I flipped back my straight tresses. I really liked Caz—a lot. He was funny and cute and sweet and tortured and I couldn't stay with him. A romantic myth in the flesh.

"Maybe she wanted a change of scenery. Wouldn't you be bored spending eternity in the same old place, seeing the same people? Especially when there are so many other places you could visit?" I suggested.

Running a hand through his glorious hair, he said, "That makes sense. But there are too many worlds; it would take us forever to search them all. Not that we don't have eternity."

"But Meg and Pollux don't."

"I do have something that will speed things up." Putting two fingers in his mouth, Caz gave a piercing whistle. Almost immediately, the most beautiful stallion I ever could imagine came galloping toward us, creating a cloud of dust. He snorted, shaking his head. Sleek yet heavily muscled, he was magnificent. His white coat practically glowed in the light.

"Hop on." Before I could protest, Caz jumped onto the horse's back and reached down a hand.

I winced. *City girl here!* "I've never been on a horse."

His beguiling smile and the chance to cuddle up intimately close with him was almost all the encouragement I needed. A helmet and seat belt would have been nice, though.

"Don't worry, I'm an expert." He pulled me up with a graceful ease. "Where to?"

Time to play Sherlock Holmes. "What interested her, besides Orpheus?"

Caz frowned. "His music and his poetry, but mostly his music. Whenever he created something new, he played it for her first."

"So we have to figure out where she'd go to enjoy music. Personally speaking, I wouldn't want to hear the same thing year after year. Heck, I get tired of it after a few weeks. So, what would she like and where would she go?"

Turning his head sideways, Caz said, "I've been here long enough to have heard it all—Italian opera, experimental grunge, New Orleans jazz. She could be in a thousand places."

I smiled broadly and wrapped my arms around his hard sculpted middle. I bet if he lay down, I could bounce a quarter off it. "I know where we should try," I purred in his ears.

He leaned back, his body against mine. A delicious warmth spread through me at the contact. I was glad he couldn't see my face because it had to be flaming red at that moment.

"Where?" he said, his voice huskier than usual. The closeness was having an effect on him as well.

"Someplace where she could get lost, and where musicians aspire to go. Eurydice's probably in a club, something small, intimate, with not too many people. Let's start out in New York. I know my way around the music venues, thanks to hanging out with Meg. If she's not there, then we'll check Los Angeles, London, and go from there. Hades has to have his own versions here. Do you know what Eurydice looks like?"

Caz pursed his lips. "There aren't too many depictions

of her. She and Orpheus are the only two people who almost got out. That kind of information is valuable."

"And dangerous," I agreed.

Caz nodded, and nudged the horse into a trot to a deserted and dirty little alley. He pointed to a little plaque on a crumbling wall. Three figures stood out in carved relief, and they were painted to look lifelike. I recognized one of them immediately from his crazy helmet.

"Hermes!"

"Yep. That's him on the left. The one with the lyre on the right is Orpheus, and the girl in the middle is Eurydice."

I stared at the carving. Eurydice had long dark hair, large doe-like eyes, and a button nose. Like all the other gods and mythical people I'd met, she was gorgeous. No wonder Orpheus was smitten.

"I've seen enough," I said. "Let's go."

We galloped into downtown New York, Tartarus style. No one blinked at the incongruity of it. It was almost like the real place, but I suspect that in the real place, a girl and a hunky guy dressed in ancient Greek attire, atop a horse of Herculean proportions, would be remarked upon. We dismounted, and Caz whispered into the horse's ear. It took off, back the way we had come.

Bustling city streets, traffic. Now I was in familiar territory. I led Caz through the city maze. We searched the smaller clubs one by one; the Black Door, the Psychedelic Garden, the Golden Goose, and others, asking people if they knew Eurydice. We came up empty, but I wasn't about to give up.

The inside of the Liar Lyre club was dark and loud and

smoky. I scanned the faces I could see, but no one resembled the girl on the plaque. Near the stage, a guy with long hair and sandals sat on one of the tables, swaying in time to the music. Under the low lights, a wraithlike man in dirty ripped jeans clutched a microphone close to his mouth, singing with a raspy voice. His messy blond hair shook as he moved his head.

"Yeah! Kurt! Wooooooo!" Rocker Dude on the table clapped his hands over his head when the song was over. I made my move.

"Excuse me," I said, tapping him on the shoulder and flashing a winning smile. "I just got here. I'm looking for my friend—maybe you know her? Eurydice?"

"Yeah," he said, still swaying although no music was playing. He peered at me through the smoke and jerked a thumb toward the backstage area. "She's hanging with the band."

Score! Let's hear it for the blonde. I snagged an obviously untouched burger off the table and took a huge bite. I'd forgotten to eat and it wasn't the first time. My stomach was protesting. I really needed some type of routine or I was going to starve to death and then I *would* be stuck here.

The burger polished off, I filched a Coke from a waitress to wash it down. No one exchanged money for anything as far as I'd seen, so technically it wasn't stealing. I turned to go, but Rocker Dude grabbed my arm.

"Wait, pretty lady! You don't want to miss the next act! Hendrix is up!"

Nodding and smiling, I pulled away without difficulty and grabbed Caz's hand. We were about to cash in. Then the watch started chiming.

Meg! Now that we knew where Eurydice was, the rest should be easy. I could tell Meg what was going on and that we'd be out of here soon. Once informed, she could work with Pollux to figure out what to do as soon as Caz and I were on the other side. I turned to go.

"You can't leave now," said Caz, his voice urgent and his grip strong on my arm.

"We know where Eurydice is. I have to talk to Meg," I said.

"She could be gone by the time you get back and then we'd have to search for her all over again. Unless…" He paused. "Unless you want me to try and get the information. But if she recognizes me, she may disappear. I don't know how she'll react."

I was torn. Could I miss my talk with Meg? After what I said to Hermes, what would she think? I bowed my head in frustration.

Caz squeezed my hand. "We have to talk to Eurydice now. The ball will be our best—and maybe only—chance to use it."

His earnest appeal and his logic convinced me. I was going to have to believe that this would work out and that Meg wouldn't abandon me.

We worked our way around back and there she was, a girl around my age, dressed all in black but with an ancient gold armband. I tried hard not to stare at Elvis and Jim Morrison chatting it up. Meg would just die if she saw this.

Remembering that the tragic heroine was trying to keep a low profile, I inched my way over.

"Eurydice?"

She started, probably not used to being recognized, and eyed me warily.

"Sorry. Don't know who you're talking about."

It was her, and I didn't need Rocker Dude to confirm it. She looked exactly like the girl on the plaque.

"A guy in the audience told us you were here," I pressed.

She closed her eyes and let out a long sigh. "I can't believe he let it spill again—" She stopped and gasped as Caz stepped up.

"Castor!" She jumped up off the speaker. Several heads turned our way and some people began easing away from us.

He nodded at her.

Her eyes were huge. "Why are *you* here?"

He gave her the *duh* look. "You know *him*—he's using Pollux and me in another power play. We need your help."

She blinked several times, like an owl. "Excuse me?"

"We. Need. To. Leave. Here." I leaned closer, to whisper, "Escape Tartarus."

Suddenly she laughed. "Oh, funny. Yeah, okay."

Hands on hips, I glared at her. "Do I look like I'm joking?" *I could take her.* Hiking on the beaches and through ancient worlds and playing with Cerberus—*oh damn, I forgot to clean up his latest mess and Hades is going to be livid again*—had gotten me in good shape. She was toast. "I need to get out of here so we can save Caz and his twin. And me, too. So how do we get out?"

She looked from me to Caz and back, numerous times.

"Like I said, I don't know who or what you're talking about," she said stubbornly.

Caz closed his eyes in defeat.

"Oh no." I grabbed her by the arm and spun her into a dark corner. "Look, we know you're Eurydice, and you almost made it out. All we want is to know where the portal, opening, stairway, *whatever* is so we can get out. It's life or death."

"I died once and I don't want to repeat the experience. That's not supposed to happen to dryads, especially not the way it happened to me. Stupid snake," she said coldly. "Don't be so quick to gamble your life, mortal. Both of us are permanently expendable if that information gets out. Goodbye."

She tried to leave again, but all my working out redeemed itself right then. She couldn't budge, and I wouldn't let her leave. "Look, I don't know what you've heard, but obviously I'm still here, so the way out doesn't exist anymore," she said desperately.

"We can do this two ways," I whispered. "If I'm stuck down here forever, I have nothing to lose by broadcasting where you are and making it so that *everyone* recognizes you. Buh-bye private life. And since Hades pretty much lets me have whatever I want ... let's just say, before you can run, I can summon him here. I could make up a pretty little story about you telling me about a way out." Of course, I didn't know if Hades would come at my bidding, but Eurydice didn't know I was nothing more than a glorified monkey in a cage, much as it pained me to make that comparison. "Or," I added, "you can tell Caz and me how to get out of Tartarus. We disappear, and I swear on my life that your identity and whereabouts stay a secret."

I could almost hear the gears in her mind, processing which risk was greater. After a furtive glance, she said, "If I tell you, you can't tell anyone, especially ... "

"Gotcha. Not planning on hanging around to blab about it. Go on," I urged.

In a voice barely loud enough to be called a whisper, she said, "And I want something." She reached over and her hands fisted on the front of Caz's toga. "I know Orpheus is in the Pit. Hades promised me we'd be reunited, but it's been three thousand years and that hasn't happened yet. I want him freed, and I want Zeus to know what I risked for you and Pollux."

"*And* me," I added gratefully.

She gave me a disgusted look. "Who cares about you?"

Scratch another name from my fan club. I was beginning to feel that Hades and Caz were the only members. And Cerberus, if I continued to play with him.

Caz nodded. "You have my word I will petition my father for Orpheus to be freed."

"And I want protection from Hades' retaliation."

That list of demands was getting longer.

"And I'm going with you."

"Oh no," I interjected. "This party is big enough."

"I'm going or no one is." She stood there, feet firmly planted, arms crossed, with a challenging glare.

"Okay," Caz agreed. Before I could mutiny, he pecked my lips with a kiss, squelching my rebellion. "We need her."

"Fine," I grumped. So much for being as unobtrusive as possible. Who'd want to go next? All the Titans?

"My uncle is having a—"

"W'Underworld Ball," Eurydice finished for him. "I've heard. Everyone wants to go, check out the new plaything." She gave me an unflattering look.

"Anyone who could be a hindrance will be there," said Caz. "It'll be a perfect time."

Eurydice nodded, seemingly mollified. "We have to go through the Pit," she said. "There's a tunnel there that leads up to the mortal world."

"I was afraid of that," said Caz. He shook his head and looked at me. "We can't. You do know who's down in the Pit, don't you?" He ran a hand through his hair, making it messier and cuter.

Focus!

"Yes, I know. The Titans. But do we have a choice? We can either sit here forever, moaning, or we can take our chance. Hades can't kill us. Or," I amended, "he can't kill you. I'm willing to risk it. Are you game?"

Putting his arm around my shoulder and giving me a good squeeze, he gave a curt nod. "Let's do it."

Eurydice leaned in close. "We'll slip away once the W'Underworld Ball is in full swing. Then…" She smiled slowly and scarily. "We go to the dark side."

MEG

Eureka, I Guess

"One hundred jumping jacks! Let's go, people!"

Mr. Rossi blew his whistle. Along with the rest of the class, I dutifully commenced the first round of calisthenics. I hated gym, but here I was, sweating, eating up my free period for the third day in a row to hammer out the dent in my GPA from missing gym class.

"Five, six, seven, eight, nine, fifty," I counted under my breath. I felt myself getting hotter and hotter. Because of Hades' little "motivation," I had no choice but to wear the bulky winter version of our gym uniform; the summer shorts pinched my scales. I was boiling, but I didn't dare complain. I bobbed up and down with the rest of the class. "Seven, eight, nine, sixty. One, two, three . . . "

As soon as we reached one hundred, Rossi barked, "Drop down! Fifty sit-ups!"

The man was a sadist. He paced up and down the rows making sure no one cheated.

"Laps!" he yelled, and I fell in line doing a slow jog—the minimal pace he allowed.

This is what happens when your Phys Ed teacher is ex-military, I thought as I chugged along. I'd actually liked Rossi when I first met him; he was my Social Studies teacher junior year. Back then he reminded me of an old hobbit with his twinkling eyes and jolly demeanor. I thought his obsession with the Battle of Normandy was just one of those old-man things. Then I got him for Phys Ed, and woe betide the little soldier who forgot her gym clothes. The only way to get back into his good graces was to attend one of his boot camp make-up sessions—or in my case, three. After my disastrous miss with Shar at the window, I was desperate for something to go right. Wednesday, Thursday, and now today I showed up for gym makeup. Rossi almost looked impressed. I really needed a gold star, and at this point I didn't care where it came from, as long as it wasn't Hades.

"That's the way!" Rossi yelled, surveying the stream of students snaking around the gym. He looked at his watch; we'd be at this for a good fifteen minutes at least.

"How are you gonna feel the burn going that slow?" said an unfamiliar voice right next to me. I turned my head to see. It was Hermes—and no one seemed to notice him.

"Uh." I gasped for breath, half from shock, half from the exercise. Hermes scowled disapprovingly and *tsked*, then took a long, admiring look down at his own muscular calves.

He slowed his pace, pulled his helmet off, and wiped his brow. Without stopping, he placed the helmet along the wall and waved a hand. It vanished, then he double-timed it to catch up with me.

"There's nothing as satisfying as a good, strenuous work-out!" he said, skipping alongside me as I panted and dripped.

"I could think of a few things," I puffed. "Let's start with a mocha latte and chocolate cake."

Hermes frowned. "Carbs, fat, and sugar. Poison."

"Caffeine, endorphins, sweet. Yum," I retorted. I loved my carbs, fat, and sugar; the way things were going, it was all I had to look forward to.

But Hermes was unimpressed. He ignored me, jogging slightly faster as if to challenge me to keep up. The moment of silence made me realize the only reason why he'd be here.

"You gave Shar my message?"

"I did." He looked at me, his eyes gleaming wickedly. "And let me tell you, she was not happy."

"What happened?" I asked, alarmed. "I mean, I know I missed our meeting, but you told her I was trying, right? You told her why I didn't get to see her?"

"I told her what you told me to say," he replied, smoothly and with no sign whatsoever of being out of breath. I, on the other hand, felt the onset of hyperventilation. I shot a glance down at his feet. The little wings on his shoes were fluttering madly. *Cheater!*

"But, you told her that you guys—you and Persephone— made me miss her, didn't you?" I pressed. Desperately.

"Huh?" He looked up from checking his vitals on a golden watch-pedometer that matched his too-tight Speedo running shorts and form-fitting tank. He wasn't listening to me, and he didn't care.

"Hermes, please!" I begged, shouting louder than I'd intended. The two girls in front of me turned and looked at me with foreheads wrinkled in aversion.

"I told her what you said to say," he huffed. "Except about running into Persephone. I'm not allowed to disclose anything about gods to mortals. But I did give her the rest."

Panicked, I tried to remember exactly what I'd said to Hermes, but the days since the concert were a blur of anxiety and Paulina.

"Did she … have a message for me?" I asked with dread. If Hermes didn't tell Shar that he and Persephone had delayed me, at least he'd told her I'd been trying—but was that enough?

"She did," said Hermes. "She said that *she* won't be at the box next time because there won't *be* a next time and *she* has a *ball* to attend. Then she told Hades to help her find a costume."

I stopped running and stumbled into the wall, clutching my sides. I could almost hear Shar, upset, scared, and mad that I didn't show, saying that. Hermes glided to a stop next to me as runners streamed by.

"Cramp, Wiley?" I heard Rossi shout.

Looking up, I saw him across the gym, standing on tiptoe and swaying so that he could see around the kids that zipped by in front of him. I nodded swiftly and gave him a thumbs-up, the sign that I just needed a minute to catch my breath and then I'd be "back in the game." I didn't need him to come over to investigate.

Hermes wiped a light sheen of sweat from his brow, then bent one knee and grabbed his raised foot in a runner's stretch.

"Come on!" he chirped cheerily, proceeding to stretch his other leg. Then he stooped to pick up his helmet, which had reappeared when I stopped him.

I grabbed him by the elbow. He couldn't flit away just yet. "You have to take another message to Shar for me."

He shook off my grip. "I don't have to do anything for you," he snipped, his voice condescending.

"You don't understand," I begged.

"*You* don't understand." He straightened up and threw out a hip, placing one well-tanned hand on it while pointing at me with the other. "First, I'm messenger to the *gods*. You," he sneered, looking me up and down, "are not a god."

"Obviously," I muttered. *And I don't want to be one. I wouldn't want to be like any of you.*

"Second," he continued, "I did you a favor by carrying your first message. I think a little gratitude is in order."

"Sorry!" Hermes was my only hope of setting this right, and giving him attitude wouldn't win him over to my side. Unfortunately, it was too late. He crossed his wiry arms over his chest and with a flick of his feet, flew out the door, over the heads of the jogging students.

I stared at him as he left, but I couldn't linger for long, not unless I wanted to face an inquisition from Mr. Rossi. Slowly, I rejoined the running parade. Would Shar really be a no-show? I had enough problems; I couldn't handle it if things got any worse.

"Hey, Window Girl." Caroline and Kate jogged past me.

It just got worse.

"What?" I ran faster to keep up with them.

"Were you practicing?" Kate sneered.

"For what?" I demanded, trying to sound as nonchalant as I could between breaths—but I knew exactly what they were talking about. They heard me talking to Hermes, but couldn't see him. Whenever I talked to Shar, I was the only one who could see her—it hadn't taken me long to figure that out. The question was, how did *they* know about Window Girl?

Rossi blew his whistle and everyone stopped.

"You're famous!" Caroline fake-gushed. Kate whispered something in her ear and then drew her away.

"It's not me!" I shouted, garnering puzzled stares. The two of them tittered all the way back to the locker room. I darted into a bathroom stall and stayed there until I was sure everyone left, then I skulked over to where I stashed my stuff and changed as fast as I could and hustled to the library. I didn't care if I was late for my next class; I needed to confirm what they were talking about. I waited patiently for a computer station, and as soon as one freed up, I nabbed it and Googled "Window Girl."

Hundreds of results popped up. I found photos of myself happily chatting with the chocolate mannequin, pointing an accusatory finger at the chocolate frog. Each image had pages of comments. There was also a video that I refused to watch. I felt my face burning. Who else had seen this stuff? My mom? Jeremy? Paulina? The video was damning evidence that I was psychotic, or ... psychotic.

I buried my head in my hands. "What am I going to do?"

"Get Paulina to wear the fleece."

Hades leaned back in the chair next to me, his feet propped up on the nearest computer station. He blew a kiss to the librarian, who blushed furiously.

"Not invisible, eh?"

He smiled expansively. "You know I show myself when the mood takes me. She wants to write the Great American Novel. Maybe I'll indulge her. I need a librarian."

"Go away," I said wearily.

"Margaret," he said in a mock-parental tone, "is that any way to talk to me?" When I didn't bother to answer, he went on, "I can't help but notice the fleece has stayed in your closet. You're never going to get her to wear it that way."

"I have other problems now," I said, pointing to the screen. "Not, of course, that you didn't know this would happen."

"I didn't." His lips cracked into a smile. "I'm immortal, not prescient. No one can predict the things you humans will do. Kind of like the squirrel dashing across the road. Will it go one way, or the other, or right under the car wheels?" He shrugged helplessly. "But I can see how you might find the spotlight distressing."

"Quite," I said, trying my best to keep my voice steady and not to overreact. That was exactly what he liked—a little drama to make his day interesting.

"You know," he continued, "accomplishing your mission will put an end to all your troubles, and not just the one about bringing Sharisse back, but the scales, your window fans, *Jeremy*."

I fought to keep silent and rubbed my forehead on the back of my arm.

"I promise you, the moment Paulina is in my keeping, everything in the mortal world as you know it will return to its original, albeit boring, state."

I lifted my head and gazed at him with slitted eyes. "What do you mean?"

"Exactly that. No more scales. No more Window Girl. No memories for Jeremy of your neglect." He smoothed an eyebrow. "And of course, Sharisse will forgive you for taking so long to complete so simple a task."

He just had to poke until he hit a nerve. "She knows I've been trying," I protested through clenched teeth.

"You weren't present to speak with her the last time. She was hurt. She felt... betrayed. But I put in a good word for you, despite my personal reservations."

I shivered, remembering what Persephone told me about Shar's activities. What was Shar thinking—or doing? The image of Hades passing by in his demi-towel flashed in my mind.

"I'm trying," I insisted. To him, and to myself.

"Take it to the next level. It's what's best for everyone." Hades' voice was silky smooth, his eyes matte-black like a shark's. He was lying. I knew he was. But what could I do?

"When I talk to Shar next time—"

"I don't know what Sharisse will decide to do, or if she is willing to listen to any excuses." He sighed blithely.

"I'm not making excuses," I whispered, but I knew I was. I wanted Shar back, but I didn't want to send Paulina to Hades. I kept trying not to be friends with Paulina, but it wasn't working. It wasn't just the fact that she'd grown on me; something wasn't right about this. My gut was rarely wrong when it came to people, and I got no chilling vibes from her. And despite all his talk of nondisclosure, Hades had been fairly free with the details of Arkady's deal while refusing to reveal anything about Paulina's.

"Well, then." Hades rose and put his hands in his pockets, à la *GQ*. "You keep pondering the whys and wherefores, Margaret. I don't mind Sharisse staying a bit—or, it looks like, *a while*—longer. I can always use *hands-on* assistants in the Underworld."

With a roguish wink, he was gone. My life was a docudrama in the Unbelievable category. I went through what was left of the afternoon in a daze with only one thought on my mind: *Would Shar show?*

The weekend plodded by, and Monday too. I spent Tuesday counting the hours until 6:55 p.m. As soon as school let out, Paulina was ready to shadow me as usual, so I told her that I had to go home to visit my mom. She tried to press me to come along.

"No, it'll be boring for you. Stay here," I snapped, not wanting a confrontation. Miraculously, she complied. I wandered around uptown, killing time.

Around six p.m., I parked myself in a cafe on the opposite side of the street from Pandora's and watched as people started to gather. First one, and then another, and still more came: men, women, little kids. A few of them had cameras. I groaned when a news van pulled up, with a videographer and a tiny woman in a dark suit who I recognized from the nightly news local-interest segment. She opened an umbrella over herself as it started to rain and freshened up her makeup.

I watched them until about 6:45, then nervously pulled up the hood of my jacket, slid on dark glasses, and walked out. Not wanting to walk into a media circus, I went down the street and crossed, slowly making my way to the back of the crowd that formed in front of the shop.

Anchorwoman was interviewing someone.

"I love Window Girl! I want to thank her personally for saving my business," said a man with a neatly trimmed, waxed, and twisted white mustache. He spoke with a friendly English lilt.

Anchorwoman eyed him shrewdly. "Mr. Coleman, some people say that this is a publicity stunt. Did you pay this mysterious Window Girl to come to your store? Rumor has it you did quite well last week, even though she didn't come. And, tonight you're running a 7:00 p.m. special—just the time that Window Girl stops talking to your displays."

"Absolutely not!" he huffed. "I don't know what possessed this young lady to come to Pandora's Box. I have no idea who she is. No one does. I don't know what she's talking about, or if the candy talks back! Chocolate does sometimes repeat on me."

He chuckled and laughter rippled through the crowd.

"Whoever she is, or whatever her reasons are, I call it divine intervention!" He grabbed the microphone and waved it at the camera. "Thank you, Window Girl! Thank you!"

"Window Girl! Window Girl!" the crowd chanted, and then started to back up, making a space in anticipation of my arrival. It was 6:54.

Did I really want to do this in front of all these people? I'd done it before, but not like this, not knowing there were cameras and news crews … but what if I missed Shar again? She'd never forgive me. Yet what if she didn't show, like Hades suggested? Although it was entirely plausible that he wanted to bait *me* into not showing, so fueling Shar's mistrust; he'd love to keep us both. I peered around the people, at the window. The wide empty space waited for Window Girl, for me. A hush fell over the crowd.

"Where is she?" I heard someone whisper, and immediately they were shushed. I had to try. Slowly I stepped forward, and the group parted like the Biblical Red Sea to let me pass. Once through, they closed in behind me. I felt trapped and embarrassed, but I couldn't fail Shar again.

The window display had changed yet again. A dark and white chocolate roulette wheel turned lazily around and around. A deck of chocolate cards sat next to stacks and stacks of chocolate poker chips. *Bet she's there, bet she's not.* It was a game of chance and I had no choice but to make a wager.

I stood in front of the window and waited … but nothing happened.

"Window Girl, what do you see?" someone shouted behind me.

"Stop! You'll wreck her concentration!" another hissed.

Suddenly, there was a bright light in the window. That had never happened before … my heart leapt up with hope. Then Anchorwoman started talking.

"This is Joy Evans, coming to you live from Pandora's Box on 57th Street. For a month now, the mysterious

Window Girl has come to this spot at five minutes to seven to talk to the displays."

There were a few moments of silence and the flash of cell phone cameras. I didn't take my eyes off the window, but I could smell the stench of Camera Guy's cigarette breath as he edged closer to me. Instantly the light was off me and Joy Evans was reporting again.

"Four minutes into today's visit and Window Girl has said nothing!"

Only one minute left? Where was Shar?

No one moved, breathed, or made a sound.

"And, seven o'clock," she announced.

There was a collected and disappointed sigh. Shar hadn't come. I felt tears welling up and slid my glasses on with shaking hands.

"It was that newswoman," someone muttered disgustedly. "She ruined the mood."

Joy Evans hustled up to me, microphone in hand and camera in tow. "Window Girl, who are you? Why do you come here?"

I looked around helplessly. Just about everyone who had been standing around had jostled close to get a view of me or hear something prophetic from me. I wanted to scream, *I'm just a girl! A scared, lonely, abandoned, duped girl. I can't help myself and I can't help Shar and I can't help you!*

"Leave her alone! Leave her alone! Can't you see she's upset?" I looked up to see Mr. Coleman, the owner, muscling in between Joy Evans and me. He was glaring at her. Then he looked down kindly at me. "Go on," he whispered.

I pushed through the group to the sounds of him arguing with Joy Evans. Shar hadn't shown; obviously she thought I abandoned her, and in a way, I did—but did I also drive her into Hades' waiting arms? Hermes reported that she wasn't going to come, and that she asked Hades to help her get a costume for that ball; she'd never asked him for anything before. Was he on the brink of getting her to give in? If Shar felt she had nothing to return to, and Hades offered her everything she could ever want ...

I couldn't let that happen. But I couldn't give Paulina to him.

Then a light dawned.

You have to stick by Shar. Put on the fleece yourself, go to Tartarus. Whatever happens next, you'll figure it out—together.

My step felt lighter, quicker; I would have skipped back to the dorm if it wasn't for the knowledge of where I'd be spending the night.

When I got to the room, Paulina was there, lounging on her bed.

"Wanna get something to eat?" she asked. She was always hungry!

I ignored her and went right to the closet and took out the garment bag. Out of the corner of my eye I saw her get up in a quick movement that was all long, black-clad legs and limbs. Shaking off my jacket, I realized that I was doing this right in front of her, and for a fraction of a second I wondered if it was the right thing to do. I decided that if she had a deal with Hades, me suddenly vanishing wouldn't surprise her, and if she didn't, then once I was down in Tartarus all memories of me would probably be erased. That's how I figured things worked—it would be too messy for Hades to leave memories of people who disappeared under mysterious circumstances.

I pulled the fleece out, shook it, and swung it around my shoulders, only to have it pulled from my hands. I whirled around; Paulina held the fleece at arm's length from herself, barely pinching it with two fingers.

"What are you doing?" she cried, gaping at me incredulously.

"I'm putting on my coat—what does it look like?"

"It's too warm. All you need is a sweater," she said. "And it's too ugly. I can't let you be seen in it." She sounded like Shar, only more gruff.

I held out my hand and wiggled my fingers, demanding its return.

Paulina eyed me cautiously, hesitating. "It makes you look fat," she mumbled, as if she didn't want to say it. As if she was desperate for... *what?* She turned around and marched over to her bed with it, and I followed on her heels.

"I'm serious, Paulina! Give—"

"You know," she interrupted, turning around, "that dance is on Saturday, right? And we're going?"

I nodded, slowly. *I won't be here, so it doesn't matter.*

She looked sad. "Can I... borrow it?"

Huh? "I... you just said it was ugly."

"Yeah." She nodded. "But looking at it again..." She turned it around, this time holding it in her whole hand. "It's not so bad. But it was definitely meant for a taller person. What're you wearing?"

I looked at the closet; the tight-fitting Edwardian dress I bought with Shar before Hades took her would never work now, with my scales. But did that matter? I turned back to Paulina, confused and with no energy left to argue. "Uh, I haven't really figured that out yet ... "

"Me neither. We can figure it out over dinner."

I managed to nod as Paulina dropped the fleece on the chair by her bed, grabbed her keys, and hustled me out the door.

SHAR

Shall We Dance?

"That, that *insect*!" I screeched. My dress had arrived from Arachne, delivered by some dead-a-long-time servant. As soon as I opened the box, I knew she'd either ratted me out to Hades or taken it upon herself to gift wrap me for him.

I'd told her I wanted to go dressed as my great-grandmother: dowdy, neutral-colored house dress; sensible, orthopedically correct shoes; and garish, flowered apron; maybe even a wooden spoon clutched in my hand. I thought I was safe.

But noooooo!

Pushing aside the silver tissue paper, I found a pearly pink high-Hollywood-glam dress suitable for the Academy Awards, something the biggest stars would wear. A diamond necklace, à la Harry Winston and most likely dripping with over ten glistening carats of stones, was cradled in a sapphire blue cushioned box. Slinky silver heels by Ferragamo—I was willing to bet handmade by Mr. Salvatore Ferragamo over in Hades' Italy of the '70s—lay waiting to be introduced to my feet.

There was nothing for it; I had to wear it. It was either that or more Grecian goddess garb, and that had gotten old fast.

Once I was dressed, I swept out and made my way through the throne room. As hostess, it was my duty to greet the guests. My heels clip-clapped on the marble floor.

"I'm speechless. What can I say, *bella*."

I stiffened, waiting for the breathing down my neck. True to form, his breath was warm as it tickled my spine, sending chills down my back.

Next come the hands. Wait for it…

His palms glided up my arms. Enough! I lifted the hem of my dress and moved away, giving him *that look*.

"I don't think I could have chosen better. You must tell me more about this Estelle. How she could go unnoticed by me is a mystery."

This outfit was sooo not Grandma! Arachne was dressing me for a sacrifice. I tapped my foot and crossed my arms over my chest to stop his rude gaping. There were a lot of bare spots; arms, back, shoulders, neck, and quite a bit of the front.

"She is my great *grandmother,* and this was NOT what I ordered from Arachne. I think you should fire her. The client is not pleased."

His tongue wet his upper lip in a way that was enticing, really, but I wasn't feeling it. "But Arachne is my employee, and I am *most* thrilled. I had to give her a bonus. A set of real legs for a while." He took a step closer and I hopped back.

"And why aren't you dressed in a costume? Just a tux?"

He shrugged. "I've decided to pass on the costume this time. Lucky for you. Can you imagine if I'd dressed as Don Juan or Romeo? This way we look breathtaking together."

Yep, Arachne ratted. He planned his wardrobe around mine. I should have worn the shower curtain—wait! Shower equals naked! Scratch that!

With a last seething look I told him, "I have duties to perform. The guests should be arriving."

"By all means, let us greet our guests." Instantly one arm snaked around my waist while the other claimed a hand, holding me prisoner. He guided me toward the front doors of the palace; at a flick of his pinky, they opened without so much as a whisper.

And there stood Caz, in a sharp blue suit and large tortoiseshell glasses.

With a date.

A stunning redhead—slim, graceful, petite, and looking sexy smart in a tweedy suit that complimented his outfit. In her hand she held a pencil and a small pad.

"Ah, nephew, good of you to come. Who are you supposed to be?" Hades' stare lingered on the girl. Should I be jealous that both Hades and Caz could easily replace me with the various flavors of the Underworld?

Get your head in the game, Sharisse.

Without even looking at me, Caz said, "Uncle, Sharisse.

May I present Lois Lane, the love of Clark Kent's life." He glanced around as if he was watching for eavesdroppers. Then he pulled open his shirt to reveal a bright tight red, yellow, and blue tee. "This is just my alter ego." He winked at Lois conspiratorially. "I'm really Superman."

Lois giggled and hung on his arm. I wanted to kick them both, but instead I stepped forward, the most perfect smile on my face. *Two can play this game.*

"Welcome, Miss Lane. Please come in and enjoy yourself. Should you require anything, you have only to ask." I turned to Caz. With the same gracious tone, I said, "What a pleasure to see you again, *Castor*. I hope you two have a wonderful time." I stepped back, next to Hades, who smiled smugly. His fingers brushed against my derrière. I refused to rise to the bait.

"Have fun," said Hades, humor dancing in his eyes. Not looking back at Caz, now known as the blond snake, I turned to greet the long line of guests.

Geez, I hope he didn't invite every single dead person in history. This ball will last an eternity.

He didn't. It seemed that Hades only invited those he called the *interesting* people: upper echelon royalty like Queen Elizabeth I—scary; twisted royalty like Vlad Dracul —mega scary; and nouveau royalty like the self-proclaimed African king with so many names I couldn't remember the first one he rattled off, but who really was a brutal dictator— scummy. There were also the typical Greek full and demi-gods, some Egyptian ones, no Romans of course, and some I'd never heard of. It was almost time to begin, judging by

Hades' growing impatience, when I spied a couple chatting amiably as they neared the doors.

"Ben and Arachne! Interesting pairing," I said, and noted that Hades had been serious about giving her human legs. She was dressed as a cheerleader to show them off. Ben came as a Redcoat.

I heard Hades' indrawn breath.

"Hello Ben, Arachne. Thank you for coming."

"Miss Sharisse, Lord Hades," Ben replied formally. "I'm so looking forward to this evening. The British have arrived! Miss Arachne has been kind enough to promise me the first dance."

"How wonderful!" I gushed. "Do enjoy yourselves."

"We do not invite the help!" Hades hissed in an aside, after they'd passed.

I feigned a shocked look. "All men are created equal and are endowed—"

"Spare me," he grumbled. "Next you'll be thinking that you're equal to us."

"Better," I replied softly.

"Hmph," he grunted as another guest came up to us. A man with long dreadlocks and dressed in a black leather jacket, jeans, and a crisp white button-down strolled up to the doors. His shirt was open, revealing amber skin and a well-developed chest.

Who was this?

"Dionysus," Hades said, tipping his head the smallest fraction of an inch.

Ah, another god.

Dionysus smiled warmly, then raised a hand to Hades

and did one of those handshake-slash-back-pat combo things that guys do with other guys.

Struggling not to laugh at Hades' almost imperceptible cringe, I put out my hand. "Welcome, Dionysus."

"I'm the god of drunkenness, dirty dancing, and debauchery." A smile spread over his lips. "No party is complete without me, but please, call me D'On." He took my hand and, quickly flipping my palm up, pressed a licky kiss dead center.

I gasped at his boldness in front of Hades. How wonderful it was that not only was I good gawking material for juvenile-acting males, but I was prime bait. And a good hostess. And a husband stealer, failed beauty queen, unmissed roomie, and pathetic mortal. Mother would be proud. So far I'd felt like a mannequin on display for everyone who knew what Hades wanted. Worse was wondering if they thought I was giving it. Still, a binding, lethal, unfair contract is a *binding, lethal, unfair* contract. I kept playing my part to storybook perfection.

"And who are you, looking so … ambrosial?" D'On's violet eyes were bright with mischief.

Hades stepped forward, partially blocking my sight of D'On and his of me, which forced him to let go of my hand. My palm was still wet from his kiss.

"This is Sharisse. Now that you're here, the festivities can begin."

With a devilish chuckle and a sly wink, D'On whispered in my ear, "I claim one dance." Without waiting for an answer, he strutted off toward the ballroom.

Hades turned and offered me his arm. "No one will

dance until after we have, then he'll liven things up. Shall we go in?"

There was no refusing him so I linked my arm through his, gathered my train, and let him guide me to the ballroom.

Glittering chandeliers gave off soft light, illuminating guests dressed in every conceivable costume: royalty, animal, monster, TV, movie, and historical. The crowd quieted and parted as Hades led me to the center of the room. He stared only at my eyes and pulled me so close I felt like I was sharing his pants. I tried to squirm away but he held me too tight. We stood there, staring at each other, waiting for the music to start. Mesmerized by his dark aura, I couldn't look away.

The waltz started. I knew it wasn't the dance lessons my mother forced upon me that enabled me to glide effortlessly around the floor; Hades swept me along in a whirling, almost dervish motion until my eyes couldn't make out anything around me but him. Heat rushed to my face and a small smile pulled at his lips, as if he knew that I was fighting an attraction to him.

"Why do you resist?" His voice was velvet. "I know you think of me, even just a little, though I suspect it's much more than that. Just admit it." His lips brushed my hair as he twirled me again.

"We both know that if I give in, you'll gloat and then I won't be anything but a joke. For you, the excitement is in the chase, not in catching the prey. And besides all that"—I paused as he twirled me around—"I don't date married men."

A laugh rumbled deep in his chest and his gaze traveled down to my lips. I tried to keep my breath even, my demeanor relaxed, but I couldn't.

"I already told you, mine and Persephone's is an open relationship. But there is some truth to your other observation. You have led me on the longest chase, and it excites me. The harder I try, the more you fight. If I should act like a gentleman, like Castor, would you give in?"

Jealous?

"No," I answered honestly. "That's not who you are—you won't change for anything or, I suspect, anyone. And as long as we're discussing this, I think the reason you're like this is because no one refuses you. Persephone wanted you to catch her." His eyes flared dangerously for a moment, but he never lost a step. "I think you're bored. It happens to married couples."

Because I know so much about that subject; me without a date for the Spring Fling, which I'm missing anyway. At least this dance will be memorable.

"*Chérie*, have you considered that maybe you like the fact that *I* chase *you*?"

I gave his words thoughtful consideration. "Possibly. It's that whole dark knight taunting the heroine. Little girls eat that up as soon as they learn about handsome, 'maybe I can save him' bad boys. But I don't think that's the case with us."

He cocked a brow. "Enlighten me."

"You have too many points against you. You're married so securely I doubt even Zeus could stop the war that would erupt if you suddenly decided you wanted out. Your wife is a powerful, immortal goddess with a possessive streak who could vaporize me and upset the entire pantheon. You live in the Underworld, and while it's amazing and spectacular, it's not my home. Eventually I might end up here, but

I have my life on the mortal plane that I want to return to."
I paused, trying to frame out my next thought before I said
something rash.

"Go on," he urged. "Say what's on your mind. Very few
get the privilege."

I turned my head, watching the crowd spin by. How
long had we been dancing?

"You're gorgeous. I have never met anyone as beautiful as
you and I doubt I ever will. I admit it's hard to resist you, but
I can, because it's wrong and because I don't like the insecu-
rity I feel around you." I refused to meet his stare. "With you
there's chaos and infidelity and guilt and lust. There's no love.
I want that. And that's the one thing you can't give me."

The music ended abruptly. Hades, his eyes smolder-
ing with some emotion, gently lifted my hand and kissed
it chastely.

"I could give love. If someone ever wanted it from me."
He spun swiftly and scooped up one of Henry VIII's wives.
In a moment he was the charming rogue once more.

Standing there like an abandoned kitten, I held my head
high. I would not slink off.

A muscular arm slipped around me and I twirled into
the midst of the crowd. "Finally, it's my turn." D'On's laughing dimples greeted me. Out of the corner of my eye I saw
Hades watching us. I ignored them. And Caz, as he whispered with his comic-book candy bar on the other side of
the dance floor.

"Waltzing is kind of reserved for you, isn't it, D'On?" I
asked.

"Oh, things will pick up soon. I wanted a few moments with you first."

"Me?" I puzzled. "Why?"

He leaned closer. "I've seen Meg. She's fine, but she has no idea what she's really dealing with. She worries about you."

He'd seen Meg! Well, that was nice to hear, but if she'd shown up to talk, she could've told me in person. A small part of me was still miffed she blew me off for a concert, but now that I knew, or thought I knew, the truth about her roommate, I felt there had to be more to it. I opened my mouth to say something; D'On seemed to know what was happening up there—or did he? *Greek god equals untrustworthy.* I decided to keep my mouth shut, and simply nodded and said nothing. D'On narrowed his eyes at me shrewdly and smiled. The music ended and he kissed my hand. "Now the fun starts. Don't drink the wine."

Waiters passed, bearing golden trays of goblets brimming with wine. I shook my head, declining, but others around me rushed over, grabbing greedily. The sedate orchestral music was replaced by progressive rock, and the crowd became a frenzied mob with Hades in the middle, the dancing wild and uninhibited.

It seemed to be the signal for me to go, and I slipped out unnoticed. Not about to try escaping in my glamorous get-up, I headed quickly to my room to change. Even if Caz had ditched the plan, I hadn't. I just had to find Eurydice.

When a shadow moved in front of me, I jumped and screamed—before I realized it was Caz.

"You scared me!" I slapped his arm.

"Sorry. Are you ready?"

Hands on hips, I glared at him. "For what? To meet your date? Oh wait, I already did. Bye." I tried to skirt around him, but he grabbed my arm and pulled me into the nearest room, which happened to be the bowling alley. Lois stood there waiting.

"Are you serious?" I spat, looking at her furiously. "What are you—"

She strode up to me, shaking her head. Then she pulled off her wig.

Eurydice!

"If I'd shown up alone, Hades would be watching us the entire night. We'd never have been able to sneak out," Caz explained.

"It would have been nice if you'd filled me in on the plan."

"There was no time," said Eurydice, "and we didn't want to make Hades suspicious. Real surprise is hard to replicate."

As I exhaled in relief, Eurydice urged, "Dionysus is revving them all up with wine and music. Even Hades is susceptible to his wantonness. But we have to hurry and get out of his reach before he realizes you're both gone."

I could hear the raucous music and voices even this far down the hall. Things were really getting wild.

"Okay, let me change first." I started toward my room again, but Caz pulled me in the opposite direction.

"No time."

I dug in my heels. "I at least need to get my purse. Female necessity." Sighing, he released my arm and waited until, purse in hand, I returned, only to find him talking to D'On.

"You saw him!" Caz said excitedly.

"He's alive and well," said D'On. "And he's in no danger from Meg." He smiled when he saw me. "I like Meg—she's got a good soul. And Pollux agrees."

The look in his eye and the tone of his voice wasn't lost on me. Pollux liked Meg. Talk about complicated. I shook my head. "It's the Siren mojo."

"I don't think so," said D'On. "He knows about the fleece, and he knows about you—what she could tell him, I expect. He understands her dilemma."

I turned to Caz. "I'm ready. Let's rock."

Caz nodded and clapped D'On on the shoulder. "Keep 'em busy, bro."

"Will do," he said, and turned back to the ballroom.

We made our way to the gothic garden. It was night in Tartarus and the plants looked even more sinister than usual. Careful not to brush up against or walk too near the deadly flora, we found the gnarly tree. Eurydice pushed aside the mangled, dead-looking branches, revealing a barely notice-able path.

It wound down, over the black rock in front of Hades' palace. I stumbled several times, cursing Arachne for the shoes and dress and Hades for being the cause of everything wrong in my life since that night on the subway. It felt more like an eternity rather than a mere few months.

The path halted at the river. Those dark waters and the drowning senator would give me nightmares for years. Caz turned an irritable eye on Eurydice.

"You never mentioned we'd have to cross or go down the Styx," he said.

"I forgot! It's been three thousand years!" Her eyes burned.

There was no time for this. "Move," I snapped. "Splendor!" I called, not too loudly. "Splendor!"

Soon I heard the slap of water on wooden oars. A shadow loomed, a boat with a darkly draped figure poised at the helm. A broad smile stretched across my face at Caz's bewilderment and Eurydice's shock.

"Who did you call? Where's Charon?" he asked.

"Watch and learn," I replied primly.

"What dirt-sucking, plebeian—" grumbled Splendor, and then stopped. "Shar? Is that you?" She docked the rocking boat at the shore.

"Hi Splendor!"

"Who's that with you?" she asked, pulling off her hood. "Castor?"

"Aglaia? What are *you* doing down *here*?" he asked.

Before Splendor could ask about Eurydice, growling and snarling came from the shadows.

"Cerberus!" Caz hissed.

I could feel him tense with fear, but still, he stepped in front of me. How brave—but not necessary. Eurydice looked like she was going to faint.

Daintily I side-stepped him and gingerly picked up a femur from a pile of bones by the lapping water. After huge piles of dog poop, a bleached bone was not daunting. First one set of eyes and then another twinkled in the darkness. Then all three slobbering heads came bounding toward me.

"Good goggy!" I called. And he stopped. One at a time, each head cocked itself at me, then sounded a friendly bark.

"Who's a good goggy?" I gushed. "Go get the bone!"

I wound up and tossed, then with yelps, Cerberus chased after it.

"Get me another one!" I urged.

Caz and Eurydice obeyed, each handing me a bone. I tucked them under my arm as I hurried over to Splendor. She gave me a questioning look, but I quickly opened my purse. "Here." I handed her my breath mints, hand sanitizer, tissue packet, hand lotion, and golden compact with the engraved *S*. "I, we, need a ride down the river."

She shook her head slightly. "The only thing down the river is the Pit. Don't you mean back the other way?"

"No," said Caz. "We need to see Kronos. We have to—"

"Deliver a message!" I interrupted. I gave his hand a squeeze, hoping he wouldn't contradict me. The fewer people who knew what we were doing, the easier it would be to keep the secret. Plus, if everything blew up in our faces, I didn't want to get Splendor in trouble for helping us. Cerberus came loping back and I threw another bone.

Splendor piled her treasures on the floor of the boat by her feet and motioned for us to come aboard. Caz nimbly lifted first me, then Eurydice, onto the boat, then hopped up himself just as Cerberus came back holding a skull in the mouth of his middle head like a squeaky ball. I picked up an arm bone with a hand still attached.

"Take this to Daddy! Good goggy!" I yelled, and hurled it into the blackness. Away went Cerberus, and Splendor started poling.

"Who's that?" she asked, twitching her head in Eurydice's direction.

"Don't ask," I said. She got the hint.

"So, Castor, visiting the relatives?" she inquired casually.

"You could say that," he responded easily. "Why the new career, Aglaia?"

We were now well down from Hades' palace and so far no one had come screaming, running, or poofing to stop us. I could relax just a bit.

"I'm keeping a low profile. Let's just say that *some* gods are a little too full of their own attractiveness."

He huffed. "My father making your life difficult?" She didn't respond right away, but she did turn bright red.

"Sometimes it's not the dog you have to worry about," she said cryptically. "It's the one holding the leash."

"So *she's* got you on the run, then."

Splendor made a face.

Sadly, I understood their references. Typical pattern. The husbands chase with kisses, the wives with knives. Zeus and Hera. I felt sorry for Hera. She'd been nice, sort of, to Meg and me.

The boat moved swiftly and silently down the river in the inky blackness. I didn't see or hear anything or anyone. We'd made it this far; maybe we'd succeed.

In the distance I saw dim lights, which grew brighter as we got closer. Suddenly Eurydice perked up. She closed her eyes and swayed in rhythm to music that got louder and louder.

Is that Elvis I hear? I'd thought he was in the Elysian Fields, appearing in some club with screaming women throwing their panties at him.

The boat ground to a halt on the rocks.

No way.

This was no dangerous squalid hole. It was lights and fountains and fancy cars...and a casino.

The Pit was the Vegas of the Underworld.

MΣG

Large-Scale Wardrobe Malfunction

On the morning of the Spring Fling, I woke to find Paulina gone. And the fleece too.

I leapt out of bed, panicked. Usually I'd find her sitting on her bed, ready to walk out the door.

Is she still in the shower? Did she take the fleece with her? Maybe she's . . . gone! I got up and padded to the edge of her side of the room, craning my neck to try and see if the fleece was shoved under the desk, rolled in her sheets, or hidden in her closet. Nothing. Under the bed? But before I could peek, I heard the key turning in the lock. I hopped back over to my desk and opened a book, trying to look nonchalant.

Paulina, fully dressed, breezed in carrying shampoo, a

fluffy black bathrobe, a towel—and no fleece. I felt my heart race. Where was it? Had she left it in the bathroom? Given it to someone? Thrown it away?

"Up early?" she asked. I looked at the clock: 8:15. I usually slept till at least 10:30 on Saturdays.

"Yeah." I slapped the book shut. "So, do you have any idea what you'd like to wear tonight?" I asked casually.

She shrugged. "Nah. I guess we should go shopping."

"Okay, but we'll want to bring my coat if you're going to use it," I said, peering around her. "Where is it?"

"Oh." She stared at me. Garbed head-to-toe in black jeans and a black billowy shirt, she looked taller and lankier than ever. She stooped by her bed. "I think it's here." She reached under the bed and dragged out the fleece. It hardly looked regal, twisted into a lump and covered in dust bunnies. Hades would freak if he saw it. Paulina didn't give it back, but tossed it onto her bed. It hit the wall and fell ungracefully next to her rolled-up comforter. She sat down next to it.

"Go ahead and get ready. I'll wait for you."

I got dressed quickly—so quickly that I didn't realize she'd left the fleece behind until we were blocks from the dorm. When I did an about-face to retrieve it, she stopped me, saying, "We don't need it. Everything goes with black, right?"

I had no fight left in me, and I didn't argue as she led me uptown. In Bloomingdale's, I walked around the women's tall department in a daze, not knowing what to do or say. I thought I'd be in the Underworld by this point, yet now I had a dance to go to.

"Think I can wear pants?" she asked, holding up four

pairs of what looked like identical black jeans. "I'm not really into dresses. Let's head over to the men's department."

"Men's?"

"Yeah, they fit better for some reason."

"Sure." I shrugged.

She selected several pairs, then ducked into the fitting room as I leaned against a pillar with a mirror bolted to each side, yawning. I felt like I was back shopping with Shar. I giggled feebly. *With Shar.* If only. My phone rang and I pulled it out. Jeremy.

"Hi."

"Hey." His voice, usually silky and capable of making my stomach do backflips, sounded flat. "Just making sure we're still on for tonight."

Did he doubt it? "Yeah, why wouldn't we be?"

Silence.

"Just checking." He paused again, then added, "Your roommate coming?"

"Yes," I answered, relieved. Maybe it was better that they meet. At least then he'd see I was telling the truth about that.

"Good," he said, sounding a little more like himself. "I'll meet you there at seven." He hung up without a goodbye.

Glumly I snapped the phone shut and waited for Paulina to come out. She bought a pair of the black jeans, a black button-down, and a glittery black headband. We went back to the dorm to get ready.

I didn't want to shower again, figuring that I might be able to throw the fleece on while she was out getting ready, but she piled the thing on top of her clothes and left for the bathroom almost as soon as we got back.

Well, I thought, walking over to my closet, *if she tries it on in the bathroom with the full-length mirror to see how it looks with those skinny jeans, she'll be going someplace other than the Spring Fling, and at least I won't have had a hand in making her do it.* But I still felt guilty for thinking how much easier that would make this; Shar would return and it wouldn't be my fault. But my hands were still not totally clean. And part of me would miss Paulina.

Alone, I stripped off the calf-length dress and socks I was wearing; the scales made it impossible to wear anything else. Since that first day when I'd discovered them in the shower, more scales had appeared. They now ran across my chest at the level of my underarms and down my back, sides, and front to my knees, like a snug-fitting strapless dress. The skirt part felt like a membrane, and it constricted my movement a bit—if it were a little lower, I'd be walking with a wiggle, and lower than that, would I sprout fins?

The scales were a few shades darker than my skin and slightly iridescent, but still, in the mirror, I looked shockingly naked. When I ran my hand down them the right way—forget going against the grain, that just hurt too much—the scales felt like no fabric I'd ever touched before; firm, but supple and slippery soft.

I went through each article of clothing that I owned. Couldn't do pants, since my legs wouldn't go in; couldn't do a skirt, since the waistbands made the scales dig into my skin. No tights, no fitted tops would accommodate my fishy torso. The choices were narrowing down to nothing.

I looked at the smocked, shapeless shift I'd thrown on the floor. How would I explain to Paulina that I was just going to wear the same thing I'd been trying to dress up for almost two weeks? Would she even care? I picked it up, shook it out, and laid it on my bed, pondering what I could do with it to make it look different. From the closet I dug out a pair of ancient silver shoes, and in my drawer found shimmery thigh-high stockings I could roll down a bit. *At least these don't pinch*, I thought, sliding them on.

I buckled my feet into the shoes and was about to put the dress back on when the door flew open. There was no time to leap behind my changing screen. Paulina stood in the doorway, all ready to go. She started for a second, looking at me in a way I'd never seen her look at me before. In a strange, unsettling way, it kind of reminded me of when I'd caught Jeremy peeking at me while I was dancing at the concert.

In the meantime, I stood frozen. *You are standing in front of Paulina in nothing but thigh-highs and heels!* We stared at each other for a long moment, and then the half-grin flickered on her lips.

She cleared her throat. "Did you just buy that?" she asked, a bit hoarsely.

"Um, no," I said, my face coloring.

"It looks … " She shook her head, her mouth working to find the right words. "That's just … rocking."

Rocking? Was she kidding?

"I'm serious," she went on, setting down her shower things and dropping the fleece on the ground. "I always thought you could pull off something like that, but you're always hiding under dark baggy clothes. *Wow*."

"I'm *not* wearing this," I said, scuttling over to my bed to get the black sack I'd had on before.

"Oh yes you are," she said, dragging me out the door before I could utter any protests—but not without the fleece. I snatched it up from the floor as we left.

The dance was being held in the school gymnasium, only a block from the dorm. I didn't want to walk down the hall and out into the streets naked, but Paulina pulled me along, reveling in the admiring stares I got from other kids, passing men and women in suits, and two policemen.

We arrived on the stroke of seven, right on time. Kate was working the admissions table.

"Oh my God, Meg," she gushed, running an appreciative eye over my scales. "Nice dress!"

She actually seemed sincere, and I looked around for Alana or Caroline; they were nowhere in sight. I made a little nod of acknowledgment, then slipped in front of Paulina; with her in back of me and the fleece in front, I was somewhat covered.

We hovered by the door, keeping an eye out for Jeremy. We didn't have to wait long. I made a little wave and at first he looked right through me, but then did a double take, his eyes lingering on my "dress."

"I'll take this," said Paulina, slipping the fleece from my hands and tucking it under her own jacket, which she'd taken off. Jeremy paid for his ticket and came over to where we stood, not taking his eyes off me—or at least, the part from my neck to my knees.

"I can't believe you're wearing something like this," he said, slipping an arm around me. "I ... uh ... what's it made of?" He ran a hand down my back and I inched away when he started to rub the scales the wrong way. I bumped into Paulina and stepped on her foot.

"Oh, Jeremy, um, I'd like you to meet my roommate, Paulina."

He dragged his gaze away from me to look at her. The two of them stood eye to eye, although it looked like Paulina was a little taller. They regarded each other for a few seconds, and I thought I could see something like a sneer forming on Paulina's face, while Jeremy's gaze was bitingly cold.

"Why don't we go inside?" I suggested, taking hold of one arm each and leading them toward the middle set of double doors that led into the gym.

They both reached for the handle at the same time. Jeremy backed off and let Paulina open it, then stepped in front of her and held it wide so I could pass through.

The gym was full of dancing kids. A mural of a garden, put together by the art club, took up one wall; couples were taking photos in front of it. A DJ was set up at one end and a few tables with food, soda, and bottles of water were at the other.

"Meg said you took her to a dance class," Jeremy said to Paulina in a not-so-nice tone. "Gonna go out there and show them how it's done?" he challenged.

Paulina said nothing for a long minute and didn't so much as sway in place in time to the music. Then, slowly, she turned to Jeremy. "And make the rest of you look like elephants with no rhythm? But I'll dance if Meg wants to."

I shook my head. Even if I hadn't been stark naked, there was no way I was going out there. I shuffled to a wall on one side of the gym. Jeremy and Paulina followed me, then planted themselves, defensively it seemed, to either side of me.

"I'm kind of cold," I said to no one in particular after a few songs had played. Neither Paulina nor Jeremy were listening to me, they were too busy staring each other down. If the looks hadn't been so obviously vile, I might have called myself jealous.

"Sorry, what was it you said you were going to school for?" Paulina asked in a derisive tone and made a smile of mock interest in Jeremy's direction.

"Film," was the clipped answer.

Paulina snorted, and an awkward, chilly silence followed. I was standing between and behind them with the wall at my back. I knew I was naked even if no one else could tell; I was trying to hide and keep warm, but so far the hiding part was the only thing that was successful. I wanted out. Spying fibers of the fleece peeking out from underneath Paulina's leather jacket, I tried to snag it but she whipped around.

"What's the matter?" she asked, peering down at me sternly.

"Um, I'm freezing," I said. My skin was a mass of goose flesh; no amount of rubbing and holding myself was going to make things better.

"You can wear my jacket," she said warmly, and started to hand it to me.

"No thanks," I tried to smile. "I think my coat'll be warmer."

"It'll ruin your outfit," she said, but I took the opportunity when she started handing me her jacket to pull the fleece free.

"Hey, when did you get that?" Jeremy asked. I looked up in horror and saw him ogling the fleece. *Not him too!* He wasn't the type to be into man-fur; the thought made me cringe. This thing had everyone in its vicinity spellbound— except Paulina. *Touché Hades.*

"This old thing?" I laughed nervously and crumpled it tighter against me. "I don't know. I have a lot of clothes."

Paulina used my distraction with Jeremy to grab a fistful of the fleece.

"It looks really cool," Jeremy went on, reaching out a hand to stroke it. "Can I see it?"

"Sure," said Paulina, turning to him and tugging hard on the fleece, as if she was going to hand it over. I felt like Alice between the Red Queen and the Mad Hatter.

"I'm the one who's about to get pneumonia if I don't put this on," I said to them, then turned to Paulina. "And I have to go to the bathroom."

"Go ahead," said Paulina. "But take my jacket. I'll keep Jeremy company until you get back."

There was no way in hell I was leaving the two of them alone with the fleece.

"Give it to me," I said, and immediately felt a tightness in my chest and stomach and legs, as if I was being squeezed, as if the scales had suddenly shrunk in some way. Paulina stared at me for a moment, her grip slowly loosening.

"Come on, P," I said softly. "I need it, and I have to go." I jerked my head toward the bathroom. I knew now there was no way she would ever wear it. I had to put it on and go to Tartarus to save us all—Paulina from Tartarus, Shar from Hades, and me from betraying them both.

She stared at me with that odd half-smile and sad, sad eyes, then uncurled her hand as if it pained her. She opened her mouth to say something, but no sound came out.

"Thanks," I said, and then peeked over at Jeremy. "Just going to the ladies' room."

He nodded.

I didn't bother to tell them I'd be back.

SHAR
Pit Stop

"This is as far as I go," said Splendor.

"Thanks," I said, and taking off my glittery shoes, I handed them to her.

Her eyes popped. They'd better. A girl doesn't give up silver, pink-studded, new-vintage *custom* Ferragamo pumps every day. She reached down, scooped up some coins, and thrust them into my hands.

"Take these. You might need to bribe your way out. And just in case, keep at least two. The next time you come back, I might not be here and Charon can't be bought off with less than gold."

I gave her a spontaneous hug, which left her speechless.

"Thanks," I whispered in her ear. "I hope everything works out for you. Really."

Caz moved forward. "I'll talk to my father about your situation," he promised. Splendor nodded gratefully.

We jumped out of the boat, waved until she started to fade, and made our way to the front of the casino, the Gorgon's Head. There were millions of little lights; it was so dazzling, I felt blinded. Caz ushered Eurydice and me in through the revolving door and smack into the ugliest, meanest, slimiest creature I'd ever seen. It was a serpent with nine heads. I flinched. *The freak show's in town.*

"Hi, Hydra," said Caz.

One of the heads nodded at us.

"Life's too short and eternity too long to look that ugly," I said, moving closer to him while Eurydice inched nearer to me.

Caz stepped right up to the monster. "I want to see my grandfather." One head kept a steady watch on us while the others monitored the patrons.

"Thisssss way," it hissed.

I clutched Caz's hand and, filled with trepidation but determined, followed, with Eurydice silent behind me.

The place was just like any casino I'd seen in movies, except there were females of various species—human, serpent, satyr, and some I couldn't make out—parading around in glitzy outfits, carrying drinks or hawking cigarettes, cigars, and other things that could kill, but hey, not a problem here, right? There were gaming tables, gamblers, dealers, and throngs of seemingly happy people and um, creatures.

Everyone looked like they were having a good time. What was so hellish about the Pit?

An argument between a Minotaur and a Cyclops broke out. Tables got smashed, chairs got thrown, and patrons quickly ducked for cover.

Then *HE* came out—easily twelve feet tall, packed with hairy gray muscle and clawed hands, one ankle tethered by a shackle and a length of mammoth black chain. He stomped over to the table, picked up the duo, and promptly *ate them*. When he started crunching the bones, I had to put fingers in my ears.

Going vegan like Meg!

"You wanted to see me?" growled the monstrosity.

Caz swallowed nervously. "Yes."

I was happy to let Caz take the lead. It was his turn anyway; I secured the boat ride and Eurydice gave the directions.

"I prefer to do business in the lounge. Follow me." The Hydra bowed and slithered off. We followed Kronos—it couldn't be anyone else, with the deference everyone showed him—into a lounge area. After he seated himself, we took chairs not too close, not too far, lest we offend.

"What do you want and what do I get out of it?" he barked.

Caz cleared his throat. "We need to get out of Tartarus, and to do that, we must pass through the Pit. We need your permission."

Kronos sat back and regarded us with an odd air.

"You have some nerve, *son* of Zeus, *nephew* of Hades."

"*Grandson* of Kronos," said Caz, shifting ever so slightly in his seat. "But you can't chose your relatives."

Kronos gave a short harsh snort. "Yes, I've learned that, to my downfall." He turned a gimlet eye on me. "You're a brave thing. Why do you want to get out of Tartarus? I hear Hades is a very cordial host—to females."

I shrugged nervously. "I don't feel the same about him. I want to go home."

He studied me critically, then glanced at Eurydice. "Back again? Some people never learn."

The stage lit up and a nice-looking man strutted out, dressed in an abominable lizard-green leisure suit. He started singing Elvis' "Hound Dog" and Kronos tapped his fingers in time to the music.

I heard the sharp intake of Eurydice's breath.

"Sings pretty good, doesn't he?" Kronos jerked his head in the direction of the stage. Lounge Lizard jiggled his hips and crooned into the microphone.

"Yes, very. He sounds just like Elvis," I said amiably.

"He just had to look back," said Eurydice, shaking her head.

Kronos' mouth twisted into a malicious grin. "That's Orpheus. Hades banished him here for being a putz and failing his test."

Oh.

Caz gently squeezed my leg. Not a grope—he wanted me to be quiet. Not a prob. If Kronos got ticked off, no sense in me becoming entrée for one.

Caz turned away from the stage. "Will you let us pass?"

After a long moment of staring, first at Caz, then at Eurydice and me, Kronos finally slammed the table and everyone in the place jumped.

"Yes," he said, with a slow, wicked smile as he leaned closer. "But passage to the mortal world is a valuable commodity. Freedom isn't free, you know."

Here it comes, I thought.

He licked his lips. "I demand a kiss."

Oh damn. He won't ask Caz to pucker. Eurydice is pretty! Pick her!

"The mortal. I want her." Kronos pointed a black nail at me.

Double damn! Why is it always me?? I wondered why I had to pay the fare for everyone. But was there any other choice? No.

"Fine," I muttered, steeling myself. What kind of kiss could he possibly want? After that last meal, a piece of skin was sticking in his front teeth.

Ewwww! *No tongue!*

Fast as lightning, Kronos bent over and placed a chaste kiss on my cheek.

That's it? I looked at him, bewildered.

"When you get to the surface, you must pass that on to your sister-Siren."

I opened my mouth to ask why when Caz squeezed my leg again.

"Um, okay."

Kronos leaned in and held me with his eyes. "Pay attention, pretty human. This is no jest. If you do not pass on the token of freedom I've just given you, both you and she will find yourselves back here, not frolicking in Hades' Elysian Fields. This will be a far less pleasant venue than what you see now—and there will be no escape."

I nodded fearfully. As soon as I saw Meg I'd plant one on her. Anything to get his rank breath out of my face.

Kronos clicked his claws like a crab and the hideous Hydra appeared at his elbow.

"Escort them to the back door."

The Hydra nodded, we rose, and before I could grudgingly thank him, Kronos disappeared.

Orpheus, finished with his song, stood to the side, wiping the sweat from his brow. He and Eurydice locked glances. He gaped as we passed and tried to say something, but one of the Hydra's heads leaned close and hissed, "Ssss-silensssse! Follow ussss!"

He nodded mutely and fell into step.

"Idiot," murmured Eurydice, but she clasped his hand tightly.

The decadent halls of the casino, the plush carpets and dripping chandeliers, gave way to cramped corridors. The elegant gold wall paper disappeared and cracked paint took its place. Here and there naked bulbs flickered in broken wall sconces.

At the end of the dingiest passage, we came to a door with a lurid red exit sign hanging askew over the top.

"Thissss isss the passssssage to the mortal world," the Hydra hissed. One head turned to Caz: "You go firssssst." Another swiveled to me: "You follow." The third moved to Eurydice: "You nexsssst," and a fourth head said, "You're lasssst thissss time, Orpheussssss."

Its gruesome body slithered and writhed so that it was poised to leave us, but then one of the heads darted back to within centimeters of Caz's face. "Don't look back! None of you! Not until all have passsssssed!" Then it wriggled away, leaving a trail of neon green slime in its wake.

Caz opened the door. I could just make out the beginning of a tunnel, craggy and foul-smelling. Bare feet. Party dress. This was going to be fun.

Caz scanned the distance. One hand on his hip, he rubbed his brow. "It was too easy."

"You try scaling rocks and jumping ship in a gown and bare feet," I retorted.

Mistrust in his eyes, he shook his head. "Kronos ate his own children to retain his power. Don't you think that giving you a peck on the cheek is too little to ask? And then"—he looked incredulous—"Orpheus can just walk out?" He shook his head. "I don't like it."

While he pondered, I wondered. What harm could come of a kiss? And maybe Kronos let Eurydice and Orpheus go as a big fat Greek "kiss my ass" to Hades. Father and sons did have an all-out I-hate-you-I'll-get-you mentality. No matter what happened, I couldn't thwart the gods—it was going to be what it was going to be.

"Let's go. We can't turn back now." Caz took my hand. "I won't look back," he said, his voice steely and controlled. "Even if any of you plead. And don't you look back, no matter what you hear, or think you hear. Got it?" His face was grave.

"Nothing is going to stop me." I returned his gaze.

"Nor me," said Eurydice. She turned to Orpheus. "Don't. Make. The. Same. Mistake. AGAIN." She gave him a fierce look and a desperate kiss.

He squared his shoulders. "I'm ready."

Quickly, Caz grabbed me to him and, finding my mouth

with his, kissed me. My head spun with the heady pleasure. It might be the last kiss I ever got if things went wrong. I put all my desperate longing into his warm, soft lips, leaving us both panting, breathless for more.

"For good luck," I said, as we pulled away.

He nodded once and started up the narrow path that only allowed a single person at a time to pass. It seemed as though the distance between us started to grow. How could that be? I was almost running up the steep, rocky path, my poor toesies feeling every pebble. The sound of Eurydice's steps behind me soon disappeared; Orpheus' were long gone.

This has to be an illusion. It's Hades' way of keeping the prisoners in.

Huffing and puffing, I could barely make out Caz up ahead, but there was a pinpoint of light which I hoped was the end of this long, dark, draining ascent. To keep my focus on climbing and not on the slithering, whispering sounds that seemed to follow me, I hummed a song that Meg played often. I couldn't remember the words or the title, but the tune was catchy.

For the first ten minutes.

Tired of that, I went through every song I'd ever heard; Christmas carols, songs learned in school, oldies my parents sang, anything. The light was getting bigger, but the sounds moved closer and every once in a while, out of the corner of my eye, I saw glowing eyes watching me. I kept the path in front of me in sight all the time, and kept climbing.

Caz was gone.

Doesn't matter. It's a trick. Keep going.

My hands were bloody and painful from the sharp

rocks, and my feet blistered. Once I almost lost my balance and nearly twisted my ankle.

I kept climbing.

My lungs burned, my heart stammered, and my legs wobbled.

I pushed on. *Almost there.*

When I thought I'd never make it, the opening was suddenly there, even if Caz wasn't. I climbed up to the light and when I stepped through, I rejoiced.

I'd made it. And so had Caz.

Kronos' tunnel opened into the mortal world inside what looked like a janitor's closet. What I thought was a boulder turned out to be a bucket on wheels with a mop; rocks were really spray bottles and rolls and rolls of TP; the pinpoint of light a naked bulb hanging from the ceiling. I threw myself into Caz's arms, feeling both our hearts pounding as we labored to catch our breaths. We stood like that until our pulses slowed.

"We made it," I whispered, brushing his smooth cheek with my dirty hand.

"Yes," he replied in a husky voice, and kissed me. As much as I adored the sweetness of his kisses, this wasn't the time, and certainly not the place, to explore each other's mouths. I gently pulled back.

We hesitated, not daring to look at the tunnel behind us—neither of us wanted to risk going back to the Underworld. Sadly, I heard no sounds from below, no one coming up. I hoped they hadn't failed the test again, but we couldn't go back in and check. Their fate was their own.

Then, through the closet door, I heard and felt the thump of heavy bass. The bulb flickered, then burned brighter. Cautiously we snuck a peek around; there was no tunnel opening anymore, only a shelf of cleaning supplies.

Caz's head dropped. "They didn't make it."

"Maybe they ended up somewhere else. I hope they're together at least," I whispered.

I opened the closet door, and gasped as we stepped out into the gymnasium of the Academically Independent High School of New York. It was nice of Kronos to send us here, not abandon us in a far-off desert, the tundra, or one of a thousand other awful places. I was *home*! And *at the Spring Fling*! It was almost enough to make me cry with joy. I rushed past astonished students and teachers, into the midst of the dance.

Caz ran over to a tall girl with an angular face and long dark hair, dressed all in black, and hugged her. Next to them was Jeremy, looking confused and angry. Where was Meg? Was there a time limit for giving that kiss?

I ran up and stopped in front of Jeremy. He backed up a step and wrinkled his nose. *Here we go again*, I thought. Then I looked down at my formerly fabulous ball gown. It was torn and streaked with mud and some oozy green stuff—probably slime from the Hydra. And it didn't smell too good. I didn't want to think about what my face looked like. Still, I smiled eagerly.

"Where's Meg?" I blurted, overly bright.

"Uh…" He hesitated and eyed me with suspicion. "She went to the bathroom."

People around us stood motionless, staring.

"Thanks!" I said and dashed away, not caring who saw or who followed.

MEG

The Naked Truth

I walked as swiftly as I could, holding the fleece in front of me, my cheeks burning. Dancing couples turned to look at me as I passed—was it my newfound exhibitionism or the fleece? I didn't care; this would all be over in minutes.

I waited in the shadows for the ladies' room to clear out. When a large group departed, I hurried in. The common area was empty, and crouching—as much as I could in the restrictive "dress"—I could see no pairs of feet in the stalls. The stage was set for me to make my grand exit, and I knew I didn't have much time.

Looking in the mirror, I was startled by my own reflection. The scales glittered under the bright overhead lights. They hugged my chest, my hips and my thighs, giving me a streamlined look. It was eye-catching and it looked … great. *If I ever get back,* I thought, *and if I ever go to another club or dance, I'm going to wear something like this again.*

The thought surprised me, then brought me back to the reason I was here in the first place—Shar. I had to get out of here and find her. I nodded at myself in the mirror, took a deep breath, and held up the fleece.

I heard fast footsteps in the hall outside. It was time; I wasn't about to do this in front of anyone.

"Here goes," I said, and swung the thing behind me to drape it over my bare shoulders.

I heard the door squeal on its hinges and prayed that the innocent people coming into the bathroom wouldn't be scarred for life if they saw what happened next. But the fleece never touched me; it was ripped out of my hands. As I turned to see who'd come in, someone crashed into me and knocked me over. My head smacked against the wall. Scales dug into my leg; spots danced before my eyes, blurring my vision; and my breath left with a whoosh.

"Meg!"

Shar's voice?

"Meg!" Someone was slapping my cheek. As soon as my eyesight cleared, I saw Shar. She was dressed in a filthy pink shimmering dress that looked like it came out of one of those cast-of-thousands MGM Technicolor movies, and her face and hands were smudged with dirt.

"Stop slapping me!"

She grabbed my face and planted a hard kiss on my cheek.

"First you hit me, then you kiss me?" I said, rubbing the

spot, laughing and crying at the same time. "I'm glad to see you, too, but how did you—"

I had to stop; my teeth were chattering so much that I could barely get any words out. If I was freezing before, I was a block of ice now. I started to get up, and Shar gasped. She scooped up the fleece from the floor, held it in front of me, and steered me into a corner. A glance in the mirror told me why; the scales were gone. I was *nekid*. For real this time!

And we weren't alone.

Three people stood behind her.

"Shar?" I heard Jeremy say uncertainly.

He walked over and looked at her, then turned to Paulina and another guy, and looked from them to Shar to me, confused and questioning. I didn't know who the stranger was; he was tall, with tousled blond hair. His blue suit was filthy, and his shirt, streaked with grime and half unbuttoned, hung out of his pants.

And why was he wearing a Superman tee underneath?

He smiled at me, with a familiar crooked grin. Paulina, standing next to him, could have been his sister; she was just as tall, with similar but not identical features. Both gazed down at me with warm gray eyes. It took everything I had not to stare at one of them, then the other. I felt my heart fluttering in my chest, butterflies in my stomach.

What the hell was wrong with me?

Paulina was a guy.

How could I have missed it? There was no mistaking it now. Gone was the scarf. Her—no, *his*—shirt was unbuttoned to the middle of his taut chest. With glasses off and hair brushed aside, I could make out the faint, bluish tint of shadowy stubble on his chin.

"I knew you'd never send me away," he said, his lips cracking into that weird half sneer, half grin.

"What?" Jeremy's eyes went from confused, to hurt, to angry in the course of about four seconds. "Okay. Now it all makes sense," he said, more to himself than anyone else. He gritted his teeth, clenched his fists, and glowered at me, his face flushed with rage. "First, I don't hear from you for days. After that it's one-word answers, week after week. You're always late—if you show at all. And you're always with your new roommate." He lowered his head and laughed mockingly. "You never really had a new roommate, did you?" He jerked his head at Paulina—or Paul, or whatever his name was—and then turned an icy stare on Shar. "Covering for Meg. Nice. Well, enjoy, man." He turned on his heel and rammed "P" in the shoulder as he left, slamming his palms against the door to open it.

"Wait! I ... I ... " I reached out a hand after Jeremy's retreating back. The door slipped shut.

Shar still held the fleece in front of me, moving her head to block my view and meet my eyes.

"It's okay," she soothed. "We'll fix it later."

I leaned my head around Shar to look at the boy formally known as Paulina. "Who *are* you?"

He finished unbuttoning his shirt, shrugged it off, and handed it to me. His chest was the same golden tone as his skin, his torso solid, muscular, and rippling.

"I'm sorry, Meg. I didn't picture things happening like this."

Crouching behind the outstretched fleece, I slid P's shirt on. It smelled of wild herbs and figs, something you'd catch a whiff of on top of a mountain looking over a span of azure sea. What was I thinking, reveling in the scent of his shirt, still warm from being next to him? He just ruined my life. I buttoned up the shirt; it fell almost to my knees, which made me feel slightly better. Or at least slightly less self-conscious. Underwear would help, but that wasn't forthcoming.

"I'm Pollux," he said. "This is—"

Daggers of realization stabbed me all over. "Let me guess. Castor, your twin." The baggy clothes, the getting up before the garbage men to be dressed, using the bathroom alone, the scarves over the Adam's apple, the lean, hard body, the big feet, the insatiable appetite. All of it screamed *Male! Male! Male!* And moron—that was for me.

"Call me Caz." The blond guy bobbed his head, then turned to Shar. "She knows her mythology."

"You have no idea," she said, linking her arm through his.

"I guess this is what you were doing in Tartarus?" I asked.

She flushed. "I didn't get this dirty and messy dancing at a ball," she quipped.

"I'm sure." I stared at the door, wondering if I should go after Jeremy. Pollux moved closer and handed me his jacket. I put it on and said to him. "There was no deal with Hades, was there? He just wanted you."

He nodded.

"We'd make a nice bargaining chip for him," agreed Caz. "If he had both of us down there he'd be able to squeeze something out of Zeus."

"But I knew you wouldn't send me there," said Pollux, flashing the lopsided smile. "From the moment when I first saw you. Look," he said, almost shyly, but reaching for me at the same time, "I wanted to talk to you, but … in a better setting than this," He looked around, and was about to continue when I held up a hand and shook my head. I had a queasy feeling that I knew what he was about to say.

"Look, Paul—I mean, Pollux—this is … just … " I glanced away for a moment, then looked up at him again, at a loss. "Awkward. That's what it is."

He took my hand in his and squeezed it, tenderly. I felt overwhelmed, but I didn't pull away. Part of me wanted to hear what he had to say; the other thought of Jeremy.

Let's go over the thousand things that are wrong with this; he hid his identity from me, he killed my relationship with Jeremy, he lived with me. He saw me naked!

"I understand," he said. "And I'm hoping you can see from the situation why I didn't … " He paused, then held me with his gaze. "Why I didn't just tell you everything right away."

There were several times when I felt the same way. I knew there was more to things than Hades revealed. And there was something else, too. A part of me … *connected* to Pollux in some way, a tie that went beyond boy, girl, friend … I shrugged the feeling away; it was too close. Unbearably, uncomfortably, exquisitely close.

I felt everyone's eyes on me, as if they were waiting for me to do or say something.

"So now what?" I looked around. "Is it over?"

There was a rumbling from the full-length mirror at

the end of the bathroom. Caz and Pollux looked at each other and nodded. The lights flickered and I thought I heard thunder.

They vanished.

Shar gasped and spun around and around. "I can't believe they left us!"

"And just in time for you-know-who," I scowled, pointing to the mirror, which enlarged to the size of a doorway with stairs leading down. The whole room shuddered and dropped like it was a giant elevator, and then Hades stepped out dressed in a rumpled tuxedo, his shirt unbuttoned, the ends of his bow tie hanging on either side of his lipstick-stained collar. He stopped in front of us, arms over his chest, one hip thrust out, shaking his head in disapproval.

"Mission *not* accomplished." He frowned. "And Sharisse, you naughty thing, sneaking out like that. How did you manage it?" His voice was quietly menacing. Shar stared at him, mutely defiant. "Very well. I'll have an eternity to persuade it out of you. I have my ways. I suspect my sire had a hand in this. *Tsk tsk*, Sharisse. You'll let that ... thing kiss you, but not me?"

I turned to Shar, horror-stricken. "What the hell were you doing down there?"

Hades leaned closer and in a soft, ominous tone, said, "Kisses from Kronos are not so easily erased, and they carry a doom. And look, you were kind enough to share it with Margaret. You'll regret this," he promised.

Shar turned her frosty eyes on Hades. "I don't think so," she said through clenched teeth. "I did what I had to do to escape."

"Then I hope you enjoyed your short visit." Hades made a sweeping motion toward the gaping doorway. Tendrils of smoke rippled along the floor. "It's time for all of us to travel down under," he said, grinning. "Ladies first."

SHAR

I'll Be Back

"At least tell me why you wanted them both," I said, standing with my fists jammed on my hips, foolish obstinacy holding the terror at bay.

"My little sweetmeat, I will be happy to explain things once we're safely snuggled in our little love nest."

Insert evil grin and lecherous hand-rubbing here, I thought.

"Oh, can't you ever just give it up?" demanded Meg. "You won, okay? We're slaves to you and your dog for eternity. Just tell us why you wanted Castor and Pollux." Her eyes were spitting ice-blue fire. Hades gave her that maddeningly sexy I've-got-dark-promises-to-keep look. After the barest of moments, he threw up his hands.

"I guess I can be a magnanimous winner. As always. Castor and Pollux separated cannot negate the powers of my minions—the Furies, the Harpies, and of course, you two Sirens. Although you might have noticed that when you were in Pollux's presence, Margaret, you weren't quite as ... alluring."

Meg narrowed her eyes at him and I made a rolling motion with my hand. "So I've heard."

Hades brushed back a stray lock. "While Zeus isn't the greatest of fathers, he seems to take exception when someone steps on his parental toes. By holding both Castor and Pollux, I could do a little collective bargaining."

"For what?" I didn't think Hades could possibly get more time with Persephone, because (a) Demeter would bring on another ice age and Zeus wouldn't allow that, (b) I didn't think he was *that* lonely; he found playmates like me to amuse him even if he had to use bribery, blackmail, and bullying, and (c) if you're going to take on the top guy, you might as well ask for something *big*, like maybe your birthright to rule Olympus. I guessed there could be tons more explanations, but who knew Hades' mind?

He exhaled and, forming a triangle with his fingers, looked coolly first at me, then at Meg.

"What I want from Zeus, I'll keep to myself. One never knows when another opportunity may present itself."

"Wouldn't it have been easier just to tell me who Pollux was?" Meg demanded. "Oh, wait—you had no deal with him, so that makes this an *illegal* take down."

Hades gave her a withering glare. "My methods for this transaction could be considered by some to be ... *unortho-*

dox. But I'll be glad to explain it all once we're back at my place. Shall we go?"

As he gallantly swept his arm toward the portal, we all heard a rumbling sound. Like thunder. Hades spun around and I think he swore in Greek.

"Hurry! Get in *now*!" He went to shove us in, but Meg did a fancy move I didn't know she could do and twirled out of his way while shoving me aside, out of his reach. Like the explosion of a silent bomb, a brilliant white light erupted, blinding me. I had to turn aside and cover my eyes. When I could sense the light had died, I opened them again. There stood Pollux, Caz, and a man who was Hades' equal in stunning looks, but golden to Hades' dark. He wore a white silk shirt, white pants, and gold sandals. On his head was a laurel wreath.

I could *feel* the power radiating off him. I gulped, looked over at Meg, and mouthed "Zeus!" She jerked her head once, her eyes large with dread.

Hades scowled. "Hello, bro-ther," he said, then looked at the twins. "Ran home to Daddy, did you?"

"Careful, Hades. I'm not happy to be here." Zeus looked around in disgust. "Do you get off on dragging people to skanky places? I can only imagine what Tartarus looks like."

"Oh, it's beautiful!" I interrupted, then slapped a hand over my ill-mannered mouth.

Zeus scowled at me. "Mortal, speak. How do you know?"

As Hades stepped forward, he gave me a shut-up-or-I'll-deal-with-you-later glare. "She's been my guest, and a difficult one at that. Cerberus hasn't been the same since she's cared for him. She'll have to return to rectify the situation."

"I didn't do anything to that slobbering—"

"You called him a good goggy," Hades said in disgust. "And now all he wants to do is cuddle! Who's going to guard my borders?"

Ignoring Hades' complaint, Zeus turned to me. "Is this true, a guest?"

"A former Siren who had no choice!" blurted Meg. Hades should have included her in his quelling look. I sent her a grateful glance. She winked.

"This is a story I must hear." Zeus snapped his fingers. We were suddenly lounging in white caftans on soft white cushions on a white boat. At least the sea was blue. Another god with a serious color phobia.

"Are we in Olympus?" I asked.

"Only gods and demi-gods are permitted on Olympus. We are currently in the Aegean Sea. Neutral territory, courtesy of Poseidon. Should anything befall me"—and he sent a distrustful glance in Hades' direction—"Poseidon is witness for the pantheon." Hades didn't even blink.

Servants in traditional white Greek chitons walked around, offering gold plates laden with fruits and some type of drink. Zeus plucked a fat ripe strawberry, tapped the beautiful maid on her tush, and turned to us.

"Begin."

Hades' mouth started to open, but Zeus, without so much as looking in his direction, wagged a finger.

"You"—he pointed at Meg—"start. Your name?"

"I'm Meg, and Shar's my friend."

"And you're Sirens?"

"Yes, but we were forced—"

He snorted. "I hear that all the time. You humans really need to come up with a better excuse when you make a bad deal." He popped a green grape into his mouth. "Continue."

Meg gave a quick rundown of her last assignment, up to the moment she was in the bathroom. Zeus nodded, Hades fumed, and I listened.

"But you didn't force the fleece on Pollux or order him to put it on," he mused.

Meg blushed. "I . . . couldn't. And I didn't know that Pollux was male, or a demi-god." She stared at her toes. "I could have ordered him to do it if I *had* known, and honestly, I might have." Then she raised her head and said defensively, "To save Shar from Hades, I was going to put the fleece on myself and go to Tartarus, but I got lucky—she escaped in time to stop me."

It was my turn to wink at her.

"Nice try, Hades, but this will not go undealt with." Zeus sucked on a juicy pear, his eyes boring into Hades' before he turned to me. "And what do you have to add to this tale?"

Then I shared what happened in my little corner of the Underworld, minus the little heart-to-heart Hades and I had during the ball. I didn't think that almost-kiss-and-tell was a need-to-know. His eyes unreadable, Hades simply stared at me.

"Hmmm." Zeus selected a fig. Didn't he eat before he left home? "For restoring my sons, your honesty to me, your loyalty to each other, and the wisdom you exhibited, I will grant each of you a boon. Speak."

"Can we confer?" I asked. No sense wasting divinely granted requests on the same thing.

He tipped his head once. "You may."

I rushed over to Meg, sat beside her, and whispered in her ear, "What do you want?"

"I want us to be done with Hades!" she hissed.

I wiped the spit from my ear. "If you ask for that, then I can ask for Eurydice, Orpheus, and Splendor to have Zeus' protection. Hades will want to get even with them for helping me."

"It's a deal." We shook on it.

"I want—" I began.

"Done!" said Zeus.

"But how did you—"

He cocked an eyebrow.

"Oh, right, omniscient," I said meekly.

Hades gave a disgruntled snort. "No, you two whisper loud enough for Poseidon to hear it under the sea."

Zeus rose, and at his pointed glare, we jumped up too.

"You are freed from your contract with Hades. Eurydice will stay reunited with Orpheus, but they must remain in the Elysian Fields."

"What happened to them?" I interrupted.

Hades tossed an olive over the side of the boat. "It was ridiculous for them to think they could make it to the mortal plane." He swallowed distastefully. "They're dead—they can never leave. However, they are reunited for all eternity, so I've kept my side of the bargain." He nodded in smug satisfaction over this small win.

"After three thousand years," I argued.

Zeus held out his hands. "It's Hades' realm, and that cannot be changed. Now, once Charon resumes his post, Aglaia will return to Olympus with the status of Favored Muse. Until that time she will be unmolested by you, brother."

Hades sighed and nodded grimly.

As I cleared my throat, Meg's mouth dropped open and she gave a barely perceptible shake of her head, begging me not to say anything apocalyptic. But I rushed on. "Sir, Aglaia has some people on Olympus who aren't fans of hers, and she's worried about, uh, upsetting the serenity of the pantheon."

Zeus roared with laughter. "Nicely put, Sharisse, but Aglaia will be under my protection and need not fear Hera. Serenity of the pantheon! Ha ha! That's a new one. You mortals are so amusing when you aren't a pain in the *ouo*." He chuckled a few more times before turning with a stern regard to Hades. "And you know the rules. You cannot approach them claiming the contract is unfulfilled or with tainted gifts. We clear?"

With a killing look, Hades did a stiff little bow.

"And keep Persephone on a short leash when she's back with you. I don't want her chasing these delightful girls. I need to have a little chat with Demeter on their behalf, and with Hera before Splendor returns to Olympus."

Before I could say thank you, Zeus was gone and we were back in the girls' bathroom in our own clothes. Zeus had thoughtfully provided Meg with jeans. Nice ones, too! He was a class act, even if intimidating.

"Shar, can I talk to you for a moment?" asked Caz. With an apprehensive glance at Hades, who seemed to be sulking in a corner, I put my hand in his outstretched one and we walked into the gym, onto the middle of the dance floor.

"I never got to ask you to dance." He gathered me close and breathed in my ear, sending chills down my spine as we swayed to the music. I snuggled closer, ignoring the gaping mouths and pointed fingers of Alana and posse.

"This is nice," I murmured, thinking, *I have a date for the Spring Fling! I'm at the Spring Fling!*

We danced for a few minutes, enjoying the closeness, before he spoke again.

"I have to leave."

Sadly, I knew that, although I'd hoped for at least an hour of mortal time with him. "I know," I mumbled into his neck. He rubbed my back, his strong hands gentle and soothing.

"Can I come back to see you?"

I pulled back to look at him. "Would you? I mean, do you want to?"

He smiled that roguish smile and my legs just wanted to give out, so I held on tighter.

"Yes. How about next week, your time? I'm going to lie low for a little bit while Hera and Zeus scream at each other. I suspect that Demeter, Persephone, Hermes, and who-knows-which gods will jump into the fight."

"Kind of like 'Celebrity Deathmatch,'" I giggled.

"You got it. But as soon as it's clear, I'll be back."

I nodded, a tear threatening to make a run for it. When it rolled, he wiped it gently with his thumb.

"It won't be that long." He bent his head to mine and kissed me, slow and sweet and deep.

I lost all track of time and space and everything else. There was only Caz and me. When my head was swimming, he pulled back.

"Gotta go." He frowned. "Be careful of Hades. He's a poor loser. And he wants you. You're the one that—"

"Says no." I laughed shortly.

He shook his head. "No, you're the one who got away; from him, from Tartarus, from your obligation to him. He'll be gunning for you especially, but Meg's in just as much danger."

I sniffed. With a brief kiss, he walked out the door into the night beyond, and was gone. I trudged back to the ladies' room.

Meg jumped. "You just left—" And then she nodded sagely. *Been there, done that.*

Pollux stepped between us, ushering Meg to the side.

"I hope I can see you again." His stormy gray eyes, identical to his brother's, pleaded with Meg, who held up her hands and backed away, shaking her head.

"I don't think I can do this now, Pollux. I need to try and make things right with Jeremy, even if it's over." She shook her head. "I can't imagine what he thinks was going on." She gulped. "There's too much…"

"Weirdness?" I supplied. If Meg's looks could kill, I'd be sizzling on Emeril's grill.

"Strangeness and secrecy and Siren juju," she said slowly. "I think we should keep it friendly."

Pollux had a cute lopsided grin that was more pronounced than Caz's. I could see that there was something between him and Meg—why couldn't she?

He held her with his eyes. "Okay, whatever you want— for now. But I don't give up easily, Meg." He stole a quick kiss before she could object. "I don't give up at all."

Oh yeah, she's feeling the love. Her blush and lack of strong objection were proof. *Jeremy is a nice, sweet guy, but he's last year's look—out of fashion and so done.*

Pollux vanished.

That left Hades.

"Now that those sappy goodbyes have been exchanged, it's my turn."

Meg reached for my hand and we held tight.

"Here it comes," she said out of the side of her mouth.

"He can't do anything to us," I whispered with a false bravado.

With a sly smile and a slow lick of his lips, Hades leaned his head between ours and murmured in our ears, "This isn't goodbye, girls. You might need *me* one of these days…"